Charlie Carroll

THE LIP

TWO
ROADS

First published in Great Britain in 2021 by Two Roads
An Imprint of John Murray Press
An Hachette UK company

This paperback edition published in 2022

3

A CIP catalogue record for this title is
available from the British Library

Paperback ISBN 9781529334180
eBook ISBN 9781529334197

Typeset in Albertina MT by Palimpsest Book Production Limited, Falkirk,
Stirlingshire

Printed and bound in Great Britain by Clays Ltd, Elcograf S.p.A.

John Murray policy is to use papers that are natural, renewable
and recyclable products and made from wood grown in sustainable
forests. The logging and manufacturing processes are expected to
conform to the environmental regulations of the country of origin.

Two Roads
Carmelite House
50 Victoria Embankment
London EC4Y 0DZ

www.tworoadsbooks.com

For my brother
Jodi

If the cold made an impression on her, she did not show it. Nor the prospect of the drop. The tide was at its lowest. No water awaited her down there, only black sand.

I have often wondered what she thought of in those last moments. I like to believe that if she thought of anything, it was of my land, of the overwhelming beauty of it from the lip. And then I hope she thought of nothing at all. Because there is peace in that.

I had no time to shout. I was halfway across the road when I realised. By my next step, she had jumped. I watched her disappear out of sight beneath the lip and, still, I did not shout. I wanted to, I wanted to scream, but something stopped me. I did not know what it was at the time, but I do now. It was already too late. She had left, her action irreversible, and the last thing she needed to hear on the drop was my scream. Then she would have known that I had seen her. Seen *it*. I could not give her that as a final thought. I wanted peace for her.

I did not shout but I did run. Her footprints remained in the grass at the lip and I nestled my own feet into them. I looked.

She lay face down on the black sand.

This is all I have.

Few ever get to see it as I do now: bathed by the rising sun behind, immaculate in this crisp morning air. There are no silhouettes in these conditions, only long shadows. The clarity is resounding. My land, my *world*, can be seen and absorbed in one long swoop.

There is no better place.

It starts from the coast path signpost: the pitted wooden needle which pierces the horizon-hanging clouds, rock steady on the western headland. And then it arcs, a jagged but perfectly curved lip, swinging back from the signpost until it reaches dead centre and then out and on again with the same slow bend, past the warning sign and towards the eastern headland, where the lip crumbles and the coast path has no barrier to separate it from the edge. That toppled into the ocean during last winter's storms. The lip forms the boundary of my land outwards but not downwards, where it continues, including the chop of Atlantic below, the sheer cliff face which rises from it, lonely Gull Rock a few metres out, standing tall and serene. And then behind, behind the lip, behind me, this field of untamed grass which swells towards the road, ends, and then surfaces again on the far side, circling the Cafy and streaming towards the woods.

All of this is Bones Break.

All of this is mine.

I know every inch of it; I know it as intimately as the seagulls. I stand at dead centre, my feet teetering on the edge of the lip. Below, the thundering tattoo of waves on rock. Wind catches the tips of my hair, lifting them above my ribs: less force than it takes to knock me down; enough to make me right myself with a step to the left, and then another back again. Here on the lip, it is vital to know where my feet are. They must have the same distance from each other as they have from the edge. For this is how she stood, nothing before her but clean and open air, her shoulders back, her bare feet flattening the blades of grass.

This is as close to her as I can get. Time and feeling separate us now, but I will not let distance do the same. I remove my sandals and picture her here. The ocean view, the sharp tang of brine at the back of the throat, the wet grass and wetter earth beneath it.

I breathe it all in, long and deep.

The swells are offshore and the wind rushes out towards the horizon, taking dawn's last clouds with it. The sun rose from behind the woods less than an hour ago: low enough to cast its river of gold across the ocean surface; high enough to begin to warm the air. The weather today will be better. That in itself is a relief.

It has been a dreadful year, worse even than what Dad called the Year of Living Dangerously. I sometimes wonder what he would have called this year, and have thought about giving it a name myself, but there is no inclination. Naming something gives it form and existence, makes it memorable. This is a year I would rather forget.

So a warm and clear day, as this morning promises, would be welcome. The cormorants are already here, jostling for position above the break line. They come when there is enough sunshine bouncing from the surface of the water to dry their outstretched wings and warm their chests. Mum once told me she found that cormorant pose 'magisterial', 'self-assured', and years later, remembering her words, I tried to imitate it on a hot day, sitting out here on the lip, cross-legged, my arms held out wide. I did not last long. Bones Break crawled with emmets that day, emmets hiking in the heat, who stopped, laughed, and pointed their fingers.

The cormorants also signal the receding of the tide: they only come when it is on its way out, exposing the rocks at the foot of the cliff face. Before long, the zawn – the tiny beach which exists at the base of Bones Break for just a few hours each day when the tide is lowest – will be visible.

This is my favourite beach in the world. The sand is black, volcanic, the same colour as the cliff face it swirls out from, and so unlike the white sand of Lantoweth further west along the coast. It astonishes me that it never washes away, is never dragged out to sea, but sits, remains, with implacable grace. I am grateful for it. It makes my zawn all the more unusual, and all the more beautiful.

That it is undisturbed is its greatest attribute. No footprints muddy the sand's perfect swirls for there is no road or path down; no boats linger at the zawn's fringes, blotting the seascape, for navigating the submerged rocks which stretch out from Bones Break would be an act of madness. It is my favourite beach because it is untouched, it is pure, and it is mine.

But if you have the stomach for it, there is a way down to the zawn, a way down which does not involve jumping. I have done it. Once. I intend never to do it again.

I come out here, to the lip, to visit the zawn as often as its rare appearances allow. I wish I could visit my second favourite beach, Porthmadden, again, but I have not been there since my eighteenth birthday. It lies far down the coast, beyond the estuary, and the trips Mum and I took down there on the morning of each of my birthdays did not recur this year.

The first was my tenth, two years before the Year of Living Dangerously. Mum woke me while it was still dark with a kiss, a smile and a promise – that this would be my best birthday present ever. We crept down the stairs so as not to wake Dad, who had stayed late at the Cafy the night before, let ourselves out of the house and climbed into the car. I remember the strange mixture of excitement and apprehension which prickled my skin as we drove out of St Petroc and towards the ocean, turning east on the coast road and passing but not stopping at the Cafy.

'Where are we going?' I asked, but Mum did not reply. Her silence only fuelled my conflicting emotions – even by the age of ten, I knew what Mum was capable of, how enlivening or terrifying she could be depending on the circumstances – and I found myself reluctant to ask again, matching her silence with mine as we crossed the estuary and then rejoined the coast road, passing through sleeping villages and around imposing moors, the sun still not yet risen.

Dawn had begun to bleach the dark sky by the time we pulled into the empty Porthmadden car park.

'Where are we?' I asked.

'We're here,' Mum said, her smile enigmatic. 'For your birthday present.'

Before locking the car, she pulled an enormous backpack from the boot. I followed her down on to the beach. Halfway between the car park and the shoreline she stopped, opened the backpack, retrieved a blanket, and the moment she began laying it on to the sand the sun appeared behind us, as if she had choreographed it perfectly.

'Sit down, Melody Janie,' she said. I did as I was told.

And then, with the flourish of a magician, she began to pull out the most magnificent breakfast I had ever seen. Croissants, butter and honey. Fresh scones, a pot of clotted cream, a jar of blackberry jam. Strawberries, apple slices, two separate bunches of grapes – one green, one red – and crescents of watermelon. A carton of pre-chilled orange juice, a flask of hot milky tea, an assortment of crisps so varied I did not know which to choose first. One packet of custard cream biscuits, two bags of jellied sweets and a large tin of chocolates. And then, the final prize, taken from a separate bag I had not even noticed her carrying and laid down in the centre of the banquet, a sponge cake topped by ten candles which spelled the letters M and J. Mum lit them with a box of matches taken from her pocket and said, 'Happy tenth birthday, Melody Janie. Double figures.'

That was when I started to laugh, started to laugh with so much giddy joy that the wind blew the candles out before I could regain enough breath to do it myself.

It was a school day, and our time was limited there at Porthmadden, but we made the most of it. Mum was electrifying, a never-ending source of jokes and hugs and gentle encouragements to *eat more*, to *try some of that*, to *just have a bit, go on, why not, it's your birthday, you're ten now*. When I could eat and drink no more of the feast, I fell back into the sand with a satisfied grunt, the blue sky above laced with streaming cloud formations.

'Don't you just love this?' Mum murmured from beside me.

'My birthday?'

'Your birthday. You. You and me and the sky and the sea and the beach. We're so lucky here I sometimes forget it. How lucky we are. How very, very lucky.'

'I wish we could swim,' I said.

'What's stopping us?' Mum propped herself up on one elbow.

'I haven't got my costume.'

'Me neither.' She began to grin. It was mesmerising. 'It doesn't matter. There's no one else here.'

I looked around me. She was right. Aside from us and our decimated picnic breakfast, the beach was deserted.

'Can we?' I said.

'We can do whatever you want. You're the birthday girl.'

We stripped to our underwear and sprinted, charged, into the waves. The April sea bit like nettles, but we did not care. We swam and we bodysurfed and we screamed laughter into the surging water and when Mum threw me I sailed high into the air and when I tried to throw her she jumped upwards and pretended it was me who sent her cascading into the bright morning wind. She taught me how to do a handstand by plunging my fingers into the sand and holding on to it like a rope against the currents, our toes pointed at the sky. She showed me how to float on my back, how not to fight the water but let it carry me aloft as if on an outstretched hand. She let me hold on to her waist as she swam us both outback, beyond the waves' break line, and then she wrapped me in her arms, perched me on her stomach and let the swells take us back in.

Mum drove us home in her underwear. I sat in the passenger seat, enfolded deep within the blanket: sandy, shivering and happy. Back in St Petroc, she dressed quickly in the car and then led me towards the house. I could see her jeans and t-shirt dampening as Dad opened the door for us.

'Happy birthday, Melody Janie!' he called, picking me up, blanket and all, and carrying me into the house, up the stairs, to my bedroom, where he finally lowered my feet to the floor. '*This*,' he exclaimed proudly, 'is your *real* birthday present.'

My eyes followed his pointed finger. At the foot of my bed, jutting out a few inches from the wall and sloping dangerously to the left, was a brand-new bookcase, the highest of its four shelves populated with ten books.

'Ten books for ten years,' Dad said. 'Next year we'll get you eleven. The year after, twelve. And so on. Every year. I promise.' It was a promise he would not keep. 'This is your birthday present. Your library. Long may it grow!'

I approached my library. Three of the books I knew from school, four I had read before, three were ones I had never heard of. Though the bookcase looked like it could collapse on to my bed at any moment, it was a wonderful gift.

'I'm sorry we tricked you, Melody Janie,' Dad said. 'But we had to get you out of the house so I could build this thing. We could have done it while you were at school, but we wanted you to have it now, on the morning of your birthday.'

I looked at Mum. She smiled. We both knew which birthday present meant more.

I was late to school that morning, and when I got there no one wished me a happy birthday. But it did not matter, because I had had the best morning of my life.

Mum collected me alone after school because Dad was working at the Cafy. She led me up to my bedroom. The bookcase, my library, no longer slouched to the left. It was as straight and solid as my legs had been that morning, thrust out from the ocean while I performed the perfect handstand that Mum showed me.

'Don't tell Dad,' she said.

We went to Porthmadden every year after that on the morning of my birthday, right up until my eighteenth. Just me and Mum. We missed this year, my nineteenth, but it does not matter. I know Mum will make up for it next year. I know she will not miss my twentieth, our ten-year anniversary.

I walk. Mornings like this are rare and the most must be made of them. I turn to my right, away from dead centre, heading east, following the graceful curve of the lip as it arcs up towards the headland where the barrier and the slice of cliff beneath it tumbled into the ocean last winter, leaving behind nothing but a sharp cleft. No one was up here at the time to fall with it.

The first village in this direction is Petherick. Bones Break does not qualify as a village. With only the Cafy, the land and the cliffs, it is lucky to have a name at all. Petherick, on the other hand, has substance: houses, shops, a school, a library, pub, chapel, harbour – as well as all the undesirable things that come with population. Litter. Noise. Fumes. Drunken fights. Worse, it has its B&Bs, its hotel, its holiday lets and second homes. In short, it has emmets. Moving in. Taking over. Bones Break may have its disadvantages, but it is free from all that.

To reach Petherick takes two hours by foot along the coast path. I do not have the inclination for such a hike today. Nevertheless, the coast path itself is rampant with life if you know where to look for it – the heather and gorse which creep back from the lip; the seagulls and cormorants and gannets and choughs and terns swooping above; the seals below, sunbathing on the zawns or floating upright in the turquoise shallows, their dog faces serene with glistening whiskers and closed eyes. It is not necessary to walk all the way to Petherick. There is plenty to watch here. Especially at Nare Point.

I skirt around the eastern headland and continue along the coast path, following its undulations as it mirrors the sweeps and folds of the lip. Nare Point lies half a mile away. Though there is no Cafy there, and though the views – sky-wide as they may be – are inferior to mine at Bones Break, Nare Point has one specific attraction. Between the road and the coast path, a large rectangular space has been cleared of gorse and gravelled over to make a small car park. People use this as a wild camper stop, and all throughout the summer Nare Point is filled with vans belonging to both locals and emmets. I have never known if this is allowed, but no one complains. The only house nearby is Mrs Perrow's, but she died last year, and aside from that there is little else but Trethewas Woods behind and the ocean beyond. A blind eye is turned to the wild campers. No one cares about them. No one but me.

I quicken my pace as I round the final bend in the coast path before Nare Point, partly from excitement and partly to warm up. Even now, with the sun full and glaring on my right, there remains a distinct chill in the air, one that causes me to shiver, to wish I had worn a coat over my dress.

I reach the car park. There before me is my prize. A single VW camper van, light green, all curtains closed and no noise coming from within. That it is the only van here this morning surprises me, but not much. The lack of custom we had at the Cafy this year is testament to how poor the season has been, the season which is now, finally, limping towards its end.

Nevertheless, this VW camper van is my favourite: the kind with the huge windscreen and the spare wheel poking from the front like the snout of a piglet. Esther's brother Nathan used to have one like this, but orange, and he would park it across the road so that I could see it from my bedroom window – until he drove it away to university one September and I never saw him, or the van, again. This one, I realise as I look closer, is a rental camper van: the company name is stencilled on to the sliding door. So there must be emmets inside. Locals do not rent camper vans, and if they do, they use them to go somewhere beyond the Tamar, out of Cornwall. I have never understood why.

I step off the path and on to the grass so that I will not be heard. Nare Point has a superb hideaway, the pocket, a sort of burrow beneath an overhang of knotted weeds. It is large enough for me to lay straight out on my side, obscured from eye level by the vegetation, the ideal vantage point for low-angle observations. Climbing in gets my dress wet, but once inside I am always surprised by how dry and warm it is. I have often wondered if a family of animals lives here, if they made it themselves, but I have never seen evidence that any life uses the pocket, any life other than myself.

I cannot see the top of the camper van from here, the weeds above me obscure it, but all else from the windows down is visible, and a few moments after I have settled into position lights come on inside the van, spilling out through the cracks in the curtains. I consider rolling out of the pocket, stalking towards the van and peeking in through the cracks to see who is inside and what they are doing. But that is not as much fun. I like the waiting: it gives me time to imagine who will face me, before they must.

One of the van's side windows is yanked open. A cloud of steam plumes out into the morning air.

Who will it be today?

I picture an older couple, childless, or grieving a lost child perhaps, touring the Cornish coast, quiet people, respectful, deserving of this landscape, simple and pleasant, worthy, discovering the medicine for their grief here, in these views, deep in these immaculate views . . .

The camper van's door slides open. I feel a pang of irritation: I could have imagined them more. But I must pause. The irritation fades as quickly as it appeared, replaced by a trill of anticipation. Now that the door is open, one or perhaps both will step out into the morning sun. I wonder who it will be. The stooped husband, worrying at his first cigarette of the day? Or the wife, her wrinkled hands rubbing at the sagging belly where once a child grew?

It is neither. Two girls climb out of the door, squinting in the sunshine. They look to be no more than a year or two older than me. They both hold mugs in their hands and one empties a steaming kettle on to the gravel. Students. Perhaps on a break from university. Best friends. I am so disgusted by them that I almost crawl out of the pocket and storm off. They are not who I wanted. But one of the girls has begun to walk towards me. She moves quickly across the car park until her feet come to a stop just a metre or two from my face. And then, right in front of me, she pulls down her pyjama bottoms, squats, and has a pee.

She does not see me. They never do.

Did you see her? Did you see *what she did*? That vile, putrid girl – pissing, *pissing* all over *my land*. The couple of my imaginings never would have done that. He would have ground his cigarette butt into the gravel beneath his shoe, and then he would have stood a while, taking in the view. She would have come out to join him, and together they would have gazed out at the ocean with the sun warming their backs. From the pocket, I would have been able to watch their hands edge towards each other and then join, witness the contact, the affection. Things were going to get better for them. Until these stupid best friends ruined it all.

I try hard not to let the emmets infuriate me, but when they behave like this it is impossible. In the Cafy, I remain professional and polite. Mum says we need them to fill our seats, to fill our cash register, to fill our lives, and I know, regardless of my own feelings, that this is true. So I bite my tongue and swallow my words and put on a brave face and do all those suppressive things I need to do at work. We are supposed to be welcoming. It is our business.

But out here, out here on my land, the rules are different.

My spying is in part an act of revenge. If they knew about Melody Janie down here, watching piss dribble down their legs, they might think twice about what they have done, and what they continue to do. They might realise that this is a place that demands respect and nurture in equal measures, not the grass-staining acid of urine, not the discarded bottles and crisp packets, not the flattening impressions of military-grade hiking boots. They might realise that the people too, the people like me, demand just as much respect and nurture as the land, that we are not here purely to serve, to give up our houses and fish and identity, to bow and beg. They might realise that they should walk, and drive, with care.

Yet it is doubtful they will ever realise these things. I make sure they never realise me. The pocket is one of many hideaways I know and frequent. At Bones Break, there is a shelf beneath the coast path signpost on the western headland. It juts out from the rock a metre down the cliff face, a flat ledge slightly longer and slightly wider than my body, so that I can lie across it on my back in perfect comfort. Because the shelf sits within an indentation of the cliff face, it is impossible to see from anywhere on the land but directly above, and nobody ever looks down. From the lip, there appears to be nothing but a sheer drop, and you would have to lean right out to look down and see me lying on the shelf, listening to you. Even the seagulls bark with surprise when they come across me there.

The greatest advantage of the shelf is that people will

stop above it. The signpost on the western headland is not just a marker for the coast path, it also signals a prime lookout – from there you can see a vast sweep of the coastline as it curves around The Warren to strike out into the ocean as Pedna Head, the surf rolling in from the horizon to crash against the miles upon miles of cliff face. Emmets always stop there. I cannot see the poses they strike for their photos, but I hear their conversations, and I absorb their words like the sun's rays. Much is banal. Clichéd platitudes. Pathetic attempts at description. Small talk and chit-chat. When something of worth comes along it is rare, and perhaps it is this which makes it all the more delicious.

The most fascinating words tend to come from those who walk alone. From the western headland, it is possible to see for miles in every direction, and the emptiness of the surroundings lends an element of privacy which only the widest of spaces can give. Solitary walkers open up when they pause on the western headland – they mumble to themselves or they shout as loud as they can or they talk to the sea as if it were an old friend. Last summer, a man who sounded young and Scottish stopped at the signpost as I lay on the shelf. I heard zips opening and closing, the rustling of paper, the clearing of his throat, and then a ten-minute monologue which began with the words 'Dear Philip'. He was reading from a letter written to his recently deceased brother. When he finished, I heard him screw up the letter, and then watched as the ball of paper sailed out above me, catching the wind and drifting ever further out to sea. I lost sight of it before it dropped into the water.

'So Philip,' the man continued, his voice softer and more hesitant, no longer reading but thinking out loud. 'You should see this. You'd have loved it. We should have got out of the city more, come to places like this. Maybe that'd have helped. You should have got to see this. It's not fair that you didn't.'

I liked that man. I felt sorry for him because he had lost his brother, and I do not like to hear anybody cry, emmet or not. But I liked him more for his kind words. He understood. He recognised how exceptional my land is. He chose it as the site to read the letter to his brother – a fitting tribute to Philip, and a fitting tribute to Bones Break too.

So I suppose that not all of them are bad. Some, like that man, I think I could even make friends with. But not these girls. They have started up the camper van's engine now and are pulling out of Nare Point, off up the coast, away, perhaps to civilisation, perhaps not. Watching them leave, I breathe a sigh of relief and crawl out from the pocket. Then I walk across to the road and stand there a while to make sure they do not come back. If they do, I'll split their heads open with a shovel.

I make my way back to the lip, skirt along the low wooden barrier until I find the place. I stand in position. Precise. Dead centre. It is vital to know where my feet are. The left an inch closer to the lip than the right, both angled slightly inwards, heels up. For this is where she stood, naked, at three o'clock in the morning.

I should have been in bed, but I was unable to sleep that night. There was no particular reason: I was not subject to some insomniac prescience, there was nothing in my gut telling me that *something was occurring*. I simply could not sleep. It had happened many times before. It has happened many times since. I got up from my bed, dressed and stepped outside the caravan, ready for a short walk to and along the lip. I hoped the night air and the brief exercise would tire my muscles and my mind, lending me the sleep I craved when I returned to the caravan.

I stepped out of the woods, rounded the Cafy, reached the road, and saw her. Her legs were pale, her bottom bony. Vertebrae rippled down her back and gleamed in the moonlight, revealing malnourishment, emaciation. She did not dive, tern-like, into the night air. She crumpled into the drop.

Her footprints lingered in the grass. I stepped into them. The tide was out. The sand black.

I ran back to the Cafy, picked up the phone and dialled 999. When asked which service I required, I vacillated between coastguard and ambulance, before choosing the former. A man spoke to me. He was emotionless. He said someone would be with us shortly. I asked how shortly. Within the hour, he said.

It was too long. The zawn had been fully visible, which meant that the tide would begin rising soon, and I knew that she could be carried out to sea before the boat or the helicopter appeared. I could not bear the thought.

I ran back out of the Cafy to dead centre. She was still there, face down in the sand. I suddenly felt very calm. I knew what I had to do. I knew that it could be done.

Rain comes, thick and urgent. I cannot stay here. I consider hurrying to the western headland and climbing down to the shelf, but soon it will be too slippery to be safe. I could return to the pocket at Nare Point, but I will be soaked by the time I get there. The best option, in weather like this, is the bush-den on the eastern headland. The rain builds. I run.

While the bush-den provides fine shelter, it is the least comfortable of all my hideaways. I can remain fully hidden there only if I squat with my knees beneath my chin – a position I find difficult to maintain for more than an hour. But an hour, perhaps, is enough, to keep watch over my land, to stay dry and, right now, to stay away from the lip.

I climb in and assume the familiar position. I rest my chin on my knees, feel the chill of them through the thin fabric of my dress. My hands, wrapped around my shins, are dry and chapped and will start to grow numb soon. I will not stay here for the full hour. If no one passes within twenty minutes, I will return to the caravan. I may even turn the gas on, light the boiler and take a hot shower. A rare luxury.

It is important no one knows of my vigilance. I must

remain unseen, must remain hidden, for only that way can I truly protect my land. Let them visit, but don't let them stay. Dad said that to me once, those exact words, told me he lived by them, and when I repeated them – *let them visit, don't let them stay, let them visit, don't let them stay* – his smile was so delighted and loving that I decided to live by them too. 'Because when they stay,' he continued, 'they never leave – they set up camp, push us out of our homes by buying them at prices we could never match, or buy our land and build their own monstrosities. Breaks my heart.'

I remember that one particular man in the Cafy all those years ago. With his fake-tan wife and entitled children. I was serving their cream teas when he began to joke about buying the Cafy, about knocking it down, about building his own 'summer palace' in its place. My hands began to shake and the cups rattled in their saucers as I placed them on the table, but he did not notice. He did not notice me at all. He kept on with his theme – where he would put the stables for his daughters' horses, the garage for his cars, the swimming pool for their parties. I stayed close as they ate and drank. Not so close as to be obvious, but close enough to listen. When they left, I watched them from the windows, and I kept watching until they had climbed into their car and driven away. I kept watching until I was sure they were gone. I have never stopped watching since. If any emmet ever steps on to my land with the intention of buying it or building on it, I will be the first to know. And I will do everything in my power to stop it happening. Everything.

The sound of footsteps catches my attention. Slow and heavy. Approaching from the west. Possibly holiday-makers from the Lantoweth chalets: holidaymakers in wellies, tramping through the mud on the coast path in a squashy, sludgy march. They sound close to dead centre, where they will likely stop to take in the view. Most do. Some continue, some turn and retreat, some cross the road and peer through the Cafy's windows, wondering if it will ever open again. I wonder which option these will choose. I listen closely, and when I recognise that the footsteps have not stopped or turned but are still heading my way, I feel oddly excited. I wonder who they will be. I hope they will talk.

All of a sudden, the footsteps speed up. They have left the path and sound like they are coming directly towards the bush-den, fast. I hold my breath, squeeze my knees tighter under my chin. There is a rustling sound: the leaves and the branches around me shiver and dance. Are they poking something in? Why? Who are they? Those two girls? Perhaps they saw me watching them. Perhaps they turned the van around, came back, tracked me from Nare Point to Bones Break. I lower my hand to the ground, searching for a stone to hit them with. A twig cracks beneath my palm. The world around the bush-den begins to shake ferociously. What are they doing? Are they trying to scare me out? *Me?*

I close my eyes, ready myself for the attack. This is my land and I will defend it to the death. I can hear breathing, close and fast. I tense my legs, ready to spring. I'll go for the throat first. I'll lift them right up over the fucking lip.

I open my eyes. There is a nose six inches away – black, dripping, its warm jets of breath reddening my cheeks. I shriek and jump backwards, out of the bush-den and on to my feet. A man rushes towards me, one arm outstretched, the other bound in a sling. His dog reappears and cautiously follows me, tail low and ears pinned back.

'Archie!' the man shouts. '*Archie!* Come here!'

The dog turns and slopes back towards the man, who stops running and wipes his free hand across his forehead. He looks as horrified to see me as I am to be seen.

'I am *so* sorry,' he says. 'So very, very sorry. Archie got a scent, you see. I thought he was after a rabbit. I didn't know . . .'

I brush down my dress and pull a leaf from my hair. I look at my feet and then back to the man. He is still in a state of distress. The dog is panting, great balloons of steam billowing from his mouth. I notice the saddle-bags attached to his sides. The man takes a few steps closer. The dog, his tail wagging now, inches along with him, but does not leave his side. I think he might want to come to me, to offer his head for a stroke.

'Are you all right?' the man asks. He has begun to stare at me: a piercing, wide-eyed stare; a weirdly intense stare; a stare I find disturbing. He is old, maybe in his sixties, and his face is as pockmarked as a cliff. I hate his stare. I hate his question. And so, rather than answer, I turn and I run, away from the man, away from Archie, back to my caravan, through the rain.

I slow from a run to a walk only once I am behind the Cafy, secure and out of sight. My heartbeat lessens. I force tranquillity by breathing, the way Mum taught me, long and deep. Reset and restore. A calm, or something akin to it, spreads.

Before me, the wildest part of Trethewas Woods begins. I slip between the trees, following the remnants of a path which is all but invisible to anybody who does not know it is there. My steps are practised, and it takes me no time at all to reach the small clearing where my home sits.

My caravan.

I open the door. It is warm inside, not as pretty as it can be when sunlight streams in through the windows to fill the interior with an alluring orange glow, but beautiful in the rain too, the gentle pattering on the roof rhythmic and soothing. My cosy caravan. I would like nothing more than to stay here, to crawl into my bed, nestle beneath the blankets and read a book. But I do not have the time. Esther is coming soon. I must get ready.

I take the kettle and the mug from the cupboard beneath the kitchenette sink. One of my large drinking water bottles is in there too. It is almost empty and will need replacing soon, but there is enough water left to fill the mug, which I then decant into the kettle. I place the kettle on to the left burner (the most powerful), open up the gas valve beneath the cooker, turn and hold down the dial and then ignite the burner with a lighter. While the kettle boils, I strip the bed of its blankets, duvets, sheets and pillows, neatly fold all but the pillows and then pack them away into the rearmost overhead storage unit. With a precise sequence of pushes, bends and pivots, I transform the bed into two couches separated by a table.

The kettle sounds its whistle and I move back to the kitchenette. I turn off the burner, reach behind the cooker and open the tin wedged there, take out one of the teabags, place it into the mug and pour the boiled water over it. I remove a spoon from the cutlery drawer between the cooker and the sink, squash the teabag against the side of the cup, watching the streaks and swirls of brown as they course through the water, stir the mixture into a whirlpool and then retrieve the teabag. I drop it into the bin and the spoon into the sink where I will wash it later or perhaps use it again.

I place the cup on the table and leave the tea to cool. I open the wardrobe door. It creaks and a gust of refrigerated air drifts out into the open. I flick through my hanging clothes and choose a dress for the day, taking it off its hanger and draping it over one of the couches. Then I remove my old dress, place it on to the newly available hanger, and put on today's. It is stiff to the touch, so cold it feels almost wet, but I know it will warm and soften soon enough. I close the wardrobe door.

I take two steps to the right of the wardrobe and slide open the door to the bathroom. It is dark inside, windowless, but I do not need to turn on the light. I know where everything is. Packets of wipes are stacked in the shower tray to the left of the door, opposite my stock of eight 5-litre water bottles. I reach forward and pluck a packet of wipes from the stack, peel back the cover, remove four wipes, then reseal the packet and place it back on to the pile. Sliding the door closed behind me, I walk to the couch and sit down. I place the four wipes on to the table next to the mug, and then I take turns between wiping my face, neck, hands, arms, feet and ankles and sipping from the tea.

And then I go to the Cafy.

The door opens. Its scrape across the floor makes my heart lurch. Two emmets step inside, expensive walking poles swinging from their clenched hands. They are dressed in pink waterproofs, mammoth boots, and bandanas already saturated with their sweat. The uniform of the rambler. They are women, women who look to be in their fifties. I keep quiet, stare at them as they take in the Cafy. One places her hand on the other's arm. They make it no further than the welcome mat before turning around and leaving. The door scrapes again as it swings shut – the rain has swollen it.

I could have told them that we are closed, but I talk to emmets only when I have to. I cannot forgive them for their intrusions into Cornwall, nor what they did to Dad. And it seems that I did not need to tell them. They left anyway. A quick look at the current condition of the Cafy would reveal to most that it is, or at least should be, closed for business. I have tried hard with it – I come in to clean most days – but it is too much for one person. All the rain and cold weather this season has encouraged patches of black mould to bloom across the walls, and no matter how hard I scrub at them they always come back. Leaks I cannot fix drip from the ceiling into carefully placed buckets. Since the electricity was cut off, it is colder and darker in here than it should be, and the stench coming from the freezers in the storeroom has grown indescribable. There is decay here, it hangs in the air, and no matter how vehemently I fight it, I worry that one day it will overwhelm me.

I sometimes wonder if, in a strange way, Dad would approve. He liked the fact the building was old, that its window frames were rotting and its paint peeling, that it made unexpected noises nobody could explain. He said it was rustic. Authentic. Homely. Right from the start. I was eight when Dad bought it. He called that year Ground Zero. Mum had just come out of the Centre. Little Sister Lucy had not yet arrived. Grandma had just passed away. The inheritance she left Dad was enough for him to buy the Cafy, which back then was called The Bones Break Diner. Dad objected to the first and last words (and especially the last, which he said was far too American for an age-old backwater like this), so he dropped them both and replaced 'Diner' with 'Cafy'. Whenever he was questioned about the unusual spelling, he would remark that he had chosen the Cornish rather than the French. I found that difficult to believe – people spoke Cornish as a first language so long ago that I doubt Cafys existed back then – but it did not matter because I liked the way Dad pronounced it, to rhyme with 'daffy', which had an upbeat sound to it, fun to say and full of joy.

The purchase came first, then the renaming, and only

after that did he tell me and Mum. I remember that morning well. Silence in the car as we pulled out of the drive, through the streets of St Petroc and on to the coast road, making our slow way through Petherick and past Nare Point to come to a stop in the car park of The Bones Break Diner. Dad switched off the engine, swivelled around in his seat so that he could see both of us – Mum up front and me in the back – and then he announced what he had done. Mum said nothing, and I was seized by the notion that this was a bad idea. The Bones Break Diner was where Dad and I used to come for cream teas after visiting Mum in the Centre. For me back then, it was a place of scones and awkward silences. I did not want to own it.

Then Mum screamed. It was so sudden and shrill that I shrunk back into my seat. Throughout the year before Ground Zero, Mum's last in the Centre, her screams had become a source of terror for me. But this one was different – with it came outspread arms which she flung around Dad's shoulders, pulling herself into him and burying her face in his neck. When she resurfaced, her scream was no longer a scream but laughter.

She leapt from the car and raced towards the Cafy – its new sign proudly gleaming on the road-facing wall – and when she reached the outdoor terrace she climbed on to one of the wooden picnic benches and pogoed up and down upon it, springing so high that her hair fanned out and her skirt revealed her knees and the bench bent so deeply beneath her weight that I thought it might break. She was shouting something, but the wind obscured her words, and all I could hear was a kind of high-pitched warbling, a strange keening noise which somehow told of her delight far more than whatever words she was hollering might.

Dad did not join her on the bench. We climbed out of the car together and stood side by side. I could tell he was happy: I could see every one of his teeth. I had not seen them all, together like that, exposed, for a long time.

I recognise the sound of her engine, know that the tyres crunching across the gravel of the car park belong to the sky-blue Ford Fiesta without looking out the window. A door opens, slams shut. Footsteps follow. Esther lets herself in through the front door. We hug for a long time.

'How are you?' she asks.

'Better,' I say.

This is Esther's fifth visit. Last week she came on Tuesday and Saturday. This week she will do the same. Next week too. We are building routines. She sets the times and I set the location. Here. Always here in the Cafy. Esther does not like it, would prefer to meet me at the house in St Petroc. She does not know that I moved out of the house and into the caravan some time ago, and I prefer to keep it that way. There is a lot I do not tell Esther. I cannot destroy our friendship again.

Her visits begin in the same manner.

How are you?

Better.

Part of the routine.

I offer her a cup of tea and am relieved when she declines. Though the gas and the water still work at the

Cafy, when the electricity was cut off a month ago – or perhaps it is longer, I cannot quite remember – any elementary form of hospitality became a rigmarole.

'I can't stay long,' she says. 'I've got a deadline this afternoon.'

'Are you ready for it?'

'No. That's why I can't stay long.'

We move into the dining room and sit at one of the tables.

'How's uni?' I ask.

'Brilliant, I love it,' she says, before tailing off. Esther has changed since school. That natural enthusiasm I so loved about her has diminished, morphed into something more considered. Either that, or she tamps it down, makes a point of being subdued around me. 'I mean,' she continues, 'it's hard, though. All my deadlines come at once. I'm pulling a lot of all-nighters lately.'

'All-nighters,' I say.

There is a pause.

'How are you?'

'Better.'

'You mean it?'

'Yes.'

We look around ourselves, at walls.

'So have you decided when you're coming to visit me?'

'I will. I promise.'

'Bristol's amazing. You'd love it, I swear. And we've got a spare room now that Lily's dropped out.'

I think of Bristol. Beyond the Tamar. Out of Cornwall. It makes my fingernails ache. I lower them beneath the table and dig them into my thighs. They throb in a way which is not unpleasant.

Esther is still talking. 'You can stay whenever you want, for however long you want. Honestly. A month, two, more. I don't mind. Charlotte won't either, she's always round at her boyfriend's anyway. It'll be just the two of us. Like the old days. Melody Janie Rowe . . .'

'. . . and Esther Leigh Harlow.' The beginning to our song, the one which never got further than that first couplet. We both laugh a little, but Esther soon composes herself and becomes serious again.

'I think it would be really good for you.'

'I know,' I say. 'I just need a little longer.'

'But why?'

'I have to keep an eye on things here. It's not even been a month yet.'

'Okay,' she says. 'Sorry, I'm sorry.' She raises her palms and faces them towards me, a gesture of calm. The gesture sparks a memory, one from school, when we were friends. Mrs Marks used to do it when somebody was talking too fast or too loud. *Easy, gently,* she would murmur as her palms floated up to chest height. Esther once said she sounded like a Buddhist monk and, after that, in the quiet of the library, we would recreate exaggerated impressions of her mantra to each other.

I mirror Esther, hold my own palms up. 'Easy,' I say. 'Gently.'

Esther's laughter is sudden and bright. It is the first time I have heard it since she started coming here to visit me. I used to love that laugh. I used to love causing it.

'Do you want to come for a walk with me?' I say, made eager by her laughter, warmed by it. 'We could go to Petherick, or Lantoweth if that's too far, or just to The Warren to see the rockfalls.' I stop talking. Esther has pulled her phone from her pocket. It vibrates in her hand. She smiles apologetically at me, stands up and walks to the back of the dining room, placing the phone against her ear. She begins to talk into it and I give her privacy by not paying attention to her words. Instead, I gaze out of the window. The two women from earlier – the ramblers, the emmets – are walking across the lip in the direction of Petherick. As they pass, they turn and look at the Cafy.

I know they are talking about me.

'I'm so sorry, Melody Janie,' Esther says, returned and hovering over the table. 'That was Nathan. Mum's been taken to hospital.'

'Is she all right?'

'I don't know. I think so. It's probably her hip again. But Nathan can't get hold of Dad. I've got to go.'

'Of course,' I say, standing up as she takes her jacket from the back of her chair and hurriedly puts it on. 'Go. I'll see you on Saturday.'

We hug again.

'I'll be back soon. Do you need anything?'

'No.'

She said that last time.

I'll be back soon. Do you need anything?

No.

We are building routines.

I stay in the Cafy all day. I clean tables. I eat crisps. I press my palms against windows.

The rain stops and the sky clears as the day comes to an end. I walk out to the lip to watch. I have not seen a sunset in weeks: the sky has always been too grey, too overcast. But now it is perfect. The sun is hanging low already, swelling out towards the horizon, that particular orange which is and always has been my favourite colour, even when I lived back in St Petroc, where the sun disappeared behind the terraced houses long before it was soft enough to look at.

There is no one on my land this evening so the view is all mine. I kick off my sandals and lower myself down to sit on the grass, legs stretched out before me, the scabs of old bramble wounds revealed where my dress hitches up. The ground is wet. An ant crawls up on to my ankle, investigating one of my hairs, testing its strength with its own leg before turning to run away and disappear through the valley between my bare toes. I yawn wide and long, like a dozing seal, and it soothes the tension in my face, around my eyes, at the corners of my lips, along my jawline.

A chough appears, settling on the coast path and

hopping into the grass. She must not have seen me; her focus is fixed on the grass and she comes closer without regard to my presence. I do not move, hoping she might come closer still. Paul Dunstan called me a chough once when I wore red tights to school. He was immensely proud of the new nickname and made sure to tell everyone about it, though it failed to catch on. To have a nickname you need to be either very popular or very unpopular, and I was neither. I seemed to pass through school largely unnoticed.

The only real friend I had, the only real friend I have ever had, is Esther.

Melody Janie Rowe . . . And Esther Leigh Harlow . . .

We lived on the same street in St Petroc and went to the same primary school, but it was a long street and a large school and we generally ignored each other. Or she ignored me. Most did. The stigma of my hospital-ised mother made other children reluctant to play with me and made their parents approve of their reluctance. To be fair, it was mostly ignorance and nothing more – except for Paul Dunstan, who found it hilarious to make faces at me, the kind with tongue out and eyes crossed and a finger circling around an ear; the kind denoting, of course, madness. I once saw him perform the same mime to his father in the playground after school before I walked home alone. Paul's father laughed harder than he did.

One of the reasons I admired Esther, even before we became friends, was that she too had her own stigma, her own black mark, and yet she rose gracefully above it and no one ever ignored or bullied her. She suffered from epilepsy. I had seen her drop to the floor in the middle of the classroom, had seen her writhe and shudder, had seen her face contort into expressions similar to the ones Paul Dunstan contrived to tease me with, and yet no one ever used it against her. No one performed cruel impressions of her seizures. No one called her Epileptic Esther. Instead, she seemed to have more friends than she needed, and when she dropped they would swarm around her, all care and concern, propping her into the position they had been taught, finding blankets and pillows and moving chairs and tables and tending to her with sweet kindness until she revived.

At first, I could not understand why. She was not stunningly beautiful, nor was she endowed with that curt sharpness so peculiarly prized at school. But, later, I came to learn why. Esther was – *is* – pure light. So radiant you felt warmed just being close to her, enlivened by her vivacity. When her focus was on you, it poured from her like a rainbow. Everyone wanted that focus. It made them feel better about themselves.

Secondary school swallowed us all up with its size and, to our tiny eyes, lawlessness. Paul Dunstan no longer ruled our year group – he was quickly supplanted by the Three Lauras, who could devastate with a look. The Three Lauras smoked, they had older boyfriends who they did things with, they set the frequently shifting trends for how long a tie should be, whether sleeves were rolled up or not, the tightness of a skirt.

Their weapons were rolled eyes and loud tuts, and if they were moved to words it meant you were in serious trouble. They were never moved as far as actions, though it was threatened more than once, and the threat alone was enough.

Esther, in the top set for everything, was no longer so noticeable, but she thrived in that way too. She kept some of her friends and lost some of her others, but only in that harmless, drifting manner which happens when something new begins and people flood together. Everything remained bright for Esther, as everything always has, because that is the kind of person she is. Bright. Pure light.

I learned that truly – I gloried in it – when Esther and I became friends.

The sun has gone. The night seems to take no time to fall these days and the temperature plunges with it. I feel the first few prickles of cold along my bare arms. I will have to return to the cosiness of my caravan soon, but I want to delay that for as long as possible. It will make the treat of warmth, when it comes, all the more sensational.

Twilight is not my favourite time: I prefer the dawn to the dusk. Yet it still brings its own kind of beauty to the lip. Bats appear from the woods behind the Cafy, swinging and swooping towards the cliff edge but never beyond. Glow-worms wink out from the heather, tantalising me into drawing close and then disappearing when I reach out to touch. Just past the signpost on the western headland, and then all the way to Lantoweth, families of rabbits dart from hole to hole at this time of day, a blur of ears and pompom tails.

I rise from the grass, stretch my legs and rotate my shoulder blades. Clicks and pops burst across my upper back. The first star of the night begins to show, close to the horizon where the sky retains its blue tinge. I move towards the low wooden barrier which separates the lip from the rest of Bones Break by a couple of feet.

The barrier itself is all but useless, a visual deterrent less than a metre high which can be stepped over with ease. Not far from dead centre, a warning sign hangs from it, black lettering on a yellow background – UNSTABLE CLIFF KEEP AWAY FROM THE EDGE – and the image of a gigantic man who looks like he is scree walking into the ocean.

Keeping away from the edge is good advice, but because this is my land I do not pay attention to the sign, day or night. I step over the barrier to the brink of the lip and then crab-walk sideways until I reach the exact spot. It was here that I first saw it.

The way down.

Down the cliffs. Down to the zawn.

I retrace my own footsteps from that night, back over the barrier, on to the coast path, across to the eastern headland, and to the lip once more. This is the jumping-off point: the start line for the way down. The drop here is only a few feet, and the grassy bowl below is soft and springy, welcoming even. Leading down from the bowl is a thin strip of grass growing on one of the shoulders of the cliff face, and this particular shoulder has a gentle downwards arc rather than a sheer drop. Because of this arc, and because the grass upon it is deep and soft, it is possible to walk down the shoulder with relative ease, though I stayed low and used my hands as well as my feet when I did it.

The most difficult part of the descent is where this shoulder of grass ends. Below that, the cliff face folds back into itself, nothing below but space and ocean. A few metres away, a second grassy shoulder begins. Getting to it, however, requires both daring and conviction, for it is necessary to climb horizontally for five or six metres to get from the end of the first grassy shoulder to the beginning of the second. Plenty of handholds and footholds exist between the two, and all faith must be put into fingers and toes. Heels dangle out into thin air.

From the second shoulder downwards, conditions improve, for this one leads comfortably all the way down to the high tide line. The grass stops there and the cliff face transforms into a gentle slope that soon levels out and scatters into rocks which, providing the tide is low enough, can be skipped across all the way to the zawn.

The night I descended, I was exhausted by the time I reached the bottom. It was not so much the exertion but the importance of it all, the imperative need to *make it*. A shower had passed over while I climbed down and I was wet through. Soaked but hot. Nauseous too. Black sand rose up between my toes. I looked at the lip above me, at the sparse tufts of grass which poked out over the edge. And then there was the drop, the sheer cliff face, the metres upon metres of wet rock which towered over me. I felt the rotation of the Earth.

Something tickled at my heels and I turned around to see the shoreline dancing back away from me over the black sand. The tide was coming in. I had to get her as far back as possible, away from the water, towards and into the low cave which arches over the sand at the base of Bones Break.

She was astonishingly light. With one arm beneath her hips and another beneath her chest I could lift her a few feet off the ground. Her legs hung down awkwardly as I carried her so that her toes coursed thin furrows through the sand, and I considered flipping her over and cradling her like a baby. But to do so would be to see her face, broken by the drop. I would not look at that; I would not remember her that way.

Halfway into the cave, I stopped and laid her gently on to the sand. We were deep enough. The sea was coming for us, that was without doubt, but it was a slow beast and I estimated I had at least an hour before the cave filled with water. I hoped the coastguard would arrive before that happened.

We waited there together on the wet black sand, the two of us, watching the sea, smelling the salt on the cave walls, and listening to the soft shore break outside. We did not have to wait long. A helicopter came, hovering low, enormous and deafening. The water whirlpooled beneath it as a beam of white light shone this way and that. I considered running out of the cave to shout and to wave, but I did not want to leave her. They would find us. I was confident of that.

Soon, the searchlight settled on the zawn, fixing its eye upon the sloppy outline of a figure imprinted in the sand, then following the footsteps and thin draglines which led from it to us. When I saw the man leap from the helicopter's open door, calm and pencil-straight, I wrapped my arms around my knees, and I rocked and I rocked and I rocked.

When I wake, I find I have been sick during the night. It is not the first time this has happened these last few weeks. The vomit has dried already, crusting across the duvet and the dress I fell asleep in. I need to shower.

I climb out of bed and peel the cover from the duvet. I will take it into the shower with me and keep my dress on, clean everything at once. I turn on the gas and depress the ignition switch until the mirror below the boiler glows with the reflection of the pilot light. I try to use the boiler as little as possible – it consumes far more gas than I would like – but the caravan's solar panels do not generate enough power to heat water and so, when needs must, this is my last resort. There are, after all, no shower facilities in the Cafy.

The boiler will take some time, perhaps half an hour, to heat. I check the weather through the window, see that it is not raining, and take the duvet outside to hang across the branches of a tree. Coming back into the caravan, out of the fresh air, the rank stench hits me and I hold my breath until I have opened all the windows and skylights.

I consider a walk to the lip – the sun will be rising soon – but it is cold outside and I do not want to wear my coat over my dress because of the vomit. So instead I pick up my book – *One Hundred Years of Solitude* – and perch on the edge of the bed. This Buendía family fascinates me, those myriad Aurelianos and Arcadios, otherworldly Remedios, staunch Úrsula, all of them versions of each other. Sometimes, I wonder what it would be like to belong to a bulbous and sprawling family like theirs, whether it would comfort or irritate. But my family is and always has been small: Dad, Mum, me and Little Sister Lucy. My parents were only children, so there are no cousins, aunties or uncles to speak of. Dad's father died long before I was born; his mother survived only until I was eight years old. My memories of her are hazy at best. The most vivid takes place at Christmas, at her house. There was a meal I could not eat and a small dog that avoided me. Grandma gave me a present – a set of pyjamas emblazoned with smiling donkey faces which I fell in love with immediately and which I changed into right there and then and which I refused to take off for the next three weeks. When I pick apart the memory, I realise that it is more about the pyjamas than about Grandma.

Mum refuses to speak about her parents.

I open the door to the bathroom and remove the toilet bucket from the shower tray. It needs emptying anyway, so I pour some bleach in, swill it around a few times, pour it all down the plughole and then put the bucket outside to dry. I turn the water pump on and open the tap, bleeding the pipes of any air that may have built up. It takes a few seconds of spluttering and spurting before the water begins to run smoothly. I remove the tap from its stand over the sink and fix it on to the head-height hook under the skylight.

I step out of the bathroom and move into the kitch-enette to test the water temperature. The tap sprays out into the sink, not scorching, but warm enough for steam to billow from it as it collects in the empty washing-up bowl. It will do. I find my towel lodged deep inside the cupboard beneath the wardrobe and then step back into the bathroom, closing the door behind me. I turn on the shower and cower at the edge of the tray until the cold water has run through and it is warm enough to step under.

And then I take my shower.

The spray works its way into my hair, plastering it to my face and shoulders and back, and I rotate my neck, massaging my scalp beneath the thin jets. It feels strange to be showering with my dress on, but not unpleasant. I may do it more often.

There is a full bottle of shampoo in the cupboard beneath the sink, so I step out of the tray momentarily to retrieve it and then, back under the shower, I apply a liberal dose first to my hair and next to the infected areas on my dress. I stand and let the shower do its job. Flecks of vomit, caught in the gloopy shampoo like flies in tree sap, peel away from my dress and drop to the tray, where they are spun in the whirlpool at my feet and sucked down the plughole. I leave the drainage tap for the waste water tank permanently open, so all this dirt should be outside soon, dripping on to the grass, soaking into the mud, fertilising the weeds.

I reach out to pick up the duvet cover from the floor and bring it into the shower, lathering it in shampoo and rinsing it through beneath the tap. Soon it is clean, and so is my dress, and so am I. I turn the shower off, reach for my towel hung on the door, and freeze. There above the towel, above the door, straddling the thin length of plastic moulding which joins the wall to the ceiling, is a spider.

It is enormous.

I breathe, long and deep. Control the panic. Remember something Dad once said. That a spider like this – not in a web, not hiding, but in full view, alone – a spider like this is not looking for food or for a place to live, but is looking for sex. Remember the impression Dad did of a randy spider. Remember how I laughed so hard that I thought I might have laughed away my fear.

I look back up at the spider above the door. My fear is as present as ever. I try to imagine Dad's face on its little head, the way his eyes squinted and his mouth puckered into a circle, imagine those long, horrible legs doing the funny bendy dance Dad did as part of the impression, but it is not funny now, if anything it is the opposite, and I have to stop imagining it because the panic is building and I know I have to do something about it.

I have two options. Fight or flight. I could blast it with water from the tap, but there is no guarantee that would kill it. It might fall into the shower tray, and then there would be nothing to stop it sprinting towards me, climbing on to my foot, crawling up my leg . . .

The thought is too painful to pursue. I must run. This

is the only option. I reach out my hand and, as gently as I can, open the door. My eyes never leave the spider. To my immense relief, it does not move. The door is open. All I have to do is step out, back into the main living space. I will shut the door behind me, seal the spider off, never think of it again. It will die long before I go back into the bathroom.

I keep breathing, long and deep. My departure must be swift, for I will pass directly beneath the spider. Smooth and silent. I take one last look at the creature, close my eyes and launch.

Something goes wrong. I should have kept my eyes open. I misjudge my trajectory and my right shoulder connects with the door frame as I pass through it. There is a thud of flesh on wood and the caravan shakes. On the thin line of scalp where my hair parts, I feel movement.

All I can do is scream and run.

I do not know how I open the caravan door, and I barely notice the duvet hanging from the tree as I race past it through the woods and alongside the Cafy, I do not check for traffic before sprinting over the road and across the grass, and once I am at the lip it is not conscious thought which makes me twirl around and around like a one-winged butterfly, not reason which makes me whip my wet hair about, lashing my face and shoulders as it flies out and around and back again, making my neck ache and my body dizzy and senseless, none of this is planned, none of this is a process. I am merely reactive. Instinctual. Unthinking. And when I finally come to a stop, panting and footsore, when I finally have not so much the courage but the exhaustion to halt and to cautiously run my fingers through my hair and then over my body, checking every inch and finding nothing, when I finally allow myself to think once more, to understand and acknowledge that the spider is no longer upon me, if it ever was in the first place, when I finally feel my heart rate slowing and my adrenaline receding and can feel the wash of relief and can look about me, it is only then that I see the emmet standing there in front of me, and it is only then that I recognise him as the same pockmarked old man wearing the same sling with the same dog, Archie, wearing the same saddlebags.

The man is staring at me. It is a replica of the stare he gave me yesterday morning, only heightened – more piercing, more wide-eyed, more intense. This time it does not bother me in the least. With all the spinning and running and whipping I feel like I have done away not just with the spider, but with my fear of it, and I begin to laugh, to laugh at myself and at the man too, laugh right in his face, my eyes locked on his, stepping closer to him and laughing louder still. This makes Archie start to bark and wag his tail, which spurs me on, and so I throw my head back and shout, 'The randy spider!' and I begin to do Dad's dance, right there on the lip.

I find it enormously gratifying when, this time, it is the man who hurries away rather than me.

I dance some more. I try to sing too. Once, when I asked Mum how she had chosen my name, she said, 'It came to us the moment we first laid eyes on you. You were our little song.'

I may be a song but I am no singer. I am comfortable within the smallest range of notes: any time I try to soar from them, from melody to harmony, my voice breaks and I have to retreat to my comfort zone. Not like Mum. Mum is an incredible singer. She can switch from one octave to another with ease, leaping back and forth between them.

I stop. My wet dress clings to my body and I begin to shiver in sudden bursts. I walk away from the lip, across the road, past the Cafy and through the woods to my caravan. I make sure the spider is definitely not in the bathroom any more and then, when I see it is gone, I lock the door behind me and change my clothes. It is Wednesday. I will stay inside today. I will do very little. Doze. Read. Remember.

At times like this, when I allow myself the luxury of memory, it surprises me that I do not immediately return to that night. Instead, that memory, the memory of the drop, of the climb down, of the helicopter searchlight, that memory comes to me unbidden and when I least expect it. More often than not, I am powerless to dispel it. But today I should like to remember the caravan itself, remember its journey to the woods and not her journey down to the black sand.

Little Sister Lucy and I moved into the caravan after Dad died and Mum disappeared. We could not stay at the house in St Petroc. It made us angry.

The caravan has been in my family – to my mind, a part of our family – for ten years, long before Little Sister Lucy came along. Dad bought it the year after Ground Zero because the season's profits had been sensational: he called that one the Year of Living Splendidly. I remember that, when we closed the Cafy in October, we were out in the caravan at every opportunity. Sometimes Mum and Dad would wait for me outside school on a Friday afternoon, the caravan already packed and hitched to the back of the car. I loved being picked up like that.

We never went far. We did not need to. Cornwall had enough to offer, some hidden gems and some not so hidden, but gems nonetheless. Whether we went over the estuary or along the tranquil south coast or to the cold lakes on the moor, it did not especially matter where we were, because the joy of it all came from being in the caravan. These were my favourite times. Not visiting old mines and museums; not charity-shopping in deserted towns; not watching Dad strip down to his pants and run towards the sea and then run faster back to his clothes after dipping no more than a foot in the waves.

All that was enjoyable, but never as enjoyable as the evenings when, after dinner around the table, we would close all the curtains, transform the couches into the bed, and watch films on Mum's laptop.

We never used the caravan again, as a family, after that winter. When the Cafy reopened the following spring, we wheeled it into our garden out of the way of the drive. That was when it became a problem. First, our next-door neighbours, the Roscarracks, decided to sell their house. Then they employed Paul Dunstan's dad to paint it before putting it up for sale. He started to make unfunny jokes about gypsies and travellers camped out in our garden – we all heard the way he cackled while they stood in their drive together looking over at the caravan. And the jokes ignited some kernel of fear in the Roscarracks, whose minds had become fixated on valuations and equity. One evening, not long after I had gone to bed, they came round to have a conversation with Mum and Dad. I crept out on to the landing and listened to it and then, after they left, I listened to the next conversation between Mum and Dad.

'Affecting the value of their property? Were they serious?'

'Ignore them, Trev. It's all nonsense.'

'I know what they're doing. Being greedy. Trying to squeeze as much money out of their house as they can.'

'Right. So don't let it get to you.'

'Probably trying to sell it as a second home. Make a fortune.'

'Exactly. When you think about it, if we *are* lowering the price, we're helping keep it affordable for a local family.'

Dad laughed at that, and I thought Mum had convinced him to ignore the Roscarracks, to put them out of his mind. She knew what she was doing. But Paul Dunstan's dad kept making his jokes, louder and louder, and then he started making them directly to Dad's face whenever he saw him outside the house, and Dad would stand there and laugh along half-heartedly with his hands in his pockets, and I realised then that adults could be bullied too. Before long, the caravan was hitched to the back of the car and driven down to the Cafy.

Dad left it in the car park. He had a plan, he told us, to transform the caravan into our very own staffroom. Though I was too young then to work there myself, I still liked the idea. There is no space for rest inside the Cafy, which has a kitchen, a bar, a dining room, two toilets, a subterranean storeroom and nothing more. I offered to help Dad clean the caravan out and make it comfortable, but he soon grew unhappy with the new location, and this time Mum agreed with him. The caravan was taking up a valuable parking space. Less parking meant less business, and that was our lifeblood. The caravan, they decided, would have to go.

By that time, I was beginning to explore and map out my land, from the nuanced contours of the lip to the extremities of Nare Point and The Warren, and deep into Trethewas Woods behind it all. I knew of a wonderful spot in these woods, a clearing just large enough to accommodate the caravan, and just close enough for us to still use it as a viable staffroom. I led Dad there.

'This is perfect, Melody Janie, absolutely perfect. But how on earth do you propose we get the caravan in here?'

'I think we need to ask Mum.'

'I think,' Dad said, 'that you're right.'

Mum likes to joke that she can solve any problem except her own. And it is true that, when she is well, I always turn to her if I am weighed down by a tough decision or dilemma. Dad was the ideas man of the family, but Mum is the solution-monger. I take after Dad too much: I have his love of stories, of the wild; but I also have his flakiness, his tendency towards flight and dreams. I wish I was more like Mum, even despite her disorder – I wish I had her boldness, her will, wish I could solve problems and make decisions with her levels of clarity and confidence.

'Easy,' she said as she looked at the clearing, one arm around Dad and the other around me. 'We can make a path.' She smiled, and we believed her.

'We'll need a machete,' Dad said.

'It's Trethewas Woods, Trev, not the Amazon.'

When she is well, Mum is the best.

We drove back to the house in St Petroc and gathered all the gardening tools we could fit into the boot of the car, a bent and rusting array of trowels and rakes and spades and hoes. Dad threw in a saw and some of the larger kitchen knives and we set off back to the Cafy and the caravan.

Clearing the path took us the best part of three days. It was hard work, and we appeared from the woods at the end of each shift with scratched arms, sore backs and our clothes drenched in sweat. But it was inescapably fun. We all agreed. We sang call and response songs made up by Dad as we hacked and stamped and chopped and uprooted; we told stupid jokes which punned on anything we could see.

'Conifer? I never even met her.'

'Leaf it out, Dad.'

'He's trying to branch out into comedy.'

The path, when we completed it, was rough and uneven and meandered its way around the immoveable trees, but the circuitous route Mum had plotted was a good one – Dad towed the caravan into and through the woods while Mum, in front of him and walking backwards, guided him on. The caravan glided through the trees without even a scratch from a circumspect twig.

The clearing was a perfect fit. It almost looked as if the caravan had grown there, grown from some strange mechanical seedling. To our dismay, we discovered that the hook-up cable was not long enough to reach the Cafy, which meant we could not plug it in and power the caravan's electrics. But Mum had a solution for that too. She piled us all into the car and drove us down to the marine store, where she bought an assortment of solar panels. Working as a team, we were able to install them on the caravan's roof, where they caught enough sunlight each day to make the electrics, and the caravan, self-sufficient. I set to work cleaning up the little gas cooker in case any of us wanted to boil a kettle or make snacks while we were on our breaks and Dad bought four large bottles of gas from the garage, all of which fitted into the storage compartment in the front of the caravan. 'This will last years,' Mum said.

And she was right. It has.

I sleep and wake and sleep and wake. Light shifts to dark, but I am rooted to my bed, made concrete by inactivity. I do not dream. I know it is raining by the soft but insistent drum roll against the caravan roof. I breathe, long and deep.

It is thirst which finally stirs me, working its way into my consciousness, sending cracks and fissures through my bones, chipping and crumbling and breaking away at the rocks which anchor me to my bed. I swing a heavy arm over the mattress – the duvet, I recall, is still hung up outside – in search of my water bottle. I find it and bring it close to my mouth. It is empty.

I have to get up.

I roll out of bed, my legs stiff and feet delicate as I plant them on the floor. I retrieve one of the 5-litre bottles from the bathroom, take it to the sink in the kitchenette, fill my small bottle, drink it in one, fill it again. I am wide awake now. I put on my coat and step outside. The night is sharp but still, the duvet wet as I pull it from the tree and toss it back inside the caravan.

A large moon is out, low – it fires up the contours of the lip, drawing me on, across the spongy grass, over the barrier, to dead centre. I stand in position, my feet fixed and unerring. Below, the tide is mid-level, its swells minimal yet enough to create a maelstrom of eddies and swirls as it washes in and out of the submerged cave at the base of the cliff. I imagine us, never found, still in there, suspended in the dark water, arms stretched out, limp bodies ripped back and forth across the roof of the cave.

That we were found was no stroke of luck: my telephone call from inside the Cafy gave them the location. But that they came in time was a marvel of fortune. They did not save her life – how could they? – but they saved mine. With the tide advancing, I had no way out, no way but up, and I do not doubt that, had I been forced to try, I would have fallen long before reaching the safety of the lip. Not that I would have left her. Never.

The helicopter neared as the man swam to shore, following him with its beam of light. Even once he reached and entered the cave, he had to shout to be heard over the whirr of the blades. But there was nothing frantic about his raised voice. His demands and orders were calm and measured, devoid of any trace of anxiety. I never felt that I was being rushed, and I recall being surprised at that even then.

'Are you hurt?' was his first question.

I shook my head.

'Who is she?' was his second.

I shook my head again.

He knelt on the black sand next to me. 'Do you know her?' He no longer needed to shout.

I kept my head still.

Gently, he placed his hand beneath one of her shoulders and began to turn her. I pounced then, grabbing his hand in my own and tearing it away from her. He made no resistance as I pushed him back and away.

'I want to help her,' he said.

'You can't.' My voice was reed-thin, an awful croak of finality.

'I want to help you too.' He moved slowly towards me and placed his hand on my forearm. 'Please,' he said. 'Who is she?'

I took his hand from my arm and placed it back on her shoulder. 'My little sister,' I whispered, sinking down into the black sand. 'She's my Little Sister Lucy.'

After Dad died and Mum disappeared, it was just Little Sister Lucy and me. We were only a month into the season, and we did our best, together, to keep the Cafy open. I should have known then the impossibility of the task. I had only recently turned nineteen, and Little Sister Lucy was just a child: a gorgeous and lovable child, but a child nonetheless. There were times when she would need more than I could give, times when I felt like I was breaking, like *she* was breaking me, and it took all my strength to shield her from that. She pushed me into an adulthood I was not quite ready for and I used to get angry, then, with Mum, for not being here. For leaving me with someone so helpless.

But we tried. As hopeless as we both were without our parents, we still tried. We told each other we were doing it for *him*, more of a ritual or tradition than an attempt to earn money, a loving but futile nod to Dad's legacy. Yet we both knew, without ever saying it to each other, that we were doing it for *her*. She would come back, come back when she was better, of that I was certain, and when she did we would be sure to have the Cafy still running for her.

Now, at the other end of the season, it strikes me as nothing short of incredible that we managed to keep it open as long as we did, though it has to be admitted that the poor weather and lack of tourists, of trade, helped in its own way. Little Sister Lucy and I could never have contended with another Year of Living Splendidly. We simply were not equipped. Without Dad, maybe. Without Mum, absolutely not.

Not that it mattered. We closed months ago.

I turn away from the lip and walk back to the Cafy. Inside, I refill my water bottle and then ghostwalk to the dining room. My favourite feature of the Cafy is and always has been the series of enormous floor-to-ceiling windows which fronts both the dining room and the bar. All my land ahead of the Cafy, the entire stretch of lip from the western to the eastern headland, is visible from these windows. Now, with the moon vanished and supplanted by cloud cover there is nothing to see but enveloping darkness, and so I retreat to remembered views, to one of the most spectacular.

The skyscapes that afternoon were exceptional. I had been cleaning tables; Little Sister Lucy had been playing with her doll in the kitchen, dreamily floating it in the towering bubbles of the filled sink. I called her to me so that we might sit together and watch the window show: watch the clouds on the horizon bulge and then burst into thick and grey sheets of rainfall; watch the seagulls as they fought the wind in the vain hope of a safe landing, their wings trembling, their sudden trajectories haphazard and impossible to predict, like the path of a bluebottle; watch the mounting swells as the waves crawled and built and broke, pure Atlantic energy, counting the sets, always seven and seven and seven more; watch the whole natural drama without a word until it was lunchtime and we were brought back to our bodies by hunger.

'Cornish Chow Mein?' I suggested.

Little Sister Lucy laughed. The story had happened before her time, but she knew it well.

Cornish Chow Mein was one of Dad's stranger brainwaves. During the Year of Living Dangerously, business became so bad that we even had to drop our perennial bestseller, the cream tea, from the menu. The clotted cream spoiled faster than we could sell it and storing it in the freezer ruined it. Dad decided we needed to change tactics. Fresh food was a waste of money. Instead, we would focus on the tinned, the dried and the frozen. Beans on toast went to the top of the mains menu (at, I remember, a discounted 'summer price'); fruit cocktail in ice cream at the top of the desserts. We got creative. Meat pies, the kind you get in a tin the shape of a Frisbee, were Flat Pasties. Meatballs, chopped frankfurters and thinly-sliced Spam constituted the Tapas Platter. Ravioli was just Ravioli, but it came with our Famous Fiery Bones Break Topping – in reality, half and half desiccated Parmesan and chilli powder. And then, at the very bottom of the barrel, came Dad's Cornish Chow Mein.

I have often wondered how we ever recovered from the Year of Living Dangerously. Perhaps it is because we have always relied mostly on passing trade, which can make things tough when the weather is poor and visitor numbers are low, but is an advantage when you do not have to worry about reputation. Of the few people who ate with us that year, fewer left satisfied. The Flat Pasties never seemed to receive any complaints, and the Famous Fiery Bones Break Topping was surprisingly popular, but, if we had ever had a local customer base, the Cornish Chow Mein surely would have been the end of it, and of us.

'Do you remember?' Little Sister Lucy said, giggling through her words. 'Do you remember that man?'

'Of course I remember,' I said, imperious, for I had been there and she had not. The Year of Living Dangerously was pre-Little Sister Lucy. But I played along, pretended she was, because she knew the story as well as if she had been a part of it. Mum had repeated it often. 'How could I forget?' I continued, before launching into my impression. 'Eight pounds? *Eight pounds?* For *this*?'

'And then Dad said . . .' The laughter began to take over, infecting me as much as it did Little Sister Lucy. 'He said . . .' But it was too much, she could not speak. I took over.

'And then Dad said, "But you get to keep the chopsticks".'

Little Sister Lucy screamed with delight. Her hair bounced over her shoulders with each heaving guffaw. 'Chopsticks!' she squealed. 'Chopsticks!'

'Let's have some,' I said. 'For lunch.'

'Really?' Little Sister Lucy's eyes widened. She loved it when I fed her.

'We might as well. We've got enough of the stuff.'

I walked through to the kitchen, where I took out two plates and then opened the drawer beneath the pile of Mum's clothes where we keep the chopsticks. I still do not know where Dad bought them from. Perhaps he ordered them online. All I know is that he spent weeks hand-painting little Cornish piskies on to each. He was convinced the Chow Mein would be a bestseller and was equally certain that people would start to come in just to buy the chopsticks themselves. That was why he ordered and then painted so many. The drawer is still full of them.

I filled and boiled the kettle before descending the stairs which lead from the kitchen to the subterranean storeroom below it. I have never liked it down there. It is cold and it is dark and the gigantic chest freezers can make a whining noise like a dying animal. Ever since the electricity was cut off, the smell has grown unbearable. I did not stay long. All I needed were the ingredients for the Cornish Chow Mein and they were as quick to locate as the dish was quick to make. I opened the designated cupboard. Inside were the five hundred beef-flavoured supermarket-brand pot noodles Dad bought all those years ago, shy of perhaps a few dozen at most.

I remember Dad proudly revealing this new stash to me and Mum for the first time, his face almost maniacal with glee as the cupboard doors swung open, the stacked rows of pots upon pots and then more pots above and beneath and behind in all their homogenous grandeur. He took three up to the kitchen, filled them with boiling water, stirred and then upended them on to three separate plates: one for him, one for Mum, one for me. 'Cornish Chow Mein,' he said as he handed us our chopsticks, pointing out the piskies upon each. Then he hoisted a knot of noodles into his mouth, smacked his lips and bellowed with theatrical delight, 'C'est magnifique!'

Mum took a smaller mouthful. 'Trev,' she said after chewing slowly. 'Are you trying to put me back in the hospital?' She and I howled with laughter.

I made the Cornish Chow Mein in the kitchen and took it through to the dining room. Little Sister Lucy was still giggling, repeating the word 'chopsticks' and shaking her head.

I have ripped my dress along the hem. It must have happened when I ran from the spider. If I do not fix it soon the tear will grow and trip me. I return to the caravan, find my sewing kit behind the first aid box in one of the overhead storage units, and take it outside.

The sun has risen. A blanket of cloud fills the sky, but there is a semblance of warmth in the air, enough at least for me to sit on one of the wooden benches in front of the Cafy. I retrieve a needle and thread from the kit and set to work on the tear. I am ambivalent about sewing – it neither interests nor irritates me – yet I find myself grateful for it when the emmet appears in silhouette on the eastern headland. The sewing allows me to observe him without appearing to. My mind, he may think, is elsewhere.

He stops and I can see that he is facing me. I know it is him, recognise the sling. I continue sewing, exaggerating the movements of my arm as the needle goes in and comes back out again to make it clear that I am occupied, that I am not watching him as he appears to be watching me. Archie emerges from a thicket of bracken and walks towards the emmet's legs, looking out to sea, studying the banks and swoops of the seagulls. The man moves forward along the coast path, stops, and then moves again, inching his way towards dead centre, his face turned always in my direction.

He reaches the road and crosses it. He is coming here. I keep on sewing. Archie sees me and breaks ahead, trotting across the road and appearing at my side with his tongue out. His tail does not wag, but he holds it up high. It is clear that he wants to be friends. I reach out my hand and he leans in to sniff it. Satisfied that I smell acceptable, he burrows his soaking nose into my palm.

'This is Archie,' the emmet says. He has stopped on the other side of the furthest wooden bench and hovers there nervously.

I do not say that I already know his name. Instead, I ask, 'What kind is he?'

'A labradoodle.'

'What?'

'A mix. Half Labrador, half poodle. Labradoodle.'

I laugh in spite of myself. Labradoodle is a funny word. I say it to Archie, who rubs his head underneath my leg. I stroke his back, running my fingers through his blond, tangled curls. He seems to like it most when I scratch around and beneath the straps of his saddlebags.

'Why does he have bags?' I ask.

'Security,' the emmet says. And then, 'Do you work here?'

'Yes.' I am still stroking Archie, who has placed his

chin on my thigh and closes his eyes when I play with his ears. 'It's my family's.'

'Is it open?'

'Would you like something?'

'No, I just . . .' He pauses. I look up from Archie to him and see that his free hand has begun to fidget, running itself up and down the zipper of his coat. 'I don't want anything. I just thought it was closed.'

'It is.'

'Ah,' he says. 'Right.'

'Are you enjoying your holiday?' I ask.

'My what?'

I do not know how to answer that question, so I try another of my own. 'Do you like it here?'

'Yes, I do. I didn't think I would at first. But it's growing on me.'

'Why did you come if you didn't think you'd like it?'

'This is where I walk Archie.'

'No, I mean . . .' His responses seem to be growing increasingly confusing. I wonder if this man is some kind of riddler, the sort that never gives a straight answer. I reword my question. 'I mean, why did you come here for a holiday if you didn't think you'd like it?'

'I'm not on holiday,' he says. 'I live here.'

'You live here?' Impossible. Nobody lives here. Bones Break is my land. I am its sole resident.

'Yes.'

'Where?'

'Look. I . . . I just wanted to check that you were all

right. After Archie found you in the bushes on Tuesday. And then, you know, after yesterday morning.' His fidgeting worsens. He cannot look at me. His gaze fixes on Archie.

'Where do you live?'

'And you clearly are. All right, I mean. I'll leave you be.'

He turns and walks away, over the road and back towards the lip. Archie reluctantly detaches himself from my stroking and scratching and trots after the man. Together they cross the western headland and push on towards Lantoweth. The man never looks back. But Archie does. More than once.

Why did he say that he lives here? He could not have meant it. Perhaps his use of 'here' is not the same as mine. For me, here is Bones Break. Who knows what here means to him? Lantoweth? Petherick? Perhaps the entire stretch of coast between both? Perhaps, simply, Cornwall?

The questions nag, crystallising into the early spikes of a headache. I need to unearth the truth. I need to know where he lives. Because if it is here, then it means that what Dad and I feared has begun. The emmets are starting to spread up from Petherick and on to my land.

I cannot let that happen.

I consider possibilities. He was on his way west, yet it is unlikely he lives in Lantoweth. There are few houses in that direction. Instead, it is more probable that he lives east, perhaps in Petherick. If so, he should be returning sometime soon, passing back through Bones Break on his walk with Archie. It has not rained at all today and the wind is low. These are perfect conditions for the shelf. If I wait there, on that particular hideaway down the cliff face, he may stop on the western headland and, like others before him, he may say something revealing. Any information, no matter how small, is important. I make my way to the western headland, past the signpost and over the barrier, sit, swing my legs over the lip and lower myself down the shelf. To wait.

I often wonder if I might be the only human to have touched this shelf, this exact piece of rock. Others have seen it, that is certain. Though it is invisible from anywhere on the lip except directly above and requires leaning right out to look down on to it, it is in full sight of any who happen to be on, or in, the water ahead. I once wore my orange dress while I sat here. A boat came past, small enough to skirt the rocks below, and then the engine was cut and I heard voices shouting and saw people on the deck waving at me. I know they were only trying to help, telling me *not to do it*, but I was angry with them notwithstanding. They had seen me. I pulled myself up on to the lip and hurried back to the caravan. Since then, I make sure to wear only dark blue or grey clothes whenever I visit the shelf.

Today, I choose to lie with my head to the west and my feet to the east. From this aspect, I have an immaculate view of Bones Break. Seabirds gather on Gull Rock, patting their orange feet over the layer of white excrement which caps the summit; settling into their regimented positions, wing to wing; staring into the wash of ocean below. One slips a little, finds its footing on the head of a lower bird and then launches from it into the air. It circles Gull Rock three times, descending with each revolution, before changing its mind and heading instead to the quieter cliff face only a few metres from me. Away from the mob, it finds its perch and tucks itself in, shaking its head from side to side as it backs into the rock. Its feathers are still brown, and as the wind ruffles them I can see the fuzz at their tips. It is young, a tired baby, unaccustomed to the territoriality of Gull Rock.

The bark makes me jump: I physically rise from the shelf by an inch. Or some of me does. An elbow and a hip.

Two more barks. I flatten on to my back, partly from instinct, partly to look upwards at the source of the noise. I recognise the head instantly. It is Archie. I smile and wave at him. He barks once more and then pants, his tongue long and speckled by black dots, dripping with stringy saliva. I can hear the emmet behind him.

'Archie. Come away from there. Archie. Come.'

I do not worry. The emmet will not look over the lip, will not see me. He will assume Archie is barking at a bird, will be concerned only that his dog has strayed too close to the edge. It will not even cross his mind that a person, me, could be down here.

'Archie, come.'

Archie whines, frustrated. I stay silent and feel guilty for it. He just wants to play, or maybe to check that I am uninjured. I like Archie. I give him another wave and this seems to satisfy him. The head disappears. Crunching footsteps slowly recede. They are leaving.

I learned nothing.

It is growing cold now. Cloud has blanketed the sky, the sun long since disappeared behind it. I begin to shiver. Movement will warm me, but I do not want to go back to the caravan. The lure of the lip is strong. The tide is high and the swells powerful, waves crashing and rolling beneath me. It is a good morning to spy.

An idea sparkles. Something I could do, something I have never done before.

I could follow. Track. Let him lead me right to his door.

Am I capable? With my network of hideaways, I have perfected the art of observation that is silent and still. But to pursue, to hunt, will demand a whole new set of skills: the ability to move unseen and unheard, to maintain the secrecy of my presence. The noise of the waves below will obscure my footsteps, but the cover is minimal. Were the emmet to turn around, to look behind, he would see and almost certainly recognise me.

I push myself to my feet, place my hands on the lip and slowly raise my head over the top, my eyes at ankle level. I can see both the emmet and Archie, the latter leading the way as they walk towards the eastern headland, saddlebags bouncing gently at his sides. He stops to sniff at some bracken and the emmet walks past him until, a few metres beyond, he turns and commands Archie to come. The emmet is facing me, but he does not see me, a disembodied head floating above the lip. My confidence swells.

I wait for them both to round the eastern headland and leave my land, disappearing from sight. As quick as I can, I heave myself up on to the lip and run, keeping to the coast path as it follows the curve of Bones Break and winds out to the edge of the eastern headland. Then I stop and crouch. I must keep low. It will be to my advantage. Archie and the emmet are still ahead, still on the path. Soon they will pass over the rise between here and Nare Point and, beyond that, will disappear from view again. When it happens, I dart forward, sprinting until I reach the rise. Once there, I sink to the ground and crawl forward to peek over the crest, the soft mud of the coast path caressing my palms and shins.

I can see them. They have almost reached Nare Point. There is a motorhome there, a large one, and I watch as they walk around and behind it. The moment they disappear, I am on my feet again, running towards Nare Point, desperate not to lose them.

I reach the motorhome. It is enormous, a giant, and it seems to have extra rooms extending out from its flanks, swellings with perfect right angles. All the windows – the dozen or more that there are – have been shut and curtains drawn, though there is noise coming from within. Music. An electric guitar, high-pitched and elaborate. I walk around the van and peer out from around it to see the emmet and Archie step out of the car park and on to the road. I feel a moment of conflict – this motorhome is new, I have never seen it before, I should observe it, for who knows who is inside and what plans they have for my land? But there is no time. I look around the van again. Archie and the emmet are out of sight. I cannot let them go. Not yet.

I must find out where he lives, even if I have to follow him all the way to Petherick. This hunt has become everything, and I must maintain it for as long as I can, no matter where it leads me.

I make my way through the car park and tiptoe out on to the road. The emmet has put a lead on Archie and the two of them walk quickly along the side of the road. A car speeds past. The emmet dips his head and pulls Archie close to his legs. Just before the road curves out of view, the pair hurry to the other side and walk through the gate which leads to Mrs Perrow's house.

Is that where they live?

The need to know overwhelms me. I charge forward, crossing the road and then keeping to its very edge in case more cars should come. I reach the house. The gate is closed but easy to open. I step through, and I look up.

And then I see him.

'You've had your fun. Let's put an end to it here.' The emmet stands in the porch, the door to the house open behind him. His free hand holds Archie on a taut lead.

'You knew I was following you?' A stupid thing to say.

'It's broad daylight. Do you think I haven't been followed before?'

'I don't know. Have you?'

He snorts. 'So now you know where I live. Wonderful. Absolutely wonderful. And I suppose you'll tell everyone.'

'Why?'

'Because that's what you do, isn't it? That's what all of you do. You can't bear to leave a man in peace.'

'I won't tell anyone. Why would I?'

He does not answer.

'I like to be left alone too,' I say.

His face softens slightly. His eyes fall from my own and travel down to my neck, to my bare, mud-stained arms. 'Aren't you cold?'

'I'm okay.'

A gust of wind punctuates the silence as we stand for a moment, looking at each other but not directly, never directly.

'Well, I can't invite you in.'

'I don't want to come in.'

'And no photos.'

'I don't want photos.'

'Then what do you want?'

I want him to leave, to leave my land now and never come back. But the words will not form. I can't find them. I wish Mum were here. She would tell him. She wouldn't hesitate.

'What do you want?' he repeats.

I try to think of something, anything, to say. When it finally comes, it surprises even me. 'Can I stroke Archie?'

The emmet pauses, caught off guard perhaps. 'I suppose so.'

I begin to walk forward, up the path which cuts through the garden, the overgrown tendrils of weeds tickling my ankles as I pass.

'No,' he says. 'Wait there. I'll bring him to you.'

I stop. They advance. Archie's tail wags harder the closer he gets. He makes little jumps with his front paws. I reach out my hand and he leaps into it, wriggling and twisting and pushing himself against me with glee, panting and licking and wrapping me up in his lead as he slaloms through my legs. I rub his head and scratch his nose and he emits a grumble of satisfaction.

'You like Archie, don't you?' the man says.

'He's nice.'

'Yes. Yes, he is.'

Archie sits down, resting his bottom on my left foot. He is warm and heavy.

'I'm Melody Janie, by the way,' I say.

'Pleased to meet you, Melody Janie. I'm Richard. Richard Brown.'

I extend my hand. He takes it, grips weakly and then lets go. Released, I bend down to stroke Archie's back.

'He likes you,' Richard says. 'That's rare.'

'I like him.'

Richard looks at me for a long time. And then he says, 'You don't recognise me, do you?'

I stare at him, deep scrutiny, searching for familiarity. Pockmarks rise from his neck to cover the lower half of his face, dotting his jaw and chin and the lines about his mouth. The closer I look at them, the more I realise how large they are, like dents left in butter by a child's fingers. If I were a man with pockmarks so striking, I would grow my beard to hide them. But perhaps he cannot – either that or he is clean-shaven. I can see no stubble at all. The hair on his head is full but short, grey all over. He is a thin man. I can see from the outline of his clothes how they hang off him. They are old clothes; his woollen jumper has rips across the belly and down the free arm. His other arm, I realise now, is not just bound by a sling, but wrapped from his wrist to his elbow in a thick, dirty-white cast. He is at least a foot taller than me and, though he is thin and no younger than sixty, I imagine him to be capable of surprising strength. He looks like how I picture Colonel Aureliano Buendía. He stands straight. His boots are filthy.

'No. I don't recognise you,' I say. 'Why? Do you recognise me?'

He looks relieved. 'I don't recognise you either. I'm pleased to say.'

I feel suddenly awkward here, not unwelcome in this space but somehow unfit for it. 'I think it's time for me to go home now,' I say. 'Goodbye, Mr Brown.'

'Goodbye, Melody Janie.'

I give Archie one final stroke, turn and walk back through the gate and on to the road. At Nare Point, I can still hear the music trilling out from the gargantuan motorhome, but I have no inclination to stop. A question haunts me.

You don't recognise me, do you?

My duvet lies in a heap at the door. I pick it up: it no longer smells of vomit but of the woods. I lay it out across the bed. I make my way to the kitchenette, find a tin of baked beans in one of the cupboards and open it, eat the beans straight from the can, cold. I think of Richard Brown, his bizarre question looping, rebounding off the cave walls of my mind like an endless set of waves.

You don't recognise me, do you?

Should I have recognised him? I try hard to, to place him, to fit that pockmarked face into some sort of context. I scan memories of past schoolteachers and old men, neighbours, from the streets and houses of St Petroc, imagine him peering out at me from backlit, ground floor windows, or encountering him on the wide sands of Lantoweth, or brushing shoulders with him as one of us entered and the other exited a Petherick shop. For a moment, I think I see him there, in the summer crowds of Petherick, one tourist in the thousands which invade the village every season. But I know it is just the reaching of a feverish brain, a brain connecting me and him, local and emmet, a brain trying to convince itself of that which it knows is not true.

What is true, what remains true, no matter how hard I try, is the implacable knowledge that I do not recognise Richard Brown. That the first time I saw him, the first time in my life, was two days ago, when Archie surprised me out of the bush-den.

So why did he ask if I recognised him?

I sigh at the impenetrability of it all. I wish that Mum were here, a sounding board to batter with my curiosity. She would have known who he was, she knows everything, and even if she did not, she would have found out. She would have stopped at nothing until she unearthed the truth. Dad, on the other hand, would have been no help whatsoever. I remember one of his favourite phrases.

'All emmets look the same to me.'

They all look the same to me too. Abominable.

I know that my hatred of emmets comes from Dad. He was pro-independence, voted Mebyon Kernow, had a tattoo of the Cornish flag – the white cross, the *Baner Peran* – on his right shoulder. He started (but never finished) an online course in beginner's Kernewek, and he had a way of spitting the word 'emmet' with such vitriol that Mum often chastised him for it.

'If you hate the tourists so much, why on earth are you in the tourism industry?'

'What else have we got down here? Everything else has gone, all that's left is to beg for scraps, pander to the emmets.'

'That's such an ugly word. At least call them holidaymakers.'

'Emmets is the perfect word for them. Do you know what it means, Melody Janie?'

'Ants,' I replied. Mum frowned; Dad beamed.

This hatred is not unique to our little family. In St Petroc, a working town for working Cornish, mass tourism has never been much of an issue, but in Petherick – where thousands of visitors descend every summer season, more and more each year, and where every other property is a holiday let or second home –

the simmering rage of the locals has spilled over into violence more than once: fights outside the pub; scuffles in the streets; even punch-ups in the sea when ignorant emmets have refused to respect the surfers' etiquette.

The most extreme incident, one which got Petherick into the national newspapers, was the time when Paul Dunstan's dad ended up in prison. A group of young men, university students in their early twenties, were renting one of the holiday lets overlooking the harbour. They were loud and they were arrogant and they drank too much and played noisy games of football on the beach. One evening in the pub, after complaining about the food and the price of the beer – yet drinking copious amounts of it nonetheless – they began to make horribly inappropriate comments to the waitress, a fifteen-year-old local girl. The comments turned into suggestions and the suggestions turned into demands and then finally one of the young men touched her. When the landlord saw her crying and found out why he told them to leave and never return. They smashed their pint glasses on the floor and pushed him on their way out.

That night, a mob of twenty locals descended on the holiday apartment. They broke in through a window and beat the young men so badly that two of them were hospitalised. The only people who admitted to taking part in the mob were the girl's father and Paul Dunstan's. They both went to court and, though they refused to name any of their accomplices, they were frank and graphic about their own involvement. The girl's father escaped a prison sentence but, due to previous trouble, Paul Dunstan's father did not.

There was plenty of hate at school too, plenty of boasts about torching cars with London registration plates, of beating up holidaymakers in Newquay, of beating up students in Treleven – but I suspect it was mostly nonsense. The one verified act of subversion was the time when Paul Dunstan – almost certainly in homage to his father, who had recently started his prison sentence – spray-painted LOCALS ONLY on Petherick's harbour wall. For the rest of that term, PSHE lessons focused on tolerance and equal rights.

'Tolerance? Equal rights?' Dad had been incensed when I told him. 'We'd bloody *welcome* equal rights down here – we're the ones without them! The poorest county in all England, and we're supposed to be *tolerant*?'

It was not mere bluster. Dad knew, as I know, that Cornwall needs tourists, that it would starve without them. But he also knew, as I know, the truth beneath that. Cornwall is impoverished, that is plain to see. But we Cornish did not bring it upon ourselves. We did not spend and consume everything and then whine for the handout of tourism. No. It was the emmets who did it to us. When they closed our mines and gave away our fishing rights they stripped us of any means of self-sufficiency, made us reliant upon their charity, so that when they turned Cornwall into their own glorified holiday park we were supposed to welcome it with simpering gratitude, and open our arms to everyone from beyond the Tamar.

That's why, although I am no fan of Petherick, I can understand why the people do what they do, why they feel how they feel. They are marginalised within their own village, too poor to keep the houses their families have lived in for generations, forced out so that some emmet and his family can have a second home by the sea and use it for four weeks a year.

A necessary evil, that's the phrase. I have even heard emmets themselves use it. 'Well, it's a shame, but we're a necessary evil.' They place the emphasis on the word 'necessary', as if the positivity of this can somehow outweigh the ultimate negativity of the word 'evil'. But it cannot. Necessary evil is still evil. That was proved when Dad died.

I eat the last mouthful of cold beans and throw the empty can into the bin. I want to walk, need the air of my land.

Stepping out of the caravan, I lock the door behind me and make my way through the woods, past the Cafy, over the road and out to the lip. This time, rather than head towards Little Sister Lucy's final footprints, I turn west, to the point where the gap between the barrier and the lip is smallest, where we scattered Dad's ashes. Two emmets pass behind me on the coast path, walking up to and then stopping at the cleft in the eastern headland.

'What do you think, Dad?' I whisper at the waves. 'Should I be nice to the emmets?'

He asked me that same question once, at the tail end of the Year of Living Dangerously, when the bad season caused him to confront the irony of our reliance upon people he despised.

The Year of Living Dangerously was our fifth season at the Cafy. I was only twelve but I remember it vividly. My parents tried to hide their burgeoning worries from me by making light of things whenever I was around – the most common joke centred on Cornish Chow Mein, or whatever other strange improvisation had appeared on that week's menu – but I could see the stress and the anxiety which lay behind it. The second bad season in a row, it was characterised by a succession of week-long rainstorms that kept the tourists locked up in their holiday lets. Mum had a lot of doctor's appointments that year. Dad aged visibly. Conversations in the car on the way back to our house in St Petroc began to follow the same pattern.

'It has to pick up soon.'

'This rain can't last forever.'

'All we need are two solid months.'

'Or just one if it's during the school holidays. A good August can make a season.'

'But a bad August can break a business . . .'

It was a bad August. It did not break us, but it came close. The summer arrived late that year, creeping into September as if it had overslept and felt guilty for it. The schools had resumed by then, mine included, but fortunately, just enough holidaymakers – mostly older couples without children, the shoulder-season crowd – passed through Bones Break and stopped at the Cafy for us to avoid bankruptcy; to see out the end of the year and limp our way into the next.

Christmas of the Year of Living Dangerously was a frugal one. We had chicken instead of turkey, a tinselled cheese plant rather than a Christmas tree. The crackers came from a pound shop and the hats tore when we tried to put them on. Mum and Dad got me plenty of presents, but they did not get each other any, so all they had to unwrap that year was the bag of mint-flavoured chocolates I had bought them from Mrs Dunstan's shop in Petherick.

Over dinner, Dad drank a bottle of wine – to himself; Mum does not drink – and then, when he finished, he opened another. 'I want to make a toast,' he said after he had filled his glass. He raised it and then gestured for us to do the same. I held my squash up, Mum lifted her water. 'To the emmets.'

Mum laughed. 'Blasphemy!'

I did not know what the word meant, but I liked it, and so I copied her. 'Blasphemy!'

'No, no, hear me out.' Dad took a gulp of wine and then shushed us. 'Hear me out. If it weren't for the emmets, we wouldn't have this chicken. If it weren't for the emmets, we wouldn't have this wine.'

'*You* wouldn't have this wine.'

'Fair enough. *I* wouldn't have this wine. But anyway, this year hasn't been easy. Last year wasn't easy either. And I've been slagging off the emmets the whole time. So maybe if I'm nice to them, they'll come back next year. They'll come back and buy our cream teas and ice cream so we can make a bit of bloody money for the first time in three years. What do you think, Melody Janie?' He leaned in close to me and winked. 'Should we be nice to the emmets?'

'Never!' I laughed.

'Melody Janie says never! What can I say? I can't argue with my own daughter!'

'Or you could teach your daughter the value of kindness,' Mum said.

'The value of kindness! You know what would be a kindness? To us, I mean? It would be a kindness if, for once, just once, we didn't even have to think about emmets. If our Cafy wasn't for them, but for locals.'

'It's Bones Break, Trev. The only locals there are Mrs Perrow and the seagulls.'

'Sounds like a band. Ladies and gentlemen! Please welcome, all the way from Cornwall, Mrs Perrow and the Seagulls!'

Mum giggled. 'Playing all the hits from their first album, *The Value of Kindness.*'

I wanted to join in with the jokes but couldn't think of anything funny.

'All right, then, how about a compromise?' Mum said. 'How about we be nice to the ones who come here on holiday? They work hard all year and they choose to spend what little time off they have in Cornwall. That can't be a bad thing, can it?'

'What's your opinion, Melody Janie?' Dad asked. 'What do you reckon to a compromise?'

'Compromises are . . .' I left a long pause for dramatic effect, '. . . good.'

'Then a compromise it is!' Dad said. 'We'll be nice to the ones on holiday. We'll be nice to the ones who visit the Bones Break Cafy and keep it afloat. But just them. As for the rest of them, as for those ones who buy up all our homes, well, they can f—' Mum caught his eye and he turned to look at me. He smiled. 'Well, they can do one.'

After Christmas dinner I offered to wash up and,

when I found Mum and Dad in the living room, he lay sprawled across the sofa, glass of wine perched precariously on his rising and falling chest. I do not like it when people are drunk. They get arrogant or violent or simply incoherent and I do not have the time for them. But I never minded drunk Dad. He became like a lazy cat, locating the most comfortable space in his immediate environment and stretching out upon it, observing the world around him through half-closed eyes, and occasionally offering his point of view between the parentheses of enormous yawns.

'I was just telling Mum how important it is.'

'How important what is?' I asked as I sat on the arm of Mum's chair.

'Our *stewardship*.' His voice was soft and low, and I had to strain to hear it. 'Our stewardship of Bones Break. Not just the Cafy, all of it. It's a gem, it is. An absolute gem. And we've got to make sure we keep it that way. We've got to take care of it.'

I nodded.

'Because, you know, when you think about it, about how beautiful Bones Break is, how pristine, because it's not all covered in hotels and bloody holiday lets, you realise how lucky we are up there.'

'I agree with your dad,' Mum said. 'We are lucky. We are very, very lucky.'

When Dad fell asleep an hour later, Mum and I drew a Christmas tree on his face, and then laughed until Boxing Day.

The two emmets linger on the eastern headland, and so I walk in the opposite direction, my feet crunching across the coast path as I make my way west. I pass The Warren and continue up and on to Pedna Head. The remains of the old engine house rise from its highest point, a hundred metres or so back from the path. The muddy track leading to it has become a canal of puddles. I teeter along its edge, over the heather and gorse flattened by years of footwear.

While I know other engine houses better preserved and far more impressive – those we would visit during our winter in the caravan, or even the few which dot the inland trail that passes, through St Petroc – this one at Pedna Head, as ramshackle and crumbling as it is, has been my favourite ever since Dad first showed it to me during Ground Zero. I remember how we circled it three times in a clockwise direction, because Dad said this was how the monks he met in Kathmandu would walk around their holy monuments as an act of worship, and when I asked him if he would take me to Kathmandu one day, he promised he would.

'We can go wherever you want,' he said. 'As long as we come back. Because this is the best place in the world.'

'Is that why you came back?' I asked.

'That's exactly why I came back. I came back for Cornwall. But I stayed for your mother.'

I smiled. Dad was always open about how fiercely he loved Mum, and I loved him for it. It made me proud. Lots of the people I knew at school had divorced parents and fathers they heard little from. That my father remained so infatuated with my mother after all their years together was one of the few things that allowed me to feel any semblance of superiority at school. The others could say what they liked about me but they could never take that away. Dad would do anything for Mum, and we all knew it.

When we completed our three circles, Dad led me to the walls of the engine house so we could feel the granite with our hands, and then lifted me up to look through a window at the derelict mess inside. He explained the vast network of mines below our feet, told me about the generations of Rowes from years before who would have worked down there or in similar mines along the coast.

'Why aren't you a miner?' I asked.

'No such thing as a Cornish miner any more. No such thing as a Cornish mine. Look at Petherick.' I turned my head to follow the direction of his pointed finger, east, past The Warren and past Bones Break and past Nare Point to Petherick. 'That whole place used to be run on mining. Mining and fishing. It was tough work, that's for sure. But they supported themselves and they looked after each other. A proper community.'

He curled his arm around my shoulders. 'And what have they got now? Nothing but tourism, tourism, tourism. No wonder they're always fighting. It's rough as hell, but who can blame them? The village is barely even theirs any more. If the same thing happened to St Petroc, I don't know what I'd do.'

'Why hasn't it happened to St Petroc?'

'No sea views.' Dad turned from Petherick to look out at the ocean. I turned with him. 'St Petroc is too far inland. The emmets just want houses with a bit of water in sight. It gives them something to boast about to their mates back in London.'

I walk around the engine house, clockwise, three times, before clambering up one of its walls and sitting in a collapsed crevice, where the edges of the exposed brickwork have weathered into soft curves. The sun is lowering, slipping gently behind the bank of cloud that stretches from one end of the horizon to the other. From up here, I can see all the way to the far end of Lantoweth, where the beach comes to an end at the Roskyn headland; and then, to the east, Petherick, the setting sun reflecting orange off a hundred tiny windows. I turn, look behind, study the undulations of Trethewas Woods as they rise and fall along the hills and dips of the land, somewhere within there, hidden and secure, a small clearing with a smaller caravan. And then, finally, connecting them all, running from Lantoweth to Petherick, bordering Trethewas Woods and passing Bones Break on its way, is the road. I can see a car pass Nare Point, brake lights shining as it follows a bend, dropping down and out of view as it makes its way towards the hairpin.

The hairpin. I cannot see it from here. Set back as it is, further inland and tucked into the folds of a hill, it is invisible from any part of the coast path. I am grateful for that. Keeping it out of sight does not keep it out of mind as such, but it helps lessen the pain of it all, the pain which ebbs and flows like the tides. I saw Little Sister Lucy jump and I stand in her footprints because I need to remember. I never visit the hairpin because I did not see what happened to Dad, and I do not want to imagine.

That afternoon. That bright, awful afternoon six months ago. The Easter holidays were over and we had given ourselves a short break, closing the Cafy for three days. It was the last of them. I had gone out for a bike ride, hoping to make it as far as the estuary but giving up halfway and turning back when I got hungry. By the time I returned, the police were already at the house. I could hear the sobs from upstairs. One police officer, young and awkward, approached me as I entered the living room. He put his hand to his chest, tried to look me in the eye but failed, looked down at the floor instead, and told me that my father, Mr Trevelyan Rowe, was dead.

He had taken the car in the morning, telling Mum before he left that he was going to Petherick to pick up some food for lunch. He had driven towards Bones Break and turned east on the coast road. He had continued on towards Petherick and then, at the hairpin bend, he had collided with another car. He had not been wearing his seat belt.

That was all the police officer could tell me. I asked him about the other car. He said there had been one person in it. His condition was critical but stable. I asked who he was. He said he did not know.

When he and his colleague left an hour later, I let them out and closed the door behind them and then I slid down on to the welcome mat with the Cornish flag on it which Dad had bought from a shop in Treleven and that's all I remember about that day.

A different police officer came to the house a few days later. She wanted to talk to us – about support systems, about grief counselling, about next steps. By then I was angry. I had suspected that the other driver was an emmet, and when the police officer confirmed it that afternoon – revealing that he had been released from hospital and was already on his way back home to Surrey – I was overwhelmed by rage. I wanted to scream and shout at every single thing the police officer said. The man had not been speeding. *How do you know?* The results of the blood test showed he had not been drinking. *What about drugs?* That corner was a danger hotspot and many accidents had happened there. *None involving my father!* Mr Rowe had not been wearing his seat belt. *So what so what so what so fucking what?*

Dad drove along that road every day and had never been in a single accident on it. The emmet, on the other hand, was on holiday, had probably been here for less than a week. Doubtless, it was the first time in his life he had driven along that road. And he had been in an accident on it. That, to me, said everything. It was all anyone needed to know to understand that it categorically must have been the emmet's fault.

I tried to explain this to the police officer, to explain that the emmet *had* to be guilty of my father's death, that when it came down to it only two facts needed to be considered, two statements of basic and irrefutable logic. Number one: Dad knew that road intimately and the emmet did not. Number two: if the emmet had never come to Cornwall, Dad would still be alive.

Mum was no help, had not been since the day Dad died. It was like she was made of sand and a wave had washed over her. I found out later that she had stopped taking her medication that day. When the police officer talked about how to contact the coroner, about inquests and death certificates, she talked to me rather than my mother. It was clear to both of us that I would need to organise Dad's funeral single-handed.

I was able to do most of it online. I took Mum's phone – she did not notice it was gone, she noticed little – to visit a few websites and fill in a few forms. Within minutes, my inbox was inundated with emails from local funeral directors. I did not want much for Dad, a simple cremation without ceremony or fuss, and stated this in my replies to each of the directors. All but one came back to me with suggestions for add-ons, with upsells, and so I discounted those and chose the one which had simply said yes, yes, we can do that for you, Miss Rowe. It was a small company in Treleven. Mum gave me her credit card and I paid over the phone. We agreed on the date to meet them at the Nankervis crematorium. They brought Dad and we took him away.

I chose to invite no one, either to the cremation or to the scattering of the ashes. There were friends of his I could have tracked down, university buddies and old neighbours and schoolmates. It would not have been difficult, but I did not have the will. Dad would have wanted only what was necessary and nothing more, and his family were all that was necessary. Nothing more. Mum kept her eyes on me the entire time we were at the crematorium. Little Sister Lucy did too. I balled my hands into fists and looked straight ahead.

A taxi brought us back here that afternoon. I held Dad in my hands on my lap. His cremains. An odd portmanteau word he would have enjoyed. We walked out to the lip and upended the urn, emptying Dad into the air. He dissolved from sight long before he hit the water.

'Say something.' I cannot remember if it was Mum or Little Sister Lucy who made the suggestion. It did not matter: it was clearly aimed at me.

'What like?'

'Something about God?'

'Dad didn't believe in God.'

'Something about that then.'

'Okay,' I said, searching for a topic. 'Once, about halfway through Year 8, a man came into school and gave an assembly about Jesus. He was pretty funny. He told jokes and had these cartoons on his PowerPoint which made us all laugh. Dad picked me up from school that afternoon and I told him about it. He was outraged. That was his word. *I'm outraged, Melody Janie! They shouldn't let people like him into schools.* I had to calm him down right there in the car, make him promise that he wouldn't go in to see Mrs Marks and have a go at her. I explained to him that just because I had enjoyed the man's talk, it didn't mean I had converted to Christianity, and he looked relieved when I said that.'

Behind me, I heard a short sob. It could have been either Mum or Little Sister Lucy, or maybe even both. I continued.

'And then Dad asked me what I did believe in. If I didn't believe in Christianity, that is. And I said I believed in evolution, that it's pretty hard to dispute when you look at all the different animals and see how common we are to each other. Dad said he agreed with me. "I had an argument with someone once," he said. "A Christian. When I told him I believed in evolution he asked if that meant I was a monkey. I told him right back that, yep, evolution says we come from monkeys, but Christianity says we're made from the soil. And I'd rather be a monkey than mud."'

That felt like the right place to end the story. Like a punchline. I'd rather be a monkey than mud.

We walked back to the waiting taxi together. It took us to the house in St Petroc. That night, Mum disappeared. A few days later, Little Sister Lucy and I moved into the caravan.

It is dark. There is a weakness in my bones. I gently lower myself down the wall of the engine house to the wet ground. Too many memories. I feel sick, as if I have binged on them. I need to sleep. I need to stop.

I place one foot in front of the other, begin the walk back along the edge of the muddy track to the coast path. I sink into the rhythm of my footsteps – the left and the right, the left and the right – letting my arms swing with the momentum and breathing in time to it all, my body a clock, ticking and tocking its way home.

At the path, I turn east and quicken my pace a little against the wind, feeling the hair swept back from my face, the first nibbles of cold on the tips of my fingers. I turn my head slightly to the left as I walk and look out to sea, counting the waves as they come in their sets of seven, always sets of seven, marking the point where each swell breaks. I pass The Warren. The wind picks up and I lean forward into it, feeling my hips flex beneath my dress. I focus on the straining muscles, the hard bones beneath them, consider the power of this, of me, consider the strength and solidity of the human body and not the brittle fragility of it.

I cross the western headland and follow the graceful

curve of the lip to dead centre, but I do not stop, do not climb over the barrier. Instead, I keep on, crossing the grass and the road and the car park and walking down the side of the Cafy and into the woods and through the woods and to the clearing and it is only when I reach the caravan that I stop and I retrieve my keys and unlock the door and let myself in.

And then I go to bed.

I wake to the moan of the wind. It careers about the caravan, shaking it from side to side and rattling the branches of the trees above. I reach up and pull open the curtains above my head. It is dark outside. Early morning. I climb out of bed, switch on the softer of the caravan's lights and find my watch. 2.55 a.m.

I throw on my coat and race out to the lip, to dead centre, root my feet into place and check my watch again. 2.58 a.m. I have two minutes. An age. Had I been this early, those two minutes would have been enough to save Little Sister Lucy. She may have fought me, but I know now that I was capable of picking her up, of carrying her. Back in the caravan, I would have held her, fed her, done whatever I could to shake that final impulse from her.

It is three o'clock. She was here and I was on the road, two minutes late. I stare down the wind, fierce, my eyes burning. Two minutes. All I needed.

I remember our argument: the terrible imprecations and the worse silences. Why did I tell her my plans? What good did I possibly think it was going to achieve? I should have kept my mouth shut and gone ahead with things without any admissions to her. If I had, she would still be here.

I should not have mentioned Mum.

Sometimes, Little Sister Lucy loved to hear about Mum; at others, she hated it. I tried to speak of her only when I was asked, when I knew it was safe, like that morning months before when we had lain huddled together in bed, her breath hot and sour on my face.

'How could she leave us like this, Mellijane?'

'Mum isn't—' I started, and then corrected myself. Little Sister Lucy liked to shorten my name, but she hated it when I did the same to our mother's. '*Mummy* isn't a well woman.'

'I don't understand her. I never have.'

'Mummy doesn't completely understand herself, and she never has either. But she'll be back. She'll be back soon. We just have to wait for her.'

'I don't think she will.'

'Don't say that.'

'But where has she gone? Why can't I find her?'

'She's gone somewhere only she knows. Somewhere to get better again.'

'I hate that she isn't here.'

'She'll be back.'

'Tell me about her. Tell me a story.'

'Now?'

'Now.' Little Sister Lucy flipped on to her front and rested her chin on her hands, wide-eyed and attentive. It frightened me how adorable I found her like this.

It was a story she wanted and so it was a story I gave her. I could never deny her anything. I loved her too much.

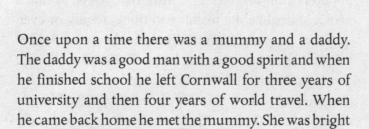

Once upon a time there was a mummy and a daddy. The daddy was a good man with a good spirit and when he finished school he left Cornwall for three years of university and then four years of world travel. When he came back home he met the mummy. She was bright and beautiful and the daddy fell in love with her instantly.

They became the best of friends and spent a year together while the mummy finished college. They learned all about each other: their loves and hates; their fractured pasts and dreamed futures. He told her everything about his travels. She told him that one day she wanted to run her own business, a seaside café. She was studying how to do so at college and already had a place secured at university to continue the same. She would learn all she could, and one day she would open that café.

What the mummy never told the daddy was that a darkness lurked inside her. She never told him because she did not know herself, not until her first term at university.

She had begun her course full of joy and expectation. She liked her new city and she liked her new studies.

Her student house was enormous and warm, and the five girls she shared it with were equally shy and equally kind. But then things began to shift for the mummy – small shifts at first like difficulty sleeping and strange flashes of anger; then larger shifts like blaming herself for everything and feeling worthless; followed by much worse shifts like the inability to think, to talk or even to move properly. And finally came the worst shift of all. She began to hear her housemates talking about her from beyond the closed door of her bedroom, the bedroom she rarely left any more. They talked loudly and they talked often. They were making plans for the mummy.

The mummy called the daddy and told him everything. The daddy drove straight to her city, picked her and all of her belongings up and drove them back to Cornwall. They visited a doctor together the following day. He used words the mummy didn't understand, words like 'auditory hallucinations', but when he explained them to her she recognised their meaning. She understood the word 'hospitalisation'. The daddy could not bear the thought, but the doctor reassured him – a new 'Centre' had opened not far from Treleven, a peaceful place, restorative and healthful. People got better there.

The mummy spent three months in the Centre, getting better. The daddy visited her every day. When it was clear that the carefully mixed medicine was beginning to work, the mummy was released from the Centre and moved in with the daddy in his small flat in St Petroc. She found a job at a bank in the centre of town and this helped give her life order and routine. She continued with her medication. She functioned. She knew she would never return to university, but this mattered less and less each day. She was happy with her life. She was better.

One year later, during a July heatwave, the mummy fell pregnant. The moment she found out, she stopped taking her medication. At first, the daddy protested, but when she told him how worried she was about the fact that it might damage their unborn baby he agreed that she was right. Together, they waited for the slightest hint of the disorder returning and when it didn't they both agreed that the child growing inside her was protecting her and keeping her strong. In the April of the next year, she gave birth to a baby girl. The daddy got a new job, a managerial position at a restaurant in Treleven which paid well, and so they took out a mortgage on a house in St Petroc and moved into it from their flat. They got married. Though the mummy had started taking her medication again after the baby was born, she began to secretly believe that maybe, just maybe, her disorder had slipped away during her pregnancy, vanished from her being – banished, perhaps, by her wonderful baby girl – so that she might lead a normal and healthy life. Her doctors had always told her the disorder was manageable but incurable, and that most sufferers fell into relapses here and there throughout the rest of their lives. But the mummy had never felt better and so, three years after her daughter was born, she decided to begin cutting down on her medication. It made no difference at all – she still felt better, she still felt happy – and within eighteen months she had come off her medication altogether.

But all it takes is one little change. That change came for the mummy the year her daughter started primary school. For the first time since her birth, the daughter was no longer with the mummy all the time. And neither was the daddy, for he worked all the hours he possibly could. The mummy was left alone every day and that was enough to start turning the tide. When the disorder returned, it came differently this time, on a wave of withdrawal.

The daughter noticed it immediately. This wasn't the mummy she knew. The brave, strong mummy. This was a different mummy altogether, and the daughter became especially aware of the mummy's silence and stillness, of how her speech and movement decreased little by little every day. And then, one Thursday afternoon when she came home from school (the mummy had stopped coming to collect her weeks before, and she tagged along with another family who walked past her house on their own way home), she found the mummy sitting in a chair in the living room, motionless. Emotionless too. The mummy's eyes were open, but they focused on nothing. She gripped the arms of the chair, her muscles tensed and her skin taut around them. The daughter spoke to her but the mummy did not reply. The daughter kept speaking to her, kept speaking to her until the daddy came home and took turns with the daughter speaking to her, turns which they maintained until the mummy's doctor arrived, and she was taken back to the Centre. She never replied.

The mummy spent two long years in the Centre. The daddy and the daughter visited whenever they could, which was all the time. The mummy did not speak for the whole of the first year. The doctors gave her a variety of treatments, but the daughter never knew which one broke her silence, which one nudged her back on to the road leading to the daughter and the daddy. Not that it mattered. The mummy began to speak again and that was all that was important. Sometimes she spoke so slowly she drooled as she talked. Sometimes she cried and slapped herself about the face. Sometimes she recognised the daughter and sometimes she didn't. Once, she fell asleep while the daddy was talking to her and snored so loudly they couldn't help but giggle. They felt very ashamed about that later.

Gradually, month by month, piece by piece, the mummy came back. She was not the same mummy as she had been before the Centre – even the daughter could see that and she was only eight – but she was a mummy and they accepted her for that. Any mummy would do, so long as she could be their mummy again. The doctors explained that they had found exactly the right balance in her medication and the daddy and the daughter made the mummy promise that she would never stop taking it again. She promised. She wanted to go home.

Sadly, while the mummy got better, the daddy's own

mother passed away. She left him an inheritance so enormous he did not know what to do with it. Until he remembered the dream which the mummy had confided in him all those years before. Her own business. A seaside café. He found the perfect place at Bones Break, a secluded stretch of clifftop paradise not far from their house in St Petroc. He used all of his inheritance to buy it for the mummy. He loved her so much, and he prayed the café would save her.

It did.

When the mummy was finally released from the Centre, the daddy took her to Bones Break and showed her the Cafy for the first time. She was so happy that she jumped up and down on a wooden picnic bench.

And she never went back to the Centre again.

The sun has risen. I should leave dead centre. I have been here too long. The memories are building; they grow too tender to bear.

I turn to my right and walk along the coast path towards and then over the eastern headland, past the cleft left by last winter's storms. Ahead of me lie two miles of lip and then, at their culmination, Petherick. I know I will not make it that far. But I keep walking.

I reach the tip of the rise halfway between the eastern headland and Nare Point and then I see them. Archie and Richard Brown are on the coast path, walking in my direction. I continue forward, slowly, gazing out to sea. I have every right to the nonchalance. This is my land.

When Archie sees me his tail soars. He rears up on his back legs and heaves himself towards me like a toddler on reins.

'It really is rather rare,' Richard Brown says as we meet. Archie plants his front paws on my dress and licks my arm. 'He doesn't usually like anyone.'

'But I bet everyone likes Archie.' I say it more to the dog than to the man. I do not like to look at Richard Brown. His returned stare makes me uneasy.

'He doesn't tend to give people the chance. He's a rescue dog, you see.'

Archie drops down and settles into an obsessive interest with my right foot. His wet nose tickles as it dances over my bare skin.

'Where did you rescue him from?'

'I didn't rescue him myself, as such. I adopted him. From a shelter in Manchester.'

'Manchester?'

'It's where I'm from. Archie needed a forever home and I needed the company. I had just . . . a relationship had ended and I was low. Poor Archie, though, he'd had it much worse.'

'What happened to him?'

'Are you sure you want to hear the story?'

I am not sure. I do not want to hear anything much at all from Richard Brown. But the story is not about him, it is about Archie, and so I nod.

'He belonged to a family who didn't care for him. I don't even know why they had him. For their own amusement, I suppose. He wasn't allowed inside their house. Lived in the back garden. Chained to an old washing machine. They hardly fed him anything so he was all skin and bone, and during the winter nights he must have nearly frozen to death out there. The neighbours could see him from their bedroom window and felt sorry for him, but they didn't do anything because, you know, they were scared of his owners. But then one of the teenage boys from the family started to torture him. He and his friends would unchain Archie and shoot at him with a BB gun as he tried to run away from them. There was nowhere he could go, the garden was walled in, you see, so they always got him. Not that that stopped them. They'd just keep shooting. Then one day they did the same, but this time they used fireworks. He was so scared that he actually tried to run up one of the walls. He fell badly. Broke both his front legs. The boys left him there, squealing with pain, unable to move. The neighbours saw it all. The next morning, he was still in the same place. He had cried and whined all night, but nobody had come to him. So the neighbours finally decided enough was enough and called the police and the RSPCA. Archie was taken away that afternoon. When I met him his legs were still healing, so I couldn't walk him. I'd just go and sit with him in his crate in the shelter, getting a little bit closer each time. He cowered from me less and less every day and after a week he let me stroke him. A week later he let me feed him and that was when we started to bond. A week after that I took him home. He's a different dog now – around me anyway. He doesn't trust anyone else. Well, except you, it seems.'

I put the heels of my palms up to my eyes to try and stop the tears, but it is no use. Richard has seen that I am crying. He stands awkwardly, looking somewhat guilty and yet also, in a way, satisfied. I crouch down and Archie steps towards me. I cup his head in my hands and rest my forehead on his so that my hair drapes over and covers us both. My tears drip on to his fur. 'I'm sorry, Archie. I'm so, so sorry.' He stands still and breathes heavily. I can feel his eyelashes blinking against my chin. 'How could anyone do that to you?'

'Some people are evil,' Richard says. He has crouched down too and is scratching Archie's rump with his free hand.

I release Archie's head and stand back up. My knees click as I rise.

'Can I help?' I ask.

'Help how?'

'Help show him that not all people are evil. Just some.'

Richard looks out to sea and then at the ground. 'Perhaps that would be good.' He keeps his gaze down. 'For Archie.'

'I could walk him.'

'I don't know.'

'Not far.'

'No, not far.' Richard's free hand lays itself on Archie's spine. 'And perhaps not alone. Not at first.'

That irritates me. I do not trust this man – it is difficult to imagine that anyone could, with his strange eyes and dirty clothes, the cleanest thing about him the sling which supports whatever is inside that cast, maybe not even an arm at all, maybe something inhuman and terrifying like the deformed flipper of a seal. No, I do not trust him. But I want him to trust me. Here is the problem to solve: Richard Brown is, I suspect, a malicious presence here and if I want to protect my land and keep it safe for Mum's return and Dad's legacy, then I need to learn as much about him as I can. Why he is here. What his plans are. Walking Archie together is the perfect ruse. I do not have to enjoy his company, I just have to endure it. This is how I will solve the problem that is Richard Brown.

'How about later?' I ask.

'We'll see. You could join us, I suppose. For his evening walk.'

'Shall I come to Mrs Perrow's house?'

'Where?'

Problem solving often requires careful language choices. 'Your house,' I say. 'Shall I meet you at your house?'

'No. Let's meet here. That would be preferable.'

'What time?'

'Six o'clock, I think. Yes. Six o'clock.'

I give Archie a final stroke. 'Bye, Archie. See you this evening.' I hold my hand out to Richard, who looks bemused at the gesture but shakes it nonetheless. 'Bye, Richard.'

'Goodbye, Melody Janie.'

I turn and walk back along the coast path, over the eastern headland and then down across the road towards the Cafy. I stop before I reach it and look back at the lip. There, beside the signpost on the western headland, is the silhouette of a lone man, his back to me as he gazes out to sea. I glance to the right. Richard and Archie materialise on the eastern headland. They appear to notice the man on the far side of Bones Break. Richard stops – I can see he is looking at the man – and Archie stops beside him. Then they turn around and disappear, back in the direction from which they came.

Richard Brown does not want to be seen. I suspect he should not be here. I will find him out.

And then I will drive him out.

I let myself into the Cafy, walk to the bar, pick up a wine glass and begin to polish, sweeping my cloth around the rim and then down into the bowl, wiping away the water marks and, after them, my own finger-prints. It is impossible to get a wine glass perfectly clean. It is impossible to keep this Cafy clean. Little Sister Lucy was never able to offer much help, but what she could offer was help nonetheless and without her the enormity of caretaking this place is overwhelming. Yet I must try; I must do my best to have it ready for when Mum comes back. Then life can begin again.

I keep up the polishing for the next hour. I think about Richard Brown and I think about Archie and then, with a mounting and peculiar insistence, I think about food. I am, I realise, very hungry.

Today I will raid the storeroom, my own personal mini-market. The choice of food is limited, but the quantity is not. The wet wipes are there too. Dad bought 500 packets to get the best possible reduction in price and thought they could even replace toilet roll, but nobody ever used them and so he bought endless toilet rolls for a similar discount. During and then after the Year of Living Dangerously, we ordered so many bulk loads of tinned and dried food that I think I could survive an entire winter living off what is in the store-room and nothing else. The notion is a comfort, for it may come to that. I do not know when Mum will return, but if it is not until next spring, when we can reopen the Cafy for the new season, I know at least that I can survive on our stocked supplies. They have long sell-by dates, which Dad always said were a myth anyway.

As the morning passes, I work my way through the various potential lunch options, creating a menu in my head, deciding what I will take from the storeroom before I descend the stairs from the kitchen and enter it. I want to spend as little time down there as possible. I dislike it more and more every day. The smell is getting worse.

I imagine the layout of the storeroom: the chest freezers, the cupboard filled with noodle pots, another with tins of beans, the enormous plastic sacks of pasta and rice, yet more cupboards filled with yet more tins, the pies and frankfurters and fruits and pickles and fish and chopped tomatoes. I mentally locate the necessary items for the meal I've built in my head. A tin of tuna. Another of tomatoes. A cup of pasta. A mixture of herbs, perhaps basil, oregano and coriander, pinched out of their kilo tubs. That will do. I finish the cleaning for the day and am in and out of the storeroom in less than a minute, returning to the caravan with my booty in my arms.

I boil a saucepan of water, pour the pasta into it and swirl it around. I open the tin of chopped tomatoes by

its ring pull, empty it into a separate pan, open the tin
of tuna, drain that into the sink, add it to the tomatoes
and then sprinkle the herbs on top of it all. I light the
other burner beneath the sauce and set it to a low heat.
Steam begins to billow, fogging the window above the
cooker. I open the overhead cupboard at the side of the
window. Inside are my stacks of paper plates and plastic
cutlery, leftovers from a wedding we hosted at the Cafy
during the Year of Living Splendidly, the only wedding
we have ever hosted. Little Sister Lucy and I used them
to save on washing-up. They helped keep our life
simple.

I take a single paper plate and lay it out on the counter
beside the sink, then take a single plastic fork and use
it to stir the pasta and the sauce. I wait for a few minutes,
and then I stab at one of the tubes of pasta, raise it out
of the water and bite into it. It is still a little firm but
cooked enough. The oil from the can of tuna has begun
to smell in the sink and so I tip the boiling water from
the pan over it, washing it down the plughole. I use the
plastic fork to hold back the pasta while the water
drains, losing a dozen tubes to the sink in the process.
The rest are upended on to the paper plate, followed
by the sauce. I turn both burners off and place the dirty
pans in the sink.

And then I eat my lunch.

Food often punctuated our time. There were days, many of them, when we just did nothing. Not the figurative nothingness of a lazy afternoon with a book or a quiet night in with a movie, not the nothingness of meditation or small talk or a morning free from plans or even sleep, but true, literal nothing. We lay together on the bed, or we lay apart on the separate couches, and we sometimes closed our eyes and we sometimes kept them open and we said not a word and we just let the day pass. It was not a game, it was not planned or decided and agreed upon. Neither of us ever said, 'Let's do nothing today.' We just did. Some days, we just did nothing.

If it had been a game, I always lost. I think that, had I stayed inert like that, immobile until Little Sister Lucy moved or said something, we both would have continued in our pursuit of nothingness until one of us, or both, quietly slipped away. But it was the hunger which always got me in the end.

It takes a long time to recover from nothing. We would rise from it in a vacant slumber, sometimes taking hours before we could relearn how to speak and walk and think again, rubbing eyes, stretching limbs, gathering consciousness like sand.

Little Sister Lucy would join me in the Cafy while I cooked tuna pasta or Cornish Chow Mein, though she did not help. She liked to sit on the kitchen floor below the sink and watch me work. We ate in the dining room together, talking mindlessly about birds and seals and our caravan. And then, fed and sated with it, we stayed there, settling back in our chairs to watch my land through the floor-to-ceiling windows as the sun set and the night crept slowly in. Sometimes, Little Sister Lucy fell asleep in her chair. Other times, she told me stories about her favourite doll. Only once did she complain.

'Bored,' she said. 'Bored bored bored bored *bored*.'

'What do you want to do?'

'I don't know.' She stood up, stretched her thin body and then plonked herself back down on to her chair.

'Well, if you're bored, let's do something.'

'Like what?'

'We could go for a walk.'

'*Huh*,' she said with a huff and a pout. 'I'm bored of walking.'

'We'll do something else then.'

'You're always walking. I'm bored of walking.'

'I just said we can do something else.'

'Walking walking walking stupid shitty walking.'

'Don't swear.'

That enlivened her. The boredom dropped from her body in a second and she stood up once more. 'Why not? You're not Mum. I can swear if I want.'

'You're right,' I said. 'You can swear if you want. But I don't like it.'

'Because you're thick.'

The sudden rush of tears surprised me even more than it surprised her. With no time to stop it, I pressed my hand to my mouth and ran from the Cafy, across the road and out to the lip. Heart pounding, flesh on fire, I stood with my shins against the wooden barrier, and I thought – *I can't do this any more.*

Little Sister Lucy appeared moments later.

'I'm sorry, Mellijane,' she said, slipping her hand into mine and stroking my finger with her thumb. 'I didn't mean it.'

We stood there together, on the lip, hand in hand, while Little Sister Lucy repeated her meek apologies and I hated how I loved her.

I raise my head to the familiar squawking from above. It is the geese, perfectly lit by the setting sun, carving their way through the mackerel sky. They spend their days at the Lantoweth Nature Reserve. Where they spend their nights, I do not know. But I see them in between, setting off in their squadrons. Bones Break is on their flight path. If I get to see them once a day, either at morning or evening, I count myself lucky. If I get to see them both on the way in and the way out, it gives me a surge of gratitude which resonates throughout my entire body.

Tonight, they seem to be leaving earlier than is normal for them, perhaps because of the cold weather. That in itself is unusual, and as I watch them I see something even more unusual, something I have never seen before. Four arrows of geese approach from separate directions to meet directly over my head, transforming into a single, larger arrow so smoothly I can barely see how. I focus on one goose in particular. It turns its head, looks at its neighbour, and then continues to look at it, focus fixed, as they fly away. That's something else I have never seen before.

I like the geese. When they disappear for the winter,

it leaves me a little sad. They are part of my land and without them it feels emptier. The seagulls have my preference because they never leave. And the choughs are my favourite of all. Because they came back – they came back and they stayed.

It is fiercely cold this evening. The wind is low yet biting, fresh off the Atlantic. The waves beat their fists against the cliffs. At dead centre I stop for a moment and look out at the furious ocean and then I push on, over the eastern headland and to the rise. I check my watch. It is five minutes past six. Richard and Archie are not here. I continue on to Nare Point, cross the road, and make my way to the door of the house. There is no bell. I knock three times, loud.

Richard opens the door. His short hair is dishevelled and his eyes red. 'I said to meet on the coast path.' There is a slur to his voice.

'You weren't there,' I say, and smile at him. I hope it makes me look charming.

'Wait here,' he says, closing the door. I stand in the porch, listening to the thuds and rattles from within. The door opens again and Archie launches through it, his tail thudding against the frame. He is wearing his saddle-bags. I accept his head, thrust as it is into my hands. Richard steps out into the porch, closing and locking the door behind him. As he begins to walk out on to the path, one foot slips beneath him and for a moment I think he will fall. He unsteadily rights himself.

I decide it is best not to draw attention to the stumble. 'Do you keep anything in the saddlebags?'

'No.' We begin to walk down the path together. 'I read a lot about dog behaviour when I was visiting Archie in the shelter. There's a technique called, I think, the Anxiety Wrap. It's a way of keeping a dog calm, as it were, the wrap of a scarf or something similar around its body. Dogs seem to like it, it makes them feel secure. I suppose it's like they're being hugged. That's what the saddlebags are. Security.'

'Is that the same reason why your arm is in a sling?'

Richard looks at me, puzzled. 'No, Melody Janie,' he says. 'My arm is in a sling because it's broken.'

That answers one of my questions, yet now I want to know how and, perhaps, why it is broken. But I will not press him immediately. I have time. If I keep my prying gentle, sporadic, he will see it all as just the occasional weird question from a weird girl.

'Here,' he says, 'you should take his lead. Get him used to it.'

Archie follows the exchange of the lead with his eyes as it passes from Richard to me. We cross the road and enter the Nare Point car park. Archie smells something and lurches away, sniffing loudly, head down. I give a soft tug on the lead and say his name. He ignores me.

'Say *Archie, come*. He understands that.'

I try it and he immediately gives up his quest and trots back to my side. The three of us walk through the car park until we reach the coast path.

'Which way would you like to walk?' I ask. 'East to Petherick? Or west to Bones Break and Lantoweth?'

'We should start small. Perhaps just to your café and back. That will do, I think.'

'It's not very far.'

'It's far enough.' His tone is sharp; the words snap.

Easy, gently.

I lead the way west, stay quiet. Richard will talk when he is ready.

He does. 'I must say that, despite the weather, this is one of the most beautiful places I've ever seen.' The wind is high and I can barely hear him. His words come erratically, punctuated by strange rhythms. He is, I am beginning to realise, drunk.

'It's my favourite place in the world,' I reply.

'Is it not different? Different now, I mean?'

'In what way?'

'I read that there was quite a tremendous storm down here last winter. That it virtually changed the shape of the entire Cornish coastline, as it were.'

'It was bad, but not that bad. Only some of the north coast was affected, nothing further west than Zennor or further east than Perranporth. A few landslides and rockfalls, but that was it. I wouldn't say it changed the shape of the coast.'

I think back to those storms. I remember them well. They were ferocious, not one storm but many, all overlapping each other with such relentless persistence that there never seemed to be a break in the heavy rains or heavier winds. It was the first time in my life that I had felt uneasy on the lip.

'Were there any around here?' Richard says. 'Landslides or rockfalls?'

'We got some of the worst,' I say. 'Up ahead, once you get over the rise and closer to the Cafy, that's where it's most vulnerable. A lot of the coast path around Bones Break sits on an overhang. Beneath it, the cliff bends back in on itself. Concave.' I make a sweeping motion downwards with my hand, curving it towards myself as it drops. 'One day, the whole thing will go, maybe as far back as the road. Not for years yet, possibly decades, but it will happen. It's certain to.'

'And where exactly did it fall last winter?'

'Little bits crumble here and there all the time, not just in winter. But those storms took down a couple of large chunks. Do you know the eastern headland?'

'Which eastern headland?'

'At Bones Break. The eastern headland.'

'I don't quite know what you mean.'

'Picture the Cafy,' I say, and I find it a little amusing the way that Richard half-closes his eyes when he does, so that I can see him drawing it on to his imagination. 'Walk towards the lip with the Cafy behind you.'

'The lip?'

'The edge. You've got the coast path, then the barrier, then the lip, then nothing.'

'I see.'

'So you're stood at the lip. Look left and you'll see the coast path signpost. See it?'

He nods.

'That's Bones Break's western headland.' I choose not

to mention the shelf. 'And then if you look right you'll see the eastern headland, sticking out on the opposite side of the bay to the western headland.'

'Ah.' He nods his head and looks at me. 'Where the barrier stops.'

'Where the barrier *fell down*,' I say. 'That was last winter's storms. A whole section of the eastern headland just crumbled one night, taking the barrier and part of the coast path with it. It was lucky it didn't happen during the day. Someone walking there wouldn't have stood a chance.'

With flawless timing, we arrive at the eastern headland, following the coast path up and on to it.

'See there,' I say, pointing to the treacherous cleft in the ground which pushes inward from the lip, the exposed rock below it black and wet, new to the light, untouched by grass or birds' nests. The thunder of the incoming tide echoes up from its base. Earlier this year, once the storms had finally blown themselves out, National Trust workers had come up here to divert the coast path, rebuilding it to give this cavernous split a wide berth. They had not repaired the barrier, only sanded down the rough wooden edges where the rest had cracked loose and fallen.

'I see this every day,' Richard says. 'It hadn't even occurred to me. I just thought the barrier had been vandalised.'

'The next one's worse.'

We had all been at the house in St Petroc the night the eastern headland crumbled. But the second collapse at The Warren had happened during the following day. We were at the Cafy that morning checking for damage. Satisfied that there was none, I had opted to take a lone walk along the lip. I had been up on the eastern head-land examining the alien cleft when I heard it, when I felt it beneath my feet.

'Where is it?' Richard asks.

'The Warren. The next bay after the western headland.'

We cross Bones Break, following the curve of the lip. Archie seems to have no fear of the drop, he walks between me and it, often trying to squirrel his way beneath the barrier, nose quivering and eyes wide. I stop while he urinates against the warning sign, and then again at dead centre.

'Say *Archie, come.*'

I do. He does. We pass dead centre.

It feels time to ask another question. I choose a direct one.

'Why did you ask if I recognised you?'

Richard stops and turns to face me, his back to the lip. He stares at me, that same stare, the one I have come to despise. I breathe in, long and deep, and I find the strength to hold the stare, to reflect it right back into his difficult eyes and, for a brief moment in that weird stand-off, I suddenly think: *one little push is all it would take* . . .

'I didn't ask you that,' Richard says.

'You said, "You don't recognise me, do you?"'

'That's a very different question.'

One little push . . . they'd find the alcohol in your blood when you washed up down at Lantoweth . . . they'd suspect a drunken stumble . . . they wouldn't suspect me . . .

Richard drops his stare, turns back to face the western headland. Did he see the violence, could he discern it flashing in the whites of my eyes? 'Show me The Warren,' he says, walking on.

I am enlivened.

I walk past and ahead of Richard. The coast path carries us on to the western headland. Richard's pace picks up as we progress. He seems eager to see the next rockfall, is perhaps already forgetting our brief confrontation: a consequence of his drunkenness. It is to my advantage. I will remember.

'You must have seen this before,' I say. 'You've walked up and down here plenty of times.'

'That's true, but I'm new here, Melody Janie. I don't see it all as you see it. That landslide on the eastern headland, I've walked past that a dozen times, but I had no idea it had only just happened. To me it was part of the landscape, part of the coastline. It could have been like that for centuries for all I knew. And I think I know now where the next one will be. Is that it? The Warren?' He is pointing forward, directly ahead.

'Yes.'

Beyond the western headland, the lip swings back into The Warren before taking the straight line which forms the eastern aspect of Pedna Head between us and Lantoweth. The Warren has been a bay for as long as I can remember, a bay like Bones Break, albeit smoother, lower, calmer and in all ways inferior to my land. But its appearance has changed dramatically since last winter's storms. Now its curve seems to cut into the lip like a forced smile, ten metres wider and another ten deeper than it had been before. The best view of The Warren, of The New Warren, is from here, from the western headland. We can see the powdery face of it, riven by the debris and detritus of thousands of tonnes of slipping and sliding stone, the lip receding ever further, crumbling slowly into the slashed chasm, the doubled-up waves at its base where the fallen rocks have created a submerged reef.

'It came down in less than five seconds,' I say. 'It shook the earth.'

'You were here?'

'I was on the eastern headland, by the cleft. I didn't see it. But the noise of it was immense. I ran across to this headland and saw what had happened. I was excited. Nature in action. But I was sad too. Because that part of the lip will never be the same again. Never.'

We stand there for a few minutes, both looking out towards the new bay. I take my memories of how The Warren was before the storms and superimpose them on top of what I see, so that both presence and absence exist simultaneously. I know that Richard cannot do that. He sees only what he sees. He lacks my context. It makes me feel sorry for him: the first semblance of pity, of anything remotely positive, I have felt for him since we met.

I turn my head slightly, enough so that I can look at

him without him noticing. He does not. He stares at
The Warren for a few more moments and then shuffles
his feet, rotating right, turning away from me and
towards Bones Break. I match his movements so that I
can see his face again. There, in his eyes, I feel certain
I can read admiration. Admiration and respect. He is
enthralled by my land. He looks at it the way many
emmets do not. Something begins to shift, grudgingly,
inside me. Perhaps I will not ask him any more questions this evening.

I leave Richard and Archie at dead centre and return to the caravan, making sure to stop beside the Cafy to watch until they are out of sight.

Inside the caravan, I eat a few spoonfuls of the tuna pasta left over in the saucepan from this afternoon and then scrape the rest into the bin, throwing in the used plate and cutlery after it. It is too early for bed and, anyway, I am not tired. Esther is coming to visit tomorrow. Saturday. I cannot wait.

Thinking about Esther makes me want to take a dark walk inland tonight, to the reservoir. I open the door and peer upwards: there are no clouds in the sky and the moon is as white and shining as a seagull's wing. A good night to be beside water that is still rather than rough, with reflections that are glassy and unbroken, where the moon will swell up from the black water like a submerged torch.

It is a fifteen-minute uphill walk to the reservoir, further and more strenuous than Nare Point, less so than Lantoweth. The night is cold: I wrap my coat around my shoulders before stepping outside. I can hear the waves crashing against the cliffs. The wind has died. I lock the caravan door and move away from the sound of the sea, deeper into Trethewas Woods. There is no path through, but I know which steps to take, where the ground is too soft, where the branches are too low. I navigate swiftly, keeping my eyes bright and alert, on the lookout for squirrels, foxes or, best of all, a badger.

The periphery of Trethewas Woods is announced by the crumbling wall which is all that remains of an ancient chapel. The moonlight is strong enough to read new graffiti etched into the moss covering the granite brickwork. TROGGY HAS ADES. I run my fingers along the words. They are shallow, cut into the moss only, the stone beneath them unscratched. The words will disappear within a week, reclaimed by the weed. Nobody will remember Troggy, or their ades. Even I may forget, some day.

A dense hedge demarcates the woods from the reservoir. To pass it, I scale the apple tree which grows from its eastern corner, climbing a quarter of the way up and then swinging from one of its lower branches to drop down on to the gravelled slope skirting the rim of the reservoir. I crab-walk down the slope until I reach the edge, crouch low, dip a hand into the dark water. Then I move back up the slope and around the rim of the reservoir until I find the point. When I do, I lower myself down and sit cross-legged, adjusting myself by fractions until everything is correct and in place. It was here, right here, that it happened, that our friendship began, six years ago, on this very spot.

I had been searching for a quiet place to eat my lunch, somewhere away from the Cafy and away from the lip which, in the summer heat, crawled with emmets. I had chosen the reservoir. Esther was there, swimming short lengths up and down parallel to the slope and ordering the seven other kids who were standing around to jump in and join her. None of them obeyed. Though they all wore their costumes, the furthest any would go was a foot dipped into the water, followed by a litany of excuses. I sat cross-legged on the slope, a few metres away from them all, and bit into my sandwich. Esther saw me and shouted my name.

'Melody! Hey, Melody Janie!'

Mouth full of bread and cheese, I could not reply, but I nodded.

'None of these lot have the guts to get in. What about you?'

I chewed and swallowed. I would have preferred not to answer, but all were looking at me now, and I could not escape the demand. 'No costume,' I said.

'So get one.' Esther bobbed in the water, her head tilted slightly in expectation. Her seven friends continued to stare at me. I had been told to get a costume and at the time it seemed like the only possible thing to do. So I stood up and started walking back to the Cafy. It did not occur to me to lie, to return and say *sorry, I couldn't find one*. Or to simply not return at all. I had a spare costume in the Cafy, and I could think of no other option than to put it on and start walking back to the reservoir again, despite the fact that I had no desire whatsoever to do so. I had been ordered and I was obeying.

I at least had the presence of mind to walk slowly, hoping that if I took long enough, Esther's seven friends would have summoned the courage to join her in the water and all would have forgotten about me. Yet by the time I arrived back at the reservoir, nobody was swimming. Even Esther had got out. She lay sunbathing on her back on the slope, talking and laughing with her friends who sprawled about her, their semi-naked bodies glowing in the sunlight. I hovered by the hedge. Esther flipped herself on to her front and spotted me.

'Melody Janie! You came back!' She was smiling.

'Just had to get my costume.'

'Where is it?' She pulled herself up on to her feet, stretched her left leg out behind her.

'Wearing it.' I pointed down at my waist. 'Under my dress.'

'Great. None of these lot will swim with me. But you will, right?'

I nodded, watching as she planted her left foot down on to the slope, spun around so that her back was to me and then swallow-dived into the water. 'Come on,' she spluttered as she resurfaced.

I looked towards her seven friends. I knew them all from school. They were not my friends. I just knew them. They stared back at me. There was no malice in the way they looked at me, only curiosity – would I or wouldn't I? – but I loathed their stares, no matter what lay behind them, and it seemed to me that the only way I could stop them was by taking off my dress and jumping into the reservoir.

To my surprise, the water was not especially cold. I had been expecting the brain-shrinking, chest-kicking freeze of a first-wave plunge down at Lantoweth or Petherick, but the reservoir was soft, welcoming, easy. And it was still too. Unnaturally still. No washing machine of currents flipped me over and about, no shattering crashes echoed above my head. I stretched out my limbs and let the beautiful water lift me slowly back to the surface. When I broke through, there was cheering.

They were cheering me.

Esther swam towards me, laughed as she wrenched one of my hands up into the air, and then high-fived it. We swam out together into the very centre of the reservoir, or what we guessed was the centre, and by the time we returned Esther's seven friends had jumped in too, paddling about at the fringes of the slope. I suppose that, once Melody Janie had done it, there were no excuses left.

I went to the reservoir every day after that, every day that summer until school started again. Esther was always there. So were her friends, though I still did not think of them as mine. As the weeks passed, more and more people joined us each day, the rumour of the reservoir rippling out along the school network, drawing in new swimmers and sunbathers. Boys soon outnumbered girls. Esther liked to swim with them and, when she did, I swam alone. But this only happened once or twice a week. Much of the time, Esther and I stuck close to one another. Nobody would swim out as far as us, not even the boys, and sometimes, when we were out so deep we could no longer hear the chatter from the slope, we would tread water and talk about the girls we did not like or the teachers we did or tell each other jokes and stories.

The weather was glorious that year. Blue skies and gentle breezes. Though the holidays ended, the summer did not, lingering into September, beyond the start of the new school year. We no longer swam at midday but in the afternoon, convoys of us spilling through the school gates at half past three and walking the two miles to the reservoir together, our costumes and towels stuffed into our bags alongside our books and pencil cases, Esther and I in the middle of it all but feeling like we were in front, that we led, for if anyone had started this craze it was us.

It would have petered out naturally if it had been allowed to. Just a few weeks later a storm came in which transformed summer to autumn in a single morning, and nobody would have thought of swimming again for another nine months. But the end was more abrupt. Mrs Marks saw to that. Parents had complained. Health and safety was an issue. Our lives at stake. An assembly was held and we were summarily informed that every single one of us was banned from swimming in the reservoir.

I was astonished when, after the ban was imposed and the reservoir deemed off-limits, Esther remained my friend. I never became part of her core social group, though the blame for that lay with me. Sometimes

Esther beckoned me over to sit with her and her friends in the playground and once I was even invited to a birthday party, but I always said no. I was a loner at school and I can blame that on the ignorance of others, but the truth is that I was often happier alone. At the very least, I never had a problem with it. Though I was grateful for Esther's friendship, it was enough for me. I needed no other.

I spent most of my free time at school, my lunches and breaks, in the library, and when Esther and I spent time together it was because she had come to seek me out there, which she did two or three times a week. Since I sometimes helped the librarian put the returned books back on the shelves, I was allowed to eat my packed lunch in the library – and, by the proxy of me, Esther was too. At the time, I thought we talked a great deal during those library lunches, but now that I look back on it I remember differently. In fact, she did most of the talking and I did most of the listening. It was no problem for me. I liked to hear her speak in those long and rolling monologues which were never selfish but simply engaging, delivered with the kind humility she oozed. I still do. Sometimes we would not even talk at all – we would sit and read or do some homework. But that was pleasant too, because we helped each other or complained in tandem about the impossibility of the task set and this made us both feel better. Once, we started to write a song together, but we could never get any further than *Melody Janie Rowe / And Esther Leigh Harlow* and so we gave up.

In Year 11 she started to drift away from me a little when she became friends with the Three Lauras. There was a school play on and, to everyone's surprise, the Three Lauras not only wanted to join in but were actually very good in it: they could act funny or serious and dance well and Laura Pearce had a singing voice that was sensational. I did not audition for the play, but Esther did – landing herself one of the leading roles – and so she told me everything about it in the library. The Three Lauras, she said, seemed to be mellowing, and she thought it was because of the play itself, because it brought together people who would not normally socialise and forced them into proximity, so that they realised how similar they all were and barriers were broken. That was what Esther said. Whether or not the Three Lauras were genuinely mellowing, they fell for Esther in the same way that anyone who gets to know her does, and soon took her under their collective wing.

I saw less and less of her after the play. She saw more and more of the Three Lauras. A part of me wanted to believe that they forbade her from coming to see me in the library, that my inclusion as friend of a friend did not sit well with their general ethos of appearance – but the truth is probably that she just liked them more than me, had more fun and excitement with them, wanted to spend more time with them. She still came to see me in the library, usually once or twice a week, and when we were together it was like nothing had changed. But I could feel her moving on, away.

The end of our friendship came when I told Esther

the secret. I have regretted it ever since. It ruined everything between us. We stopped speaking and she began to spend all her time with the Three Lauras. Soon we would not even look at each other when we passed in the corridor. One afternoon, she told me that my tie was too long.

When school finished, Esther went to college in Treleven and I started working full-time at the Cafy. We occasionally bumped into each other on our shared street in St Petroc and she might ask how I was or if the Cafy was busy, but she always had somewhere to be. She always had someone to see. A year later, her family sold their house in St Petroc and moved to Treleven. I assumed then that she was gone from my life for good.

Until she reappeared two weeks ago. I was in the Cafy cleaning the bar when I looked up and saw her there in the doorway. She had heard the news, she said. She strode forward and hugged me so hard I thought I might dissolve into her chest. Then we sat and drank tea together and talked for the whole day. She told me about her new life, a student in Bristol. I did not say much. I did not need to. I was happy just to listen.

Since that day, Esther has said she will visit me every Tuesday (when she has no lectures) and Saturday (when she drives her sky-blue Ford Fiesta down to spend the weekend with her parents in Treleven). So far she has stuck to her word. After the second visit she began suggesting that I come to see her in Bristol, that perhaps I could spend a month or two or even more there with her. I have tried to explain to her the impossibility of me spending so long away from Bones Break. If I am not here to look after it, who knows what will happen? Without my presence, this whole place could be stolen out from under me by scheming developers and emmets hungry for their sea view. I try to explain all of this, but whenever I do she looks bemused as if she does not understand and, when I think about it, it is probable she does not.

No matter. So long as her visits continue, I can be content with that. We have the same conversations each time.

How are you?

Better.

Melody Janie Rowe . . .

. . . and Esther Leigh Harlow.

I'll be back soon. Do you need anything?

No.

Tomorrow, though – tomorrow I will change our conversation. There are some things I have not told Esther, private things that are better kept to myself. I do not want secrets to ruin our friendship again. But there is one secret I want to share. Tomorrow, I will tell Esther about Richard Brown.

It is not my biggest secret, but it is big enough.

It grows colder and colder. I light the two burners in the kitchenette for some temporary respite. They make a noticeable difference to the temperature in the caravan, but I know it will be short-lived. I should not leave them on while I sleep. I stand beside them for a while, warming my blood. And then, safety outweighing reluctance, I turn each off, climb into bed, bury myself beneath the duvet and breathe into my hands.

This might be the coldest night yet. Autumn is beginning to bite.

I have two sources of heating in the caravan and I try to use both as little as possible. The first is a gas-powered heater, embedded in the sideboard below the wardrobe as part of the original conversion. It takes a long time to warm up, but once it does it fills the entire caravan with a fug of heat which makes my eyes heavy. Its problem is that it gulps up my gas, can consume an entire bottle in one week and, even though I still have full bottles remaining in the front storage compartment, I do not know when I will be able to replace them.

The second source of heating is my portable electric fan heater. This is small and quick to work, but its heat is quick to dissipate too. Turn it off on a cold night and the caravan will settle back into refrigeration within ten minutes. It can also prove to be a powerful drain on my solar panels, causing the lights to dim and the inverter to squeal its alarm in protest. On days when there has been little sun it can suck up all the available energy in less than an hour, and today there has been little sun.

It would be unwise to use either heater tonight, and so instead I dart out from the duvet to take my coat, a thick pair of leggings and an even thicker pair of socks from the wardrobe. I rush them on and dive back into bed. If this cold persists, then perhaps I will retrieve the second duvet, the extra blankets and the two hot water bottles from the compartment beneath the bed. I will place the second duvet underneath the first and sleep between them like the filling of a sandwich. The extra blankets will go on top, the hot water bottles inside with me, down by my feet. This will surely suffice for even the coldest of nights. Winter approaches and I must survive it, transcend it, while I wait for Mum.

It was warmer when Little Sister Lucy was here, in bed with me, even though she liked to sleep down by my feet. When we moved from the house to the caravan, from separate bedrooms to a shared bed, I thought she might enjoy our new nightly proximity. But, in fact, though she rarely left my side during the day, once we were tucked up and the lights were out, she would pull as far away from me as possible, sliding down beneath the duvet, retreating to her corner at the bottom of the bed, her feet poking out and the rest of her covered. My softly snoring lump.

Only once, after I had been crying about Dad, did she let me spoon her until we fell asleep. When I woke in the morning she seemed to sense it immediately and wriggled out of my arms and on to her back and then on to her left side so that she faced me. I put my arms around her once more, but I kept the embrace loose. I did not like the thought of her wriggling away again.

'You scared me yesterday, Mellijane. You wouldn't stop crying.'

'I miss Dad.'

'I miss him too.'

'I know you do.' I moved my left hand up her body to stroke her hair.

'Do you miss Mum as much as Dad?' she said.

'Yes.' I had to look away from her gaze for a moment. I thought I might cry again. 'Don't you?' I whispered, not looking at her.

'I don't think she's coming back.'

I shook my head. 'Don't,' I said. 'Don't ever say that.'

'Let me go.'

I did as I was told, taking my arms from around her and pushing myself up into a sitting position. She shimmied over the bedsheets and planted her head on my lap to stare up into my face. She did not say anything.

Her enormous wet eyes were too much. I cried again. I did not stop for a long time.

Sunlight filters through the cracks in the curtains, cutting shards from my visible breath. My eyelashes are crusty with sleep. I step out of bed, pulling my coat tighter around me, and pad over to the bathroom, opening the door and taking a packet of wipes from the shower tray. I trace one across my eyes. It stings like frost.

I have woken late. I hope Esther has not arrived already, arrived and then left. Keeping my coat and leggings on, I slip my trainers over my socks and open the door. A gust of wind wrenches it from my hand, slamming it against the side of the caravan. The morning is a squall. Dead leaves pirouette through the air. As I step out of the doorway, there is a crunch beneath my foot. I look down. Ice. I have broken through the thin membrane covering a shallow puddle. Brown water sloshes up through the cracks to dirty my trainer. The plate of ice begins to sink. I smash it six, seven times with my heel. Muddy droplets splatter up and over my leggings.

I close and lock the door and make my way through the woods. The sky-blue Ford Fiesta is not in the car park. I have not missed her.

I let myself into the Cafy and walk through to the kitchen to test the gas. It still works. I locate the crockery and ingredients necessary to make a pot of tea for two, fill the enormous whistling kettle with water from the tap and then put it on the stove to boil. As I work, the crunch of tyres on gravel reaches me from outside, then the footsteps and finally the swing of the front door. I walk out into the bar area to meet her.

'How are you?'

'Better.'

I lead her into the kitchen, where we wait next to the stove for the kettle to boil.

'Are these yours?' Esther asks. She is pointing at the pile of spare clothes Mum likes to keep on one of the worktops, a full and comprehensive set, even including socks and underwear, all folded neatly and stacked into a shallow cube, topped by a pair of faded green slip-on shoes.

'Mum's,' I say.

Esther nods slowly. 'What's that smell?'

'The storeroom.'

'It must be a full-time job, trying to keep this place clean.'

The whistle of the kettle sounds. I pour the boiled water into the pot, drowning the two teabags.

'I wanted to say sorry for last time,' Esther says while I mix and stir.

'Is your mum all right?'

'She's fine, she's just lost a lot of confidence ever since her . . .' She stops. I know the word she wants to say. She wants to say *fall*. Her mother fell in her house a few months ago and injured her hip. But Esther is too sensitive to use that word around me. '. . . ever since she hurt her hip. She calls me all the time. I don't know why it's always me. She leaves Nathan and Maggie alone, but I seem to be on the phone to her every day. She even suggested that I move back in with her and Dad, that I commute to Bristol!'

'Imagine that,' I say. 'Someone trying to get you to move in with them. The horror.'

Esther's eyes widen in mock surprise and then we both laugh in unison. 'So cheeky!' she says. 'Fine, I'll never extend my love and care towards you again.'

'You're even beginning to sound like a mother.'

'Fuck that, I'm never having kids,' Esther snorts, and this makes me laugh harder. It was a funny thing for her to say. I am not precisely sure why. 'That's the first time,' she says.

'The first time what?'

Esther looks at me. She does not blink. 'The first time I've heard you laugh.'

'It's not been easy.'

'Of course not. But you know I'm here for you, don't you?' She takes both my hands in hers.

'I do,' I say. 'Thank you.'

'You've not really talked about it all, not with me anyway.'

Some things are better left unsaid. 'I haven't talked about it with anyone.'

'Well, just know that you can. With me. If you want to. And whenever you want to. Now. Later. Whenever.'

'Later.' I squeeze her hands, drop them and take a sip of tea. 'I will talk to you later. Soon. I promise.'

'Okay,' Esther says. 'I won't push. It's nice to be talking to you like this again.'

'How do you mean?'

'Like we used to. Laughing. It's nice to see you smile. Oh God, it sounds like I'm criticising you for—'

'No,' I interrupt her. 'I understand. When you come, we talk but we don't really say anything. But I like this too. Us joking together. It's good for me.'

Esther beams and takes a sip of her tea. We walk from the kitchen through to the dining room and sit at a table.

'I do have some news, though,' I say. 'I've met someone.'

'Oh, yeah?' Esther raises a single eyebrow, and I hit her gently on the knee.

'Not like *that*. There's an emmet here. An old man with a dog. He's moved into Mrs Perrow's house.'

'Mrs Perrow's . . . ?'

'The cottage just down the road from here. Opposite Nare Point.'

Esther nods. 'You've been making friends? That's not like you.'

'He's not my friend. The dog – Archie – he's lovely, but the emmet isn't. Pretty much the opposite, in fact. Do you know what he said not long after we first met?'

'What?'

'"*You don't recognise me, do you?*"'

'Is he a celebrity?'

'I don't know. I don't know what he is. I didn't recognise him but I got the feeling that I should. There's something not right about him and I'm trying to find out what it is.'

'Do you know his name?'

'Richard Brown.'

'Why don't you just Google him?'

'I don't have a phone.'

'Why not?'

'I don't like them.' I could tell her why, but that would begin a conversation I do not want to have.

Esther shakes her head and removes her phone from her pocket. 'Melody Janie Rowe,' she says. 'Cornwall's youngest Luddite.'

She begins to tap away at her phone screen and I move my chair closer to hers to watch. She switches between search engines and social media platforms with astonishing speed, here and there filling the screen with a profile picture and asking, 'Is this him? Is this?' The answer is always no.

Esther sighs and stops her browsing. 'Trust you to want information on a man with one of the most common names in the country. We'll never find him with just this, there's too many Richard Browns. What else do you know about him?'

'He's from Manchester,' I say. 'He has a broken arm. His dog is a rescued labradoodle called Archie.'

'It's not really narrowing things down.' Esther continues to tap away. 'Anything else?'

'He's tall. Over six foot. Short grey hair.'

'Personal information is better.'

'That's it. He doesn't tell me anything. He's too guarded.'

'Impossible,' Esther says, switching off the phone and placing it in her lap. 'Do you see him often?'

'Most days. I've started to walk Archie with him.'

'And are you sure he's . . . safe to be around?'

'I'm not scared of him,' I say.

Esther gazes out of the window towards my land. 'You should have a phone.'

'They're not for me.'

Esther ignores my words and faces me again. 'I'm going to get you a phone.' It is not an offer. It is a declaration.

Before I can thank her, we are interrupted by the sound of her own phone. The word MUM flashes up on the screen. Esther answers. I know she is being summoned back to Treleven.

I take the teapot and cups and saucers and spoons back to the kitchen and when I return to the bar area Esther is putting on her coat. We hug as we usually do, but this time our parting conversation is different. Esther does not ask if I need anything. Instead, she says, 'I'm getting you a phone.'

I do not want a phone. Not after last time. But perhaps Esther is right. Perhaps I should have one. If only so that I can call her. And so, instead of saying no, I say, 'Okay.'

'There's an old one at home that still works. I'll charge it up overnight and drop it off here tomorrow afternoon on my way back to Bristol.'

'What time?'

'Late afternoon. I usually set off at about five o'clock.'

'Thank you,' I say. The thought of having my own phone again leaves me uneasy. But knowing that I will see Esther tomorrow tempers the trepidation immaculately.

Esther's comment about the storeroom rankles. I need to clean it. But it is a big job and I am not sure I have the strength today. Instead, I retrieve the surface cleaner and a cloth from the kitchen and make my way back to the dining room to wipe down the tables. It all helps.

The circular motion of the cloth across the surface of the table is hypnotic and I find myself thinking back to the first time I came here, to the Cafy, all those years ago. Dad and I had spent the morning visiting Mum in the Centre, but she had been dazed and vacant and I had left her room feeling angry with her. Dr Trenoweth had seen me stomping down the corridor and had asked if I was all right. I had wanted to reply that I was not all right and that neither was my mother, and that if he had been any good at his job then he would have seen this and done something about it rather than asking stupid questions – but I was far too young and overwhelmed with rage to articulate all that and so I began to cry frustrated tears instead. Dad found me like that, eyes screwed up, mouth wide and howling, with poor flustered Dr Trenoweth trying to calm me down and only making things worse.

Dad took me away from the Centre and, instead of

going home, we came out here to the Cafy – back then, The Bones Break Diner. We walked along the lip for a while, along the very land which would one day become mine, and then Dad suggested a cream tea. We crossed the road and entered. To this day, I cannot remember if it was busy inside or if we were the only two there.

'Do you like Dr Trenoweth?' I asked Dad.

'I like him a lot.' He cut his scone in half, smeared jam across it and began to dab little spoonfuls of clotted cream on top. 'Mum's in good hands. I'm grateful that he's her doctor.'

'Why?'

'Because I think he knows what he's doing. And I trust him. We want Mum to get better, don't we, Melody Janie?'

My mouth was full of clotted cream, so I nodded instead of replying.

'Well, Dr Trenoweth will help Mum get better. That's what he does. He helps people who aren't feeling normal feel normal again.'

I swallowed the cream. 'Why doesn't Mum feel normal?'

Dad reached across the table to pick up my cup of tea and took a large gulp from it. I did not like tea back then and Dad could see I had left mine untouched. 'Right, I've got a question for you,' he said. 'And you have to answer me completely honestly. Will you do that?'

I nodded.

'You won't lie?'

I shook my head.

'Good. So this is my question. Is there a part of you – anything at all, no matter how big or small – that you don't like? Something that, if you could, you would change?'

I thought about it, taking a small bite from my scone.

'Here, I'll help,' Dad said. 'There's a part of me I've never liked. Never ever. I've always wanted it to be different. Since I was your age and still now.'

'What is it?' I was suddenly desperate to know. What on earth did Dad not like about himself? He was perfect!

'My hair,' he said.

'What's wrong with your hair?'

'I hate it. Absolutely hate it. It's curly and it sticks out from my head and I can't ever seem to do anything with it to make it look good. I wish I had hair like yours – all nice and soft and straight.'

'But I *love* your hair!'

'Ah, well, there you go. That's the thing. You love my hair because it's a part of me and you love me and I wouldn't be me without this hair. Right? Imagine if I had long straight hair like yours. What would I look like?'

'You'd look stupid!' I giggled.

'And imagine if I didn't have hair at all.'

'Then you'd be bald! And you'd look even stupider!' I giggled louder and Dad joined in. It felt good to laugh with him.

'Okay then,' he said, composing himself with another sip of my tea. 'So that's what I hate about myself. My hair. Now, what about you?'

I had come up with an answer while he had been talking about his hair. 'I don't like my fingers.'

'Why not?'

'They look like boys' fingers.'

'What makes you say that?'

'Paul Dunstan said that girls should have long fingers with long nails at the end, and that mine are stumpy and fat.'

'I love your fingers. I don't think they're stumpy or fat, but I don't care because I love them anyway. They're a part of you. And I love you. If you had different fingers you wouldn't be my Melody Janie. And I love my Melody Janie.'

I thought it would be funny then to put my fingers in his hair, but Dad must have thought I meant something else because he held my hands in his own and pressed my fingers down on to his scalp for a few moments. Then he let them go and I used them to dip my spoon into the jam and slip a dollop of it into my mouth.

'So you hate your fingers and I hate my hair,' he said. 'But I love your fingers and you love my hair. Because they're a part of us. And we love each other. And I wouldn't be me if I didn't have my hair. And you wouldn't be you if you didn't have your fingers. Right?'

I nodded, tonguing the jam's seeds from my teeth.

'Well, Mum also has something about her that she hates. It's not something you can see, like fingers or hair, it's inside her, but just because we can't see it, that doesn't mean it isn't real. And we love her even though she has it. We love her *because* she has it. Without it, Mum wouldn't be Mum.'

'So is she in the Centre to get it changed?'

Dad thought about this for a while. 'No. She's in the Centre so that she can come to terms with it. To stop hating it. To realise it's a part of herself just like fingers or hair.'

'So she's in the Centre because she wants to stop hating herself?'

Dad smiled at me. Sometimes, I think I miss that smile more than anything else in the world. 'Exactly,' he said. '*Exactly*. She's in the Centre to learn to love herself just as much as we love her.'

I remember those words perfectly. I repeat them to myself, out loud, as I clean the table. *She's in the Centre to learn to love herself just as much as we love her.* I say it again, mimicking Dad's voice, soft and deep.

'I love you, Mum,' I say in my own voice. To no one. 'I love you so much. And I know you love me too. I know you'll come back.'

The caravan smells damp inside. I hope it has not developed a leak. I open one of the side windows, the smallest, and a bluebottle surfs in on a wave of cold air. It flies directly to the opposite window and grows frantic, beating its head and wings against the plastic, trying to break its way through to the outside. I approach with slow and quiet stealth, extending my arms and cupping my hands. The fly strikes the window again and again. It does not understand. All it wants – which is everything – lies beyond that invisible barrier. Seen but out of reach. The frustration must be insufferable. 'Come on, little fly,' I say. 'Let me help you.' With one swift move, I make a sphere with my hands and wrap them around the fly, locking them tight to shut off exits, to shut out light. The fly, sensing either help or death – either the beginning or the end – falls still. I can feel its legs on the crease of my palm, quivering. I walk it back to the open window, careful to keep my hands steady, to neither jolt nor roll the fly as we move, and when I hold my hands outside and open them it stays for a second or two in my palm before launching up and away, the wind carrying it deep into the woods.

I check my watch. 5.45 p.m. Richard will start to walk

Archie soon. I do not want to miss them. I need more information: something specific, indicative; something to anchor him down amongst the swirling waves of the internet; the beacon light of a key word or phrase.

I put on a pair of socks and my boots and then step outside. I make my way to the lip, seabirds circling overhead, their wings steady and stiff as they lower to circumnavigate Gull Rock. All of a sudden, courses change as they aim their beaks out to sea. Those already settled rise into the air and, as one, the birds zoom into the distance. My gaze follows their trajectory. Coming around the eastern headland, far enough out to avoid the submerged rocks yet close enough for the hands and the faces of the men on deck to be visible, is a fishing boat. The gulls flock to its rear, scrapping and charging and diving along its deck and into its wake. There is no elegance to the drama, only bolshiness, determination. This is not a murmuration but a vicious sky fight. The men on the boat pay little heed. They live their working lives to this chorus.

I make my way along the lip to dead centre, cross the barrier and step into position, but it feels wrong. With the fishermen in full view, with my feet not bare but wrapped in socks and shoes, there is a disconnect. I cannot feel Little Sister Lucy like this. Voices rise up the cliff face to meet me: shouts and calls which pierce through the fug of screaming gulls and a thrumming engine. The voices are not directed at me, but the fact I can hear them is enough. I am too exposed. It needs to be just me and her. I step out of position.

Walking towards the eastern headland takes me in the opposite direction from the boat – soon it is out of sight, soon after that it is out of earshot too. I welcome the peace as I pass the cleft and follow the coast path east. At the rise, there is no sign of Richard or Archie and so I continue on to Nare Point, through the car park, across the road and up the pathway to the house.

I knock on the door. Archie begins to bark from inside but the door remains closed. Surprised a little at my temerity, I try the handle. It is locked. I knock again. Archie barks louder.

'*Shup, Arch.*' The voice is heavy and slurred but it is unmistakeably Richard's.

I crouch down and open the letterbox with my fingers. 'Richard,' I call into it. 'Are you there?'

'Leave me alone!' His voice is close and, startled, I jump back from the letterbox. 'Why can't you all just leave me alone?' The question is a demand, angry and drunken.

I do not open the letterbox again, but I know he can hear me. 'It's me, Richard.'

'Richard who?'

'No, Richard, it's me, Melody Janie.'

'Melody Janie?'

'Melody Janie, from Bones Break, from the Cafy.'

'Oh,' he says. 'Melody Janie.' There is a long pause. And then, 'Fuck off.'

A door slams from inside the house. I knock a few more times, but there is no response. Even Archie does not bark.

The clouds race across the sky. They are thin, slaves to the wind. I watch one as it streams in from the horizon, crossing the moon, backlit and broken up, dissolving into streaks and swirls. It vanishes into the darkness before it reaches me.

This walk is aimless. Without Richard and Archie, I have continued alone, east, all the way to Petherick's western headland. I stop and, for a moment, consider walking down into the village. But the moment passes quickly. From the headland I can see it all below, street-lit, bright and busy. Live music drifts up from the pub, followed by the thin clouds made by the smokers huddled in the doorway. Somewhere a bottle smashes and somewhere else a woman howls – I cannot tell if it is a laugh or a scream. Teenagers have built a bonfire on the beach and proudly taunt any dog walkers who stray too close. A parked car, blocked in by a van, sounds its horn for an age but no one comes to move the offending vehicle. Someone swears and someone swears back louder. Saturday night in Petherick.

On the far side of the village, the new estate is virtually empty, just three windows weakly lit in stark contrast to the surrounding darkness. It will be like that until next spring, all those empty homes and no locals rich enough to occupy them.

A fight begins outside the pub, brief but loud. I hear the bellows and the screeches. From here it looks like they are dancing. Others arrive to pull them apart and there follows a roared argument which lasts far longer than the fight itself. I remember once asking Dad why it was so violent here. 'They're being backed into a corner,' he told me. 'And they're going down fighting.'

I stand and watch for a long time, safe on my coast path. Soon the pub closes. The bonfire goes out. Roads clear. Houses darken. There is nothing left to watch. I turn and begin the long trek west back to Bones Break. It is cold but I am not tired. I am not tired at all. Once I reach Bones Break, I may continue walking, walking around my land. A late-night patrol or an early-morning perimeter check.

A seagull swoops low, directly overhead, and I duck instinctively. Its face comes close to mine. I see the terror in its eyes. It did not intend this proximity. It is fighting the wind, fighting it with a determined fury, its feathers dishevelled and buffeted as it tries to land somewhere below the lip. It must be exhausted, should not be out so late. Perhaps it was carried far out to sea and has only just fought its way back. An updraft catches it from beneath and it soars high into the air, its flapping and banking useless. It will find no rest tonight.

The grass is dry and stiff beneath my feet. Strands of hair stick to my eyelashes. A sharp gust blows, bouncing off my shoulder and making me lurch to the left. I brush past a bank of thistles, scratching the bare skin on my right calf. I wince and squat low to examine the damage. There is no blood, only two red lines swelling into angry welts. I lick my finger and rub the saliva gently over the wound. I am not sure why. Something about antiseptic. It seems to work: the sting lessens.

I make out the silhouette of Richard's house as I draw near. The lights are not on but I can hear something. I walk forward a few more metres, pause, turn my head and cup a hand over my left ear to protect it from the wind. There it is. Human noise. A beat. Faint but regular, indecipherable but unmistakeable. A kick drum, synthesised and slow. I doubt it is coming from Richard's house. Far more likely is that it comes from Nare Point. A van. Campers, emmets probably. Someone to spy on.

I dart from the coast path into the scrub and push forward through thickets of gorse. The music means that the emmets are awake, could even be stood out on the lip, and I need to approach without being seen. Ahead, between me and Nare Point, stands a wild hedge. The beat grows louder, impenetrable words rapped above it. I sidle into the hedge, try to find a way through or over it, but it is too dense. A sharp branch pokes its way into the side of my dress and refuses to let go. I lurch back and away from it without thinking. Stupid of me. The rip is audible. I can feel the cold air rushing in through the fresh opening, numbing my ribs.

I make my way down along the hedge towards the road, testing it here and there for openings until I find one. I squeeze my way into it and try to shimmy through, but my dress gets caught again and when I reach down to free it, something sharp – a thistle or broken branch – stabs into my cheek and slashes across as I jerk my head back in pain. While the rest of me freezes, my hand instinctively goes to my face. I can feel the fresh blood through my fingers.

I breathe, long and deep.

Taking my hand from my face and moving with the utmost care, I extricate my dress from the hedge. Then, protecting my face with both hands – I can feel them smearing the blood over my cheeks and mouth – I gently but firmly push forward.

I appear from the hedge, a mess. Torn dress and bloodied face. But it is all forgotten in an instant when I look across the car park and see the source of the music. A VW camper van, light green, spare wheel poking from the front like the snout of a piglet.

I cannot believe they have come back. I warned them. They ignored me.

One of the side windows is open. Light, music and smoke pour out to be dispersed by the wind. A hand appears through the window, a long rolled-up cigarette drooping between its fingers. The thumb flicks and a spark of ash flashes and then disintegrates into the night. The hand vanishes back inside.

I need to be closer. I can smell and hear them. I want to see and feel them too. I want to watch their eyes as they talk, study their mouths. I want to eavesdrop on their language, their private language which they use when alone, the words and the gestures, the movements, flinches and smiles. I want to pay them careful attention.

I approach the van. Not too close. Slowly, steadily, I move into position, a few feet away from the side door, my head level with the open window. It takes a second or two for my eyes to adjust to the light, to the thick smoke which swirls around inside. Two heads bob and sway through the fog. One is laughing or maybe coughing, I cannot tell.

'Lay the fucking card, will you?'

'It's my go?'

More laughing or coughing or both. 'It's always your go!'

The one who pissed all over my land takes a long drag of the oversized cigarette. Her lips pucker. She is so ugly. She exhales, smoke billowing from her pig nostrils, directing it towards and then out of the open window.

She screams: nails driven into my eardrums.

The other follows her friend's gaze. 'What—' She sees me. Her screams are louder.

I do not move. Their eyes and mouths are so wide. I realise how I must look to them, gazing in through their open window, my torn dress and bloodstained face, my hair unkempt, half-lit by their orange light and half-shrouded by their smoke, in the middle of the night in the middle of nowhere. I must look like a ghost. Or a murderer. The thought makes me want to smile, but I do not. One of them has frozen, but the other pushes herself back, away from the window. I picture her fingernails digging into the cushioning beneath her. I look at them both in turn, stare each in the eyes for two or maybe three seconds and then I take a deep breath and I scream back at them.

I can no longer hear them. All I can hear is my own roar. But they are screaming too. I can see them, even through the tears which have begun to well in my eyes. My head pounds. I do not have much scream left. Before it ends, I raise it a pitch, and then I charge the van. The speed with which they slam the window shut and close the curtain is astonishing. They manage it before I reach the side panels and beat upon them with my fists. The lights are extinguished. I stop screaming. I can still hear them inside, their low, moaning cries. I lean close to the window and stage-whisper garbled nonsense into the seams. I scratch my nails down the metal.

'Go away!' one of them shrieks from inside. '*Go away go away go away go away!*' Her cries turn into thick and phlegmy sobs, the wails of an infant. My job here is done. I tiptoe to the grass and then sprint silently away, making sure to reach at least dead centre before allowing the howls of laughter to burst from me.

Sunlight wakes me and I peer out from under the duvet. My dress, torn and dirty, lies crumpled on the floor beside the bed. Fire ripples across my cheek as I move and stretch, and I gently explore the thin scab beginning to form over the long cut with my finger. I get out of bed and step into the bathroom to peer into the mirror. The face that looks back is ludicrous: the sallow, blood-stained cheeks; the bright eyes. I tilt my head to the left and tenderly clean around the wound with a wipe. It takes twenty more before I am satisfied. I smile at myself in the mirror. It hurts.

Closing the bathroom door behind me, I move to the wardrobe to retrieve a clean and intact dress. I gaze out of the window as I put it on. The sun is out, the air looks warm. I do not need my coat. The dress and my sandals will suffice. I help myself to some water biscuits and tinned sardine paste, step out of the caravan and immediately make my way towards Nare Point. I want to see if the girls are still there.

They are not. Of course. Nare Point car park is empty. I suspect they got no sleep last night. Their drive must have been dangerous. Perhaps they crashed. Or perhaps they are still driving at this very moment. Perhaps their accident is just a junction away.

I look over to the road: Archie and Richard are approaching. When they reach the car park, Richard releases Archie, who breaks into an open sprint and bounds towards me. I think he is about to knock me down, but he comes to an expert stop inches from my feet and rears up, planting two paws on my belly and dangling his tongue at me. I scratch him behind his left ear and he leans into it, eyes half-closed in bliss.

'Good God, what happened to your face?'

My hand lifts to my cheek and lightly fingers the long thin scab. 'Nothing.' I want to change the subject. 'So you remember me this time?'

'Yes. Look.' Richard adjusts his sling with his free hand. 'I'm so very sorry about last night.'

'You told me to fuck off.'

'I did. And I can only apologise. I'm very, very sorry. I wasn't myself.'

'Then who were you? Not Richard Brown?'

There is the stare: the uncomfortable, piercing stare. I hate it. 'I'm afraid I had a little too much to drink. I'm sorry.'

'Well,' I say, looking away from his strange eyes and down at the car park's oil-stained gravel. 'I forgive you.' It is a lie. I do not forgive him. But if I am to find out what I need to know about him, he must believe we are friends.

'Can I join you for your walk?' I ask.

Richard thinks for a moment. 'Archie would like that,' he finally says.

We set off together through the car park until we reach the lip. 'East or west?' I ask.

'I'm in the mood for a long walk today. To clear my head. Perhaps we could go all the way to Lantoweth?'

'Perfect.'

We turn left on the coast path and make our way towards the rise. I gaze at the horizon. The sun is out and the ocean is calm: sky and water echoing blue. It occurs to me that it is a beautiful morning.

'May I ask you something, Melody Janie?'

'If you like.' I welcome his questions. They will make the ones I want to ask not intrusive but reciprocal.

'Were you,' he pauses, searches for the right way to ask, 'were you out here very late last night?'

He knows. 'When?'

'It was about three o'clock.'

'What was?'

'The screams.'

I must answer before this silence gives me away. 'And you think that was me?' I say.

'No. I don't know. Maybe. It sounded like a girl.' He stutters and corrects himself. 'Young woman.'

'Well, it definitely wasn't me.' I suddenly remember that Richard does not know I live in the caravan. 'I was back home and in bed long before that. But I wouldn't worry about it. Kids come up here from Petherick and St Petroc to mess around all the time.'

Richard looks at me. That searching intensity again.

'Honestly, Richard,' I say to hide my discomfort, 'I wouldn't worry about it.'

We walk on in silence, to and then past the cleft on the eastern headland, along the mesmerising sweep of Bones Break to the western headland and then yet further, pushing towards The Warren. The void left by the rockfall grows before us until we reach its lip. Richard creeps up close to the edge but I stay back. When he returns to me, we move on towards Pedna Head. We have not said a word since the rise. I will wait for Richard to speak first. I own this silence. He will be the one to break it.

Where Pedna Head ends Lantoweth begins. Three miles of wide sand which come to an abrupt stop against the imposing girth of the Roskyn headland. We follow the coast path behind the beach until we reach the steps carved into the brown cliffs. Richard latches the lead on to Archie's collar for the descent. Archie's saddlebags scrape against the walls as he passes, sediment crumbling in his wake.

Richard speaks. 'The first time I came here, I thought I might have found the most beautiful beach in the world.'

'There's better,' I reply.

We stride towards the shoreline. The tide is high and we do not have to walk far. Richard detaches Archie's lead and then plucks a mussel shell from the sand. Archie watches him closely. He throws it towards the water, but it is empty and feather-light and the wind carries it over his head and behind him. Archie looks at his master and I swear I can see disdain in those eyes. I love Archie. Richard finds a stone, flat and the size of his palm, and tries again. The stone sails through the air, landing a few metres out into the water, swallowed by an incoming wave. Archie speeds after it into the sea, then skids to a halt, turns and retreats as the advancing wave nears him.

'I try to get him a little further out each time. But he'll never go deeper than his knees.'

'At least it keeps the saddlebags dry.'

'Quite.'

We walk slowly with the sea on our right, darting inland each time a renegade wave breaches the shoreline. A slight mist hangs over the far end of the beach, the Roskyn headland barely visible behind and through it. Archie sloshes along in the water beside us. Never deeper than his knees.

'There's something else I should like to ask you, Melody Janie,' Richard says. 'If I may.'

'So many questions today.' I like my answer, the sense of authority it conveys.

'May I?'

'Okay.'

Richard takes a deep breath. 'Have you told anyone about me?'

'No,' I lie. 'Why?'

He ignores my question and we continue down the beach, westward, the sand hard and wet beneath our feet. Our footprints are shallow. Firm.

'That's two questions you've asked me,' I say.

'I didn't realise we were keeping count.'

'And I answered both honestly,' I continue. 'But whenever I ask you anything, you avoid giving me a proper answer. You're very good at that.'

'Practice,' he says, picking up another stone and throwing it into the sea for Archie.

'So, may I ask you a question?'

'Yes,' he says. 'One more, because that was your first, and apparently we only have two each.'

I smile in spite of myself. As slippery as Richard is, I cannot help but begin to enjoy this game. 'Are you famous?' I ask.

'Why do you ask that?'

'It would explain a lot.'

'Such as?'

'In general, everything. In particular, when you asked if I recognised you. You're a celebrity.'

'I'm not a celebrity.'

'But you're . . . you're *known*. Aren't you?'

'Yes.' He sighs. 'I'm known.'

'Why? What for? What did you do?'

'That's just it,' Richard says. 'I didn't do anything.'

We walk a few steps further, in silence. 'Is that why you're here?' I ask.

'Yes. I didn't move here, as such. I was relocated.'

'Do you want to . . . to talk about it?' The question feels alien to my tongue, this trite but meaningful offer, both generic and gentle, within it the reassurance of friendship, as false as it is.

'No,' Richard says.

'Because you can't?'

'No, I can. I just don't want to. And I think that's enough questions.' His tone is final. He throws another stone for Archie. I say nothing. And then, to my surprise, he speaks again. 'You know, all you have to do is look in any newspaper from the last couple of months.'

'I don't read the newspapers.'

'Of course you don't. Online, then.'

'I don't have Wi-Fi.'

'You must have mobile data on your phone. Everyone does. Even me.'

'I don't have a phone.'

'Why not?'

'I don't like them.'

We reach the headland. The tide surges forward, its currents swelling and swirling as they rush into Roskyn's caves, building banks and whirlpools. A tern nosedives after a fish and re-emerges with its beak empty. My hands and face are wet, droplets sparkle from the wisps of my hair. Archie sniffs at the incoming water, turns and saunters to Richard's side. He is getting tired. We have walked a long way.

'We should head back,' Richard says.

I nod. For now, the questions can stop. I have a new piece of information.

Look in any newspaper from the last couple of months.

We turn away from the headland, begin the long march east, retracing our steps back through the sand, back towards the coast path. We walk in silence, enter our downtime. A lull in conversation and in the thoughts behind it. Walking long and smooth, our steps synchronising, finding the rhythm of heart and breath and falling into its automation. This is good country for wordlessness.

We come to the foot of the cliff staircase. Richard looks up the rising steps.

'We can stop for a while if you like,' I say.

'Maybe at the top.' He begins the climb. Archie follows. I take the rear. Richard has to rest every dozen steps or so, but it is never long before he starts again and we reach the lip in minutes.

'How are you doing?' I ask.

'Never better.' He is panting heavily. He sounds like Archie.

'Shall we push on?'

'Absolutely.'

There is a slight incline in the coast path as it wends its way behind the remainder of Lantoweth. It levels out once we reach Pedna Head. On its far side, the curve of my land comes into view.

'Whatever the reason,' I say, 'you chose the best place in the world to relocate.'

Richard sneers. It ages him terribly. 'I didn't choose,' he says. 'Bones Break. A notorious suicide spot. And they put me in a house a stone's throw away from it. It's a sick joke.'

A chill creeps over me. 'Suicide spot?'

'You must know that. You work here. People jump all the time.'

'Who?'

'I don't know, Melody Janie. People. Just look at the name. It's written on the side of your café.'

'That's not why it's called Bones Break.'

'Of course it is.'

'No, it's not even the name of the place. Not really. It's the wave. Surfers named it, named the wave, the break. Bones Break. Because it's impossible to surf. Too many rocks.'

'Perhaps the surfers meant the wave broke on the bones of suicide victims.'

'No, Richard,' I snap. 'That's not what it means at all.'

Richard, castigated, does not reply.

We are approaching dead centre. I feel angry and

force myself to breathe, long and deep. When I have calmed, I stop walking. 'I had better go now,' I say.

'Yes,' Richard says. 'Me too.'

I take Archie's head in my hands and rub his nose. 'Are you walking again tonight?'

'Yes.'

'Six o'clock?'

'Yes.'

'I'll see you then.'

'Okay.'

I walk back to the Cafy, let myself in and then watch through the windows as Richard and Archie disappear over the eastern headland. I will give them a few minutes more, and then I will head back out. In search of a newspaper.

It is time to go down into Petherick.

In the caravan, I change my dress, eat a packet of crisps, drink some water, ready myself for the walk and, at the end of it, Petherick. I am dreading it. I consider stalling, waiting for Esther who is coming this evening and who, if she keeps her promise, will bring me a mobile phone. Last time, we only had a common name to search for, but this time we will be able to search the newspaper websites themselves, within which Richard has assured me I will find him and his story.

I had a phone once. It was during the last year of school. Everyone else had one. Even the youngest kids, the Year 7s, would bump into each other in the playground because they were gazing deep into their phones. I had seen the same on my land, the endless emmets who could not seem to sufficiently admire the view without taking it in through the filters of their screens. When I was feeling kind I laughed at their ignorance; when I was feeling less so I imagined them so enthralled by their little devices that they air-walked right off the lip, snapping terrified selfies as they plummeted into the ocean.

I made vows to myself that I would never become like those emmets, like all the others at school. I preferred to read books in the library; I preferred to trust in my eyes and my memories for their panoramas of Bones Break. And so, when I was fifteen years old and Mum upgraded her phone and offered me her old one, I took the thing with a shrug, promising I would use it to call her in an emergency, promising myself I would use it for nothing more.

I stayed true to my word for a week, never once looking at it. I did not even take it to school with me, and when I asked Esther for her number one lunchtime in the library she laughed at me because I had to write it in my notebook. The following Saturday morning I tried to turn the phone on but the battery had already run out. Using Mum's old charger I powered it back up and, while I waited, I added in Esther's number and then deleted all the other contacts except for the numbers of my parents. I was surprised to discover that this, such a small act of engagement, gave me a brief but unmistakeable thrill. There was a sort of magnetic power to the phone, and for the first time in my life I glimpsed why and how people could become so mesmerised by these little gadgets. Once it was fully charged I put the phone in my pocket and took it to work with me that afternoon.

It was a quiet Saturday at the Cafy and, during a lull, I felt the urge to sit on one of the picnic benches with a cup of tea and play with my new phone. There was no Wi-Fi at the Cafy, so Mum showed me how to turn on the mobile data and then left me to enjoy it. I was no stranger to the internet: I was allowed to use Mum's laptop at home and had regular IT lessons at school. They had left me familiar enough with the skills of working a computer to transfer them easily to this phone. Unsure what to do first, I opened the web browser and logged into my school email account. It was filled only with messages from Mrs Marks and homework assignments from various other teachers, homework I always completed by hand when I could and on the computers in the school library at lunchtime when I could not.

I closed the browser and opened the phone's app store to find Facebook. I knew exactly what it was; conversations about it were so prevalent at school that it was impossible to ignore. I was never involved in the conversations, but I heard them often enough. I downloaded the app and created an account for myself, using a photo of Bones Break as my profile picture. Once I was in, I was presented with a scrolling list of people I might know, all of them classmates from school. Esther was there. I added her as a friend first and then tried a few others, keeping my choices minimal, sticking to the ones who, like me, were neither the most nor the least popular, and therefore likely to accept my requests.

Knowing it would take some time for them to respond, I typed ideas into the search bar. The Cafy had no page or group and nor did Bones Break itself, but my school had a multitude: the whole school, my year group and even my tutor group. I joined them all.

There was a ping. Esther's profile picture appeared

in a speech bubble at the bottom of the screen. I tapped
it to reveal a message.

Melody Janie Rowe . . . it said.

. . . and Esther Leigh Harlow, I replied.

Another ping. *You on FB now? O happy day!*

Mum gave me her old phone, I wrote back.

A tiny video appeared on my screen showing a rolling
loop of a man popping a bottle of champagne while a
woman danced in the spray and screamed wildly.

Ha ha, I typed.

At Esther's insistence, I downloaded a different
messaging app. She explained that she suspected her
sister Maggie was secretly snooping on her Facebook
account through their shared laptop, but that this
app was tied only to Esther's phone and was therefore inaccessible to Maggie. Once the new app was
installed, I sent a *Hello?* to Esther's number, she replied
with a *Yes yes,* and from there a volley of messages
unravelled between us, a back and forth so relentless
I began to wonder how my fingers kept up. Esther was
a genius at expressing herself in weird and wonderful
ways, and I was given a whirlwind education in acro-
nyms, emojis, links and gifs. I liked how we would
sometimes overlap each other, asking questions and
then forgetting to answer them because more messages
appeared and needed to be addressed; how we would
circle back to tangents long ago abandoned; how we
could sometimes think and write the same thing at
the same time; how we seemed to cover both
everything and nothing at all.

'Looks like we've got an addict.' Mum was stood beside me, coffee in her hand, wind in her hair. I had not heard her approach.

'I'm not an addict,' I said.

'Good, because we're closing. Come in and help me clean the bar.'

I looked at the clock in the corner of the phone. An hour and a half had passed. Mum saw my look of disbelief, interpreted it correctly.

'Addict!' she sang, and I chased her into the Cafy, both of us giggling. But not before I messaged Esther that I had to go.

Mum was wrong. I was not addicted. I used the phone for little other than communicating with Esther. Sometimes I explored Facebook, but those who had accepted my friend requests rarely posted anything interesting, and the groups I had joined tended towards nastiness too much for my liking. Once, I saw a post from Paul Dunstan on the school group which said, *What do you call a line of freaks? A Melody Janie Rowe.* It had three likes. I expect he was disappointed by that.

As Year 11 passed and Esther became friendly with the Three Lauras, our lunchtimes together in the library grew fewer and so did our messages to each other. Sometimes, I would write something to Esther and a day or even two would pass before she replied. Once or twice she did not reply at all. If I am completely honest with myself, I think I told her the secret because I was beginning to miss her and I knew that sympathy was one way of getting Esther's attention.

It was not, of course, the primary reason. Fundamentally, I told Esther the secret because I was frightened and I was angry and I was confused and I needed to confide in a friend.

It was the week before my sixteenth birthday. There was one term of school left and all focus had been put on to the impending exams. Lunchtimes in the library were always busier at that time of year. The Cafy was open but Mum and Dad forbade me from working until the exams were over. All my free time needed to go into my revision. They wanted me to do well and so did I. And so, with that pressure and with the library often too noisy for work, I began to stay up later and later each night revising – sometimes hours after I had already said goodnight to Mum and Dad. It was during one of these nights that I heard them talking. About me.

I knew they had not heard me crossing the landing between my bedroom and the bathroom – if they had, they would have stopped talking immediately. Perhaps even shouted something up to me. Asked why I hadn't gone to sleep yet. Told me to go back to bed. But, instead, I heard Mum say, 'She's starting to worry me.'

I froze.

'You shouldn't worry. She's a good girl. She's going to be fine.' Dad's words were ever so slightly slurred. I guessed he was some point through a bottle of wine.

'She'll be sixteen next week.'

If there had been any uncertainty over the subject of their conversation, it was gone. I lowered myself to the landing floor, kept quiet and still, and listened.

'So?'

'So it's going so fast. It's going *too* fast.'

'I know. Seems like only yesterday she was—'

'No, Trev, that's not the point, that's not what I mean.'

'I know what you mean, but I don't agree. She's half me too.'

'But which half? Which half? Sometimes I think I can see it in her. The things she says. The way she looks at me.'

'You forget that I was there, I was there through it all—'

'On the outside—'

'On the outside looking in. Just like I am with Melody Janie. And I don't see any of it.'

'It's too subtle now. Even I didn't notice it when I was sixteen. It wasn't until I was nineteen.'

'You shouldn't be saying this.'

'That's three years, Trev. Three short years. What if that's all she's got left? Until it happens to her? What if—'

'Stop it. Stop it now.'

'What if she's just like me?'

I heard Dad stand and walk out of the living room into the kitchen. Mum followed. The door closed behind them. I could not hear the rest of their conversation. I did not know if I wanted to.

Mum thought I was turning into her. That was the secret she and Dad kept from me. Now knowing their secret was the secret I had to keep from them.

I crept back to my bedroom. Sat on the edge of my bed. Picked up my phone. It was too late to call Esther, but I needed to tell her the secret. It was too heavy for me to carry alone. Too heavy, too sharp, too terrifying, too nauseating. I had to communicate it, in some way, to someone. I began to type out a message to Esther, spilling it all out, everything Mum had said, everything she feared, everything that meant. I deleted it and started again, and then again and then yet again. It took me almost an hour and dozens of attempts before I got it right. Or right enough. I hit send. And then I tried to sleep.

When light through the windows woke me the next morning, I checked my phone. Esther had not replied. I got up, dressed and went downstairs. Dad looked hungover. Mum asked what I wanted for breakfast – a little too loudly? A little too quickly? – and I said toast. I checked my phone while I ate. Still no reply. I went to school and completed practice tests in lessons. At break I opened my messages and then also at lunchtime in the library when Esther didn't come. Nothing. I did more practice tests in the last two lessons and looked at my phone on the way home. Still nothing. I revised and checked my phone and revised again and checked my phone again and ate dinner and checked my phone and revised some more and then went to bed and checked my phone. Esther had not replied. Twenty-four hours had passed since I had told her the secret, and she had said not a word.

The next day was the same, and the day after that. And then it was the weekend. Nothing from Esther. On Saturday I cried, but then Mum came home early from the Cafy and saw me and the look on her face left me cold. I did not cry on Sunday.

On Monday, Esther came to see me in the library. She sat down next to me and, without a word of explanation or apology for her silence over the past five days, she began to talk about her weekend with the Three Lauras. I let her talk for a few moments, and then I closed my books, put them into my bag, stood up, walked to another table, sat down and resumed my studies.

'What the fuck, Melody Janie?' Esther swivelled around in her seat to look at me. I did not reply. I did not look up from my books. She came and sat on the chair next to me. 'Are you taking the piss?' she said.

I did exactly the same again – closed my books, put them away, moved to another table, opened my books and put my head down.

'Fine,' was all I heard her say before she left the

library. She never came to see me there again. Perhaps she assumed that our friendship ended that day, but I knew better. I knew it had ended the moment I told her my secret and she ignored it.

Mum was wrong. I was not like her. I know what she feared, but there is so much of her I wish I had in me. Her courage. Her determination. If I were more like Mum, I would have confronted Esther that afternoon in the library, asked her why she had never replied to me, told her how hurt I was, told her how I had never needed her more than when I sent her that message, told her how much she had let me down by never replying to it.

But I never said those things, not that lunchtime in the library, not when we passed each other in the corridor, not when she told me my tie was too long. If I had, it would have given Esther the chance to tell me that she had lost her phone a week before. It would have given her the chance to tell me that she had never seen my message, that she had no idea about my secret nor that I had confided it to her. She could have told me all that in the library that lunchtime and I could have forgiven her instantly and we could have talked and, most importantly, we could have stayed friends.

I worked it all out when, later, I saw her post on Facebook, the one which said *Back online! New phone. New number.* But by then it was too late. I had ignored her for too long. I did not know how to go back on that, how to explain myself and try to make it up to her. I did not have the vocabulary for it. I was too ashamed, and the shame locked my lips shut whenever I was around her.

One way of dealing with the shame, the shame and the guilt and the sheer despair of losing my only friend, was to shift the blame. I began to see that it was not just me at fault. It was my phone. Moreover, it was all phones. I had put too much trust, too much confidence in them. Become too reliant. This never would have happened if Esther and I had simply talked to each other, talked like real people. I blamed my phone, blamed it until I hated it. One evening not long before the start of my exams, I handed the phone back to Mum and told her I no longer wanted it. That night, I went to bed early and stuffed toilet paper into my ears. I knew Mum and Dad would be talking about me again. I did not want to hear a word.

I have never wanted another phone since. I do not still. I will take Esther's phone, but I will use it only to call her, as I once promised myself I would use Mum's old phone only for emergencies. I will not use it for secrets. I will not rely upon it to communicate for me. I will be more like Mum. I will not rely on anyone. I will do what needs to be done myself.

I will go to Petherick.

We never emptied the cash register after we closed the Cafy, and ever since I have used it as my personal bank account. Not that my dipping in is frequent. I rarely need money.

I remove three £5 notes from their niche in the till. Plenty remain, alongside more tens, fewer twenties and a rash of coins.

Before Little Sister Lucy jumped, the two of us had scant need for money. We closed the Cafy, we cancelled all future orders. We did not need anything fresh, especially not in those quantities. We lived off the food from the subterranean storeroom – Dad's endless investments for a future he would never see – and the water from the taps. Our home was the caravan, self-sufficient, and for leisure we had my land and we had each other.

As I step out of the Cafy and begin to make my way east, I wonder how long it has been since I last went into Petherick. When Dad died and Mum disappeared and Little Sister Lucy and I moved into the caravan, we rarely left even Bones Break together. She did not have my love of walking, and the lip inspired no joy in her. One day we made it all the way to Lantoweth, but we never returned there. She grudgingly preferred the inland trail to the reservoir, though she would complain about climbing the hedge at the periphery of the woods.

We never went to Petherick. I did not mind so much. At school, people used to say that there was a rivalry between Petherick and St Petroc, and gangs of teenagers from both endlessly organised mass fights and endlessly failed to turn up to them. Whenever I disparaged Petherick, Esther blamed it on the rivalry, called me a St Petroc girl, once even told me to grow up, but I have always known that the rivalry is ludicrous. The reality is that I do not like Petherick because it can be violent and it can be frightening. It is, after all, the place where Paul Dunstan's father was able to encourage a mob of men to beat a group of emmets so badly that two of them were hospitalised.

I may not have been down there, inside Petherick, for some time, but I have stood and watched from the coast path on the headland. Last night was the first time since Little Sister Lucy jumped, but before that I would go often, many Saturday nights, leaving her curled up in a softly snoring lump beneath the duvet, and walking east along the coast path to stand sentinel on the headland, observing. There were always fights, every time, and if I did not see them I heard them.

It was because of those fights that I did not go down into Petherick, because of the consistency of the violence that I remained instead on the headland, merely watching. I had no desire whatsoever to walk through – to be amongst and within – a place where a brawling, screaming scrap was just a part of the weekend. It terrified me, it still does, and the only way I can keep moving towards it, knowing that, this time, I will not stop at the headland but will continue down the coast path and into the village, the only way I can bring myself to go down and into Petherick is if I think of other things.

Reaching, my mind settles on Richard – on his secret, on his story – probing about for possible details and avenues. Why is he here? If he did nothing, was it something he saw? A robbery, a scandal, a murder even? Is it connected to his broken arm? I picture a map of Manchester dotted with the bright heads of red pins, mafia hitmen on the hunt for Richard Brown, interrogating hapless bartenders and delivery drivers, issuing threats and following up on them, cracking fingers, bursting kneecaps, moving on to the next taxi rank or dive bar.

I smile to myself. I don't even know what a dive bar is.

I walk, and think, some more.

Petherick is quiet. A few families walk miserably along the beach. A fisherman sits on the harbour wall, as still and silent as a heron. The amusement arcade, all flashing lights and squealing techno, is being cleaned by a bleary-eyed woman in a baggy uniform. In the corner, a toddler, despite the noise, sleeps in a push-chair. The fish and chip shop is closed. Smells of roast pork and woodsmoke drift out of the pub on a tide of instrumental folk music, but when I pass and look through the window, only three or four old men in enormous sweaters perch at the bar. The rest is empty.

I turn away from the seafront and make my way into the centre, past the primary school with its murals of engine houses and surfboards painted on to the walls, across the stone bridge over the bulging river which rushes towards the ocean, and then down the cobbled street to find, between the pasty shop and the Methodist chapel, the newsagent.

A bell sounds as I enter. Paul Dunstan's mum stands behind the counter. It is, after all, her shop. She looks up with a smile. When she sees me, the smile drops, and her face settles into an expression I cannot quite read. Is it suspicion? Sorrow? Fear?

'Hi,' I say.

'Good morning.' Her eyes flutter nervously, never settling on my own for long before darting off again to land on a wall or window.

'I'd like a paper, please.'

'Which one?'

'All of them.'

She coughs timidly, holds her hand up to her mouth and, keeping it there, says, 'Do you need a bag?'

I look at the rack of newspapers. They are thick and heavy, gigantic. I remember that it is Sunday. I nod and accept the large canvas bag passed over the counter to me, then begin filling it with one copy of each paper. When I am finished, I pass the bag back to Paul Dunstan's mum, who removes each paper in turn and scans them through her till.

She tells me the price.

I pay her.

She counts the change and, though I hold out my hand to accept it, she places the coins on the counter instead. As if she does not want to touch me.

'Thank you,' I say.

She does not reply.

The remembered realisation that it is Sunday hampers my plans for the rest of the afternoon somewhat. I had intended to take my collection of newspapers to the library, scour them for any sign or detail of Richard Brown and then, if that failed, use the internet to work my way through any recent issues I could find online. But the library will be closed today, and that means that there is no need for me to remain in Petherick for any longer. I can walk west back to my land and read the papers in the comfort and privacy of my caravan.

I am glad to leave Petherick. The encounter with Paul Dunstan's mum has unsettled me. Was it rudeness or just awkwardness? Did she not want to speak to me or could she just not think what to say? Fright or fluster, care or concern? I do not know and I will put it to the back of my mind. I do not have the space for her.

I follow my route out of the centre and back towards the seafront, where I can join the coast path to rise up the headland. As I draw close, the door of the pub swings open in a blast of violins and hand drums. A young man appears, pint of ale in one hand, unlit cigarette in the other. His hair is long and bushy, falling over his forehead and eyes, and perhaps this is the

reason why it takes me so long to recognise Paul
Dunstan. When I do, I have a few moments to note
how tall he has grown, how tall and ugly, before his
eyes lock on to mine and the recognition is mutual. I
want to keep walking, keep moving, but we have seen
each other, and we have seen each other see each other,
and without any conscious thought or motivation I
am stopping, and he is walking towards me, and all
of a sudden we are talking.

'Melody Janie?' He lifts his hand for me to shake and
then, perhaps deciding the gesture is too peculiar, transforms it into a low wave.

'Hi, Paul. I just saw your mum.'

Nodding, he lights his cigarette and sucks in. The
action is swift and devoid of thought, so unlike that
time at school when I saw him smoking up the tennis
courts and his movements were as forced and conscious
as a bad actor. Now, he is practised. 'She's always
working,' he says, exhaling the smoke with his words,
then taking a gulp from his pint. 'Heard what happened.
Sorry.'

I feel a sudden twist in my stomach. It is familiar.
The few people I have seen since Dad died have all
offered this kind of casual apology. My reaction, the
twist in my stomach, is always the same, and so are my
words. 'Thank you.'

'Say you were there when it happened.'

Paul is not talking about my father, I realise. He is
talking about Little Sister Lucy. I look at him as he
breathes out, smoke pouring from his mouth and nose

as if he is opening up his whole head to release the fumes. 'Who says that?' I ask.

Another gulp of ale. 'Everyone.'

'How do they know?'

'Don't know. Only rumours.'

'Rumours.'

'All rumours. Don't listen to them myself.'

All rumours? What other rumours are there? I look at Paul again. He is still demolishing his cigarette and pint, but he has begun to turn away a little, as if he wants to head back to the safety of the pub. Perhaps he regrets starting this conversation. Perhaps he should. 'What else do they say?' I ask.

'Silly stuff. You know what this place is like. Chinese whispers.'

'Tell me a Chinese whisper. Tell me some silly stuff.'

'Don't listen to them myself.'

'What do they say?'

Paul is noticeably uncomfortable now. He flicks the cigarette on to the ground, crushes it beneath his trainer and takes a step back.

'What do they say?' I repeat.

He looks back over his shoulder, and then over mine. 'That you were there . . .' he mumbles. 'There . . . you know . . .'

'I don't know. Tell me.'

'You were there the . . . the whole time.'

'And?'

'Come on, Melody Janie, all nonsense, don't listen to them myself.'

'And?'

Paul sighs. I stare deep into his eyes. I can see the defeat. He knows he has to say it. He does. 'And that maybe . . . you know . . . *they* say that maybe she didn't . . . maybe she didn't jump.'

I should never leave Bones Break. Never ever ever. It is safe there, safe on my land *because* it is my land, because I can protect it and keep the bad people out. Emmets. Paul Dunstan. His mum. All of them. All of them and their Chinese whispers. Stuck in their unfulfilling routines in their unfulfilling lives in their unfulfilling stupid fucking little village. Bones Break has everything I need. I never have to leave it again, never return to Petherick or St Petroc or Treleven or Three Stones or anywhere. I will fix myself to Bones Break, a limpet to its safety, and wait for Mum. Alone.

I quicken my pace as I reach the peak of the headland above Petherick where the coast path begins to flatten out, but the swift steps and the sky-wide views cannot wrench my mind from Paul Dunstan. From his insin-uations. He never said it explicitly, but I know precisely what he meant. He meant that I pushed her. He meant that I pushed my Little Sister Lucy off the lip.

Hot tears blur my vision and my cheeks burn rage-red. My fingernails bite into my palms, fists which swing by my sides with the heaviness of rocks. I imagine slamming one of them into Paul Dunstan's ugly mouth, imagine the sound of it – like a can of beans being opened, like

the first puncture of a ring pull, the dull *fot* and the gasp
of air – as his lips burst and his teeth shatter, imagine him
crumpling, falling, dissolving to the ground, imagine
kicking him in the stomach and stamping on his ribs and
crushing his balls and breaking his fingers and finishing
him off with one final, resounding boot to the face.

I walk quicker still, breathe long and deep, but it is
no use. How could he say that? How could he think
that? How could any of them? From the moment she
first entered my life, I did nothing but care for my Little
Sister Lucy. I nurtured her and protected her and loved
her with all the force of my heart. I would never have
hurt her. Never.

The worst that ever happened, between Dad's death
and hers, was the one time, the one single time, when
I lost her. It was, before the drop, the darkest hour of
my life. I had woken later than usual that morning, and
when I looked down the bed for the familiar softly
snoring lump, there was nothing but the peaks of my
own feet.

Terror engulfed me in an instant.

I remember leaping out of bed, running out of the
caravan and making straight for the Cafy. It was the
most likely place to find her – Little Sister Lucy adored
the Cafy – but when I raced through and around it,
searching the dining room and bar area and toilets and
kitchen and the subterranean storeroom (and even, hot
needles piercing my skin as I lifted open the doors, the
chest freezers), when I raced through and around them
all, I found her nowhere.

I sprinted out and over the road to the lip. Four emmets stood at dead centre while another two made their way towards the western headland. They all turned to face me when they heard my approach, the thudding of my feet on the bare grass. I considered imploring them for information, asking each and all if they had seen a little girl, but something stopped me. Later, I reasoned why. I could have asked for their help, and it is possible they would have given it, but it would have come with consequences. Should we not have found Little Sister Lucy, they would never have left me alone. They might have offered to go on looking with me, or to call the police on my behalf, or, worst of all, they might have formed a search party, roaming far and wide, perhaps into Trethewas Woods, perhaps to our caravan. I could not allow that.

So instead I sprinted past them, frantic. They all watched me with something between fascination and unease, but they said nothing. Or, if they did, I did not hear it. I ran to the western headland first, where the view led all the way out to The Warren and Pedna Head behind. Little Sister Lucy was not there. I turned and ran back across Bones Break, over the eastern headland and to the rise. I still could not see her. The few remaining rational thoughts I could muster told me that she would not have strayed any further. She had no love for the lip. If she was anywhere, it was the woods.

I took the road back, for speed. Loose pebbles of chipped tarmac sliced their way into the soles of my bare feet, but I did not feel them, not then. Not until later. Once I reached the Cafy, I ran into the woods along the overgrown pathway to the caravan, and then I began to walk in ever-expanding circles out from it.

Rationality began to disappear altogether. One thought rebounded about the squeezing panic of my mind.

I can't lose her.

Keeping to the circles was difficult: trees and stinging nettles and deep patches of undergrowth marred my way. But I fought through them all. I stuck to my system. It was the only thing I could do.

I roamed far, past Mrs Perrow's old house in one direction and level with The Warren in the other. Still I could not find her, nor any sign of her. My feet began to bleed. The only footprints on the ground were my own: they streaked red over the browns and greens.

I can't lose her.

But nor could I continue, not without shoes. I hobbled back to the caravan. I had left the door open in my haste to leave. I stepped inside, and that was when I heard her. Gentle giggles. I opened the bathroom door. She had made a small fort from the packs of wipes and sat cross-legged behind them in the shower tray.

'You found me!' she said, grinning her simple congratulations.

'Please don't ever do that again.' I slumped against the door frame.

'Why?' Little Sister Lucy was suddenly all concern, her grin gone.

'Because,' I said, 'because I can't lose you.'

She stood up and came to me, wrapping her arms around my waist and burying her head in my muddy, sweat-stained dress. 'I'm sorry, Mellijane,' she said. 'I won't do it again.'

'Promise?'

'Promise.'

I stumbled to the bed and fell down on to it. Little Sister Lucy, silent now, gently inspected my feet. 'They're broken,' she said.

'They'll be all right.'

She padded back to the bathroom, retrieved an unopened packet of wipes and then returned to tend to my feet while I closed my eyes. It hurt like madness, but she was careful, deft, and I said nothing, did not even cry, as she picked the sharp pebbles and wooden shards from my skin. It took her hours, but she continued with intent patience, only occasionally breaking her silence to softly sing, 'Sticks and stones may break my bones . . .'

I sit in the Cafy. I can barely remember arriving here. Whirlpooling thoughts drag me lower and lower. I must distract myself. Eating something will help, I know, but I do not want to go down to the storeroom, so I make my way to the kitchen and search its cupboards. There are some surviving packets of plain crisps. I retrieve three and carry them back with me to the dining room, placing them beside the stack of newspapers on the table. Eating crisps with my left hand and methodically making my way through the first newspaper with my right, I continue in the same fashion until all the crisps are eaten and all the news-papers read. It takes hours, but the distraction works. I start again, from the first paper, scanning the articles for the name Richard Brown, but this time paying more attention to the pictures. Image after image of people I do not recognise – politicians, models, celebrities, actors, musicians, criminals, victims – pass through my fingers. Richard's face never appears.

A new frustration begins to ache, one I am grateful for. I embrace it, use it to push Paul Dunstan and Little Sister Lucy out of my brain. I want to know who Richard is. I want to know what he did. Or, according to him, what he didn't do. Knowing his story will help me evaluate the potential danger of his presence here, what he is up to and why. The more I know, the better equipped I will be to protect my land from him. I let the desire for knowledge overwhelm me, and I read through the newspapers one final time. But they tell me nothing.

I throw the last newspaper on top of the pile on the table, stand up and stretch my legs. I need to think. I have been approaching this the wrong way, relying on chance, on the unlikely possibility of spotting his face or name in a single day's batch of papers. Those odds are less than slim.

I have my questions, of course. I will see Richard again in a couple of hours for Archie's walk and I can subtly insert some more into our conversation. But are my questions even working? What have I truly found out? That he is from Manchester. That he was relocated here for something he didn't do. Little else. I know more about Archie than I do about Richard Brown.

I cannot keep returning to Petherick every day to check the newspapers. I never want to go there again: the thought alone makes me anxious. I need to pin Richard down here, on my land. Somehow. Perhaps I could tell him I know, tell him that I found out everything. Maybe then he might open up, tricked by my false knowledge into spilling it all – if I already know, why keep hiding? Or perhaps I could invite him into some sort of shared secrecy. A trade-off. Mine for his and his for mine. Offer a confession so private he would be compelled to reciprocate. An intimate revelation, something I have never told anyone, would never tell anyone . . .

No. I will not do that.

What I want, I am beginning to understand, is help. I am not sure I can do this alone. I need my friend.

'Oh my God, what happened to you?' Esther does not initiate our ritual when I open the door. Instead, she is all concern.

'I slipped in some mud,' I lie.

'Are you okay? Does it hurt?' She reaches out towards the wound on my cheek but I gently divert her hand with my own.

'It looks worse than it feels,' I say.

We sit. Before I can ask for her help, she reaches into her bag and produces a phone. 'For you,' she says, passing it to me. 'I've entered my number. You can call me any time you like. There's credit.'

The phone is heavy in my hand. 'Thank you,' I manage to say.

'It's my old phone from last year. Not much, I know, but it works fine. It's got mobile data, but I'd stick to Wi-Fi if I were you. The rates are pretty high. Pay as you go.'

I press the button at the bottom of the phone and it comes to life in my hand.

'No password,' Esther says, 'but I can show you how to set one.'

The screen is large and bright, filled with apps of different colours and designs.

'I didn't know what you'd want to use, so I just left it all on there.'

'Thank you,' I say again, pressing another button on the top which turns the screen black. 'But I think I'll just use it as a phone. For emergencies.'

'It's yours, use it however you like. Just make sure you call me. Whenever you need to.'

'I will.' I lay the phone on top of the newspapers still piled on the table. It surprises me that Esther has not mentioned them. I decide to, if only to move the focus of our conversation away from the phone. 'I went into Petherick this afternoon.'

'Your favourite place in the world.'

'It's worse than ever.'

'Says the St Petroc girl.'

I ignore the label. 'I saw Paul Dunstan.'

Esther groans. 'And how is the dickhead?'

I have not heard that word since primary school. It makes me laugh. 'Still a dickhead. I bumped into him after I bought the Sunday papers. I've been looking for him.'

'For Paul Dunstan?'

'For Richard Brown.'

'Oh. Your age-inappropriate friend.'

'He's not my friend.'

'Did you find anything about him?'

'Nothing.' I sigh. 'I'm getting nowhere.'

'So what are you going to do?'

'I need some help.'

Esther looks at me, and a slow smile begins to

spread across her face. Within that one smile, within those pink lips and white teeth, is all the charm, all the joy, all the mischief and intimacy and playfulness that I remember and love about Esther Leigh Harlow. She used to be my best friend. How beautiful it would be to call her that again. 'What can I do?' she says.

Esther cannot stay long. The drive up to Bristol is three hours and it will be getting dark soon. But she can stay long enough to see Richard while I walk with him. We hope she will recognise him. Unlike me, Esther keeps up with the news.

'What time are you meeting him?'

'Six o'clock.'

'Where?'

'At the rise between here and Nare Point.'

'Which way will you walk?'

'Probably west. Towards the Cafy, and maybe further to Lantoweth. It's the way we usually go.'

'How about I give you a ten-minute head start, and then I'll start walking east towards you? We'll pass each other on the coast path, pretend we don't know each other.'

'I've seen Richard turn around to avoid people. He might do the same if he sees you coming.'

'So what should we do?'

'I've got an idea.'

Locking the Cafy behind us, I lead Esther out to dead centre and then we follow the coast path on to the eastern headland, past the cleft, across to the rise, and

then finally to the Nare Point car park. 'Over here,' I
say, and Esther follows me to the periphery of the
gravel. I point out the pocket to her.

'What is it?'

'A hideaway. You can crawl in and watch us from
there. Richard will never see you.'

'You want me to get into that?'

'Don't get all precious, it's fine.'

Esther looks at me with a smile. '*Precious?* I like that.'
She lowers herself to her hands and knees. The ground
is muddy, and the little squeals she makes as she backs
herself into the pocket are half from horror and half
from delight.

'Can you see all right?' I ask.

'I can see everything,' she says. 'Are you sure he won't
see me?'

'He won't see you,' I say.

They never do.

Richard opens the door after one knock. 'Well, this is a surprise.' He bends down, picks a tumbler of whisky up from the floor with his free hand and then stares at me while he takes a sip. I can hear Archie behind him, shut in a room, thudding against a closed door.

'Sorry, I know you prefer us to meet on the rise,' I say, holding his horrible stare.

'That's not what I meant.'

'I don't understand.'

'Don't you?' He swirls the whisky and then takes another drink, this one longer than the last. 'I didn't think I'd see you at all. Ever again.'

'Why not?'

Does he know? Did he see me walking to Petherick? Or, worse, did he see me walking back, arms laden with thick newspapers?

'Maybe you don't understand. You're very innocent, aren't you?'

I cannot tell if the question is genuine or sarcastic. I consider asking but know it would do me no favours. I *want* him to think me innocent. I change the subject. 'Are you walking Archie? Can I come?'

He laughs. It is neither pleasant nor unpleasant. It is just a laugh. 'Give me a minute.' He closes the door.

I look back at the car park, but the pocket is out of sight. I wonder how long Esther can manage in there.

The door opens again. Archie races out to welcome me with all the gorgeous love so characteristic of his greetings. Richard steps out after him and grabs him from behind. It makes Archie flinch in a way I do not like. He puts the saddlebags and lead on while Archie waits, anxiety immediately forgotten. Then the door is closed and locked and we walk down through the garden and on to the road.

We are silent as we cross the car park. I can feel Richard's attention on me. I know he is monitoring me, I can tell by the way his eyes are down and his head is angled slightly towards me, by the way he mirrors my footsteps so deliberately that when I slow, his pace matches mine with an immediacy which must be conscious. His breathing has become heavy, like he has forgotten about it. His focus has narrowed. I stand at the end of his telescope.

'Maybe we'll see the most beautiful beach in the world,' I say.

Richard looks at me, confused eyes.

'This morning,' I tell him, 'you said that you thought Lantoweth might be the most beautiful beach in the world, and I told you there was better.'

'Quite.'

'Well, there is. At the bottom of Bones Break. It's

rare. You can only see it during the lowest tide. Have you seen it yet?'

Richard shakes his head.

'Thought not. Most people don't even know it exists. I do. It's beautiful. The most beautiful little zawn you'll ever see in your life.'

'The most beautiful what?'

'Zawn. You know, a type of beach. Like a bay or a cove.'

'I know bays and coves. But I've never heard of a zawn before. Another of your odd Cornish words?'

We are approaching the pocket, and it astonishes me to realise that Esther is partially visible. I can see her shoes, one of her hands and the hair which hangs over her face. How have I never been noticed there? Or have I? Does everyone see me, and simply choose to ignore me? To continue as if I were not there, because the pretence is far easier than the acknowledgement of a strange girl lying half in and half out of a thicket of bracken?

I look across at Richard. It is clear he has not seen Esther. His gaze flits between me and the sea. Even Archie does not notice her. Perhaps I do only because I know, because I know she is there. Perhaps that is all it takes.

I feel a tremendous rush of exhilaration at this explicit act of espionage. Esther is a spy! *My* spy! We can begin to work together; she can help me monitor my land, help me keep it safe for Mum's return. I felt so empty after Little Sister Lucy jumped, but now I do not have to any more. My friend is here with me, *for* me. I will show her the bush-den next, teach her how to sit and wait and watch there too. And then maybe even the shelf . . .

No. Not the shelf. Some things I must keep for myself.

We continue on, towards and over the rise, making our way to Bones Break. Our shared silence pervades, but that does not matter. The purpose for this walk – that Esther see Richard Brown – is complete. I need go no further today.

We reach dead centre and stop. I call Archie, who lumbers towards me, sniffing the air as he approaches. I take his head in my hands and crouch before him. 'I'm going home now, Archie,' I say. 'I'll see you tomorrow.'

'You're going home now?' Richard asks. It is clear he is surprised. Surprised and, I think, a little upset.

'Yes.'

'But you haven't shown me your favourite beach. The shawn.'

'*Zawn*,' I say, trying hard not to hiss the word. I lean out over the lip and look down the cliff face. 'The tide's not low enough yet. It won't be visible for at least another hour.'

'Then let's keep walking and we can see it on the way back.'

'You want to walk for another hour?'

'Yes, of course. Why? Don't you?'

I do not. I want to get back to Esther, to find out if she recognised Richard – though, of course, I cannot tell him that.

'We don't have to go as far as this morning,' he is saying, 'but it's a lovely evening. It would be a shame to call it a day now, so soon.'

He seems desperate to continue, to continue walking with me. A word flashes into my mind, one the Three Lauras liked to overuse. Clingy. Is he being *clingy*?

'I'm sorry, Richard,' I say. 'I'm tired. I shouldn't have come calling for you. I think I'd better go home.'

'Okay,' he says. 'That's okay.' He looks so upset that I find myself feeling sorry for him. It surprises me a little.

'I'll walk back to your house with you, if you like.'

'Why? Aren't you too tired?'

'It seems like you want the company.'

Richard smiles at that. 'Do you know,' he says, 'I think I do.'

We turn around and begin the walk towards his house. I look out over the sea. A bank of grey flows forward from the horizon, its faint streaks and lines revealing rain in the distance. It is not a lovely evening. Not by any stretch of the imagination.

'Did you always live in Manchester?' I ask.

Richard's eyebrows drop and his jaw sags. 'Why are you asking me that?'

'You want company. Conversation usually comes with it.'

Archie trots over to Richard, who strokes him on the back between the straps of the saddlebags. Sensing the uneasiness in the air, Archie lowers his tail and glances beseechingly from one of us to the other. Richard is the first to break the silence.

'Most of my life was spent in London.' His tone is troubled, uneasy.

'I'm sorry,' I say. 'I shouldn't pry. It's just something I thought we could talk about. While we walked.'

Richard sighs. 'I'm being defensive,' he says. 'I shouldn't be.'

'It's okay.'

'Maybe it's not. You asked me a harmless question. I snapped at you.'

'It's okay.'

We pass the eastern headland. Archie trots ahead: tail high, nose low.

'I was born and brought up in Manchester,' Richard says. 'I moved to London when I was in my twenties. But I always wanted to go back. It took thirty years, but I got there eventually.'

'You retired?'

'No. I got into property. Renting.'

'Then you must be rich.'

'I wouldn't say I was rich exactly.'

'You were a landlord. Landlords are rich. How many houses did you own?'

'Six. Six *properties,* technically. Four student houses and two flats.'

And now another in Cornwall, I think. *Not even a second home, but a seventh.* I decide not to voice that, and instead repeat, 'Rich.'

'Maybe you're right. It was all about timing. Timing

and location. I moved to London in the early 1980s, bought a house, and by the time I was fifty its value had rocketed. Enough for me to sell it and buy the six properties in Manchester. One for me to live in, the other five to rent out.'

'You make it sound so easy,' I say, 'when there are families down here who'll never be able to afford their own home.'

Richard either ignores or fails to pick up on the derision. 'Timing and location, that's all there is to it,' he says. 'It's not like I did anything on purpose. It was just timing and location. I bought in London when a single, young man *could* buy in London. The house would have appreciated in value exactly the same whether it had been mine or someone else's. It was just the house. I didn't even work that hard. I was little more than a mediocre accountant in the City.'

I do not like the way he says *the* city, as if London is the only city in the world. 'So lucky,' I mutter.

Richard looks at me with something like shame, though it does not last long. 'I was, I won't deny that. Very, very lucky. But I've had my fair share of bad luck too, Melody Janie. Believe me.'

We reach the rise. I look over towards Nare Point, wondering if perhaps I might see Esther fleeing from the car park. I do not.

Richard seems to notice the direction of my stare, and so I try another question to distract him. 'Did you like London?'

'Not particularly, no. It was never my home. Not in

the way Manchester was. Is.' He looks out to sea, directing his words to the water rather than my ears. I have to strain forward to hear him. 'Like I said, I was born in Manchester. Grew up there. Studied there too. Fine university. My family had always lived in Manchester and most still do. All the friends I had there, few ever left. Not that any of them speak to me any more.'

'I can't imagine ever leaving my home.'

'I'm not even sure now why I did. Some vague notion I had that to make anything of yourself, to be *successful*, London was the place to do it. And, I suppose, in a way, I was right all along. I could have taken a similar job in Manchester, I could have bought a similar house, but the property boom up there was no match for London's. So maybe there *was* a small part of me that knew, that knew *precisely* what I was doing. Maybe that's why I didn't go back until I had made enough money to be able to retire. Maybe I could smell it in the wind. I don't know. Even if that is the case, the way I used to miss Manchester was painful. Physical, in fact. Have you ever been?'

I shake my head but he does not see me. His stare remains ocean-bound. 'No,' I say.

'You should. Marvellous city. Magnificent. So much culture. So much energy. And a good size. Not like London at all. London is far too big for one man.'

His gaze still on the sea, he has veered from the path. I can see he is about to step into a puddle. I let him. It splashes up around his ankle and he smiles clumsily at me.

'Maybe I'm being too kind to Manchester. Maybe I should treat London with greater respect. I could have stayed anonymous in London. Everyone is anonymous in London.'

We arrive at Nare Point. I look down at the pocket as we pass. Esther has gone. I must too.

'I'm going to go back now,' I say.

Richard stops, turns, looks at me and smiles. It is pleasant. A kind smile. 'Thank you, Melody Janie.'

'What for?'

'For the company. For the conversation. It was a tonic.'

I smile back at him.

'Speaking of which,' he continues, 'would you like to come in for a drink?'

'Maybe some other time,' I say, before crouching down to hug Archie. His breath is fetid and meaty. I stand back up, wish them both a nice evening and return to the coast path.

Esther is waiting on one of the wooden picnic benches in front of the Caty. She rises when she sees me approach and marches forward, gripping me by the arms when we come together.

'Promise me you'll never see that man again,' she says.

'Why? Did you recognise him? Who is he?'

'He's Nicholas Cartwright,' she hisses.

The name means nothing to me.

Esther hurries us inside the Cafy and makes me lock the door. I follow her into the kitchen.

'Let's sit in the dining room,' I say.

'No. He can see us through the windows.'

'He's at home now.'

'He could be watching you without you knowing it.'

'Esther, just tell me, who is he?'

Esther reaches into her pocket and takes out her phone. 'There was a murder,' she says as she taps at the screen. 'A few months ago. A young man. Caleb Hawkins. Twenty-four years old. He was raped and stabbed, repeatedly, inside his flat. Your friend was his landlord.'

I do not know what to say. I say nothing.

'Christ, Melody Janie, it's been all over the news for months. How do you not know about this?'

'I . . . I don't . . .' I cannot speak because I cannot think. The sudden violence of it all dries my throat and scratches at any tenderness I felt for Richard. Esther thrusts her phone at me.

'This is him. Caleb Hawkins.'

I take the phone and see him. His graduation picture. He stands on green grass before a white building. His gown drifts out to his left in what must have been a light

wind. He has removed his hat. Long, straight dark hair
flows down to his shoulders. The rectangle of face poking
out from beneath it is pale and thin. His eyes are blue.

'Nicholas Cartwright raped and killed him,' Esther
says.

I swipe back to the dozens of thumbnails which fill
the screen in an infinite scroll. Most are the same graduation picture – it seems that this is the portrait that the
public took to their hearts. Yet there are plenty of others.
Drinking bottles of beer with friends at a beach bar, Caleb
Hawkins' bare skin red while that of his companions is
nut-brown. Formal school photos, his shirt white, his
blazer green, his hair styled differently with each passing
year. Caleb Hawkins and another man, almost a foot
shorter than him, their arms around each other; then
the exact same photo but with a rainbow superimposed
over it. Caleb Hawkins as a toddler, pedalling a plastic
go-kart. Caleb Hawkins as a teacher, sat proudly in front
and centre of his class of beaming, toothy eight-year-olds.
Caleb Hawkins as a rock climber, clad in small shorts
and a big helmet, rope coiled and twined around him.
Caleb Hawkins as a cyclist, red-faced and mud-spattered,
standing beside his bike on a grey hill.

And then, amongst the thumbnails, an image of
Richard. I click on it to enlarge. With his white beard,
his long and dishevelled hair, with his thick glasses, he
looks different in the picture, somehow younger,
somehow shorter, like he has not just changed his
appearance but also his posture since then. Regardless,
this man in the picture is Richard Brown. Or, as the

caption below informs me, Nicholas Cartwright. The same man. The photograph has the slight blurring of lines, the lack of definition, of the zoom, and Richard appears to have seen the photographer and is hurrying away. His left arm is raised up to his chest, like he is about to hide his face, and beneath it is revealed a long, vertical rip in his duffel coat. His light brown trousers are stained and thin around the knees; his shoes, dirty-white trainers, are splattered with paint. He is unkempt, harried, gaunt. He looks, and I cannot deny this, like a rapist and a murderer.

'But I don't understand,' I say. 'Why is he here? Why isn't he in prison?'

'He got off. I don't know how. Everyone knows he did it. The whole country knows.'

I remember this morning's conversation. 'He said he was relocated,' I say. 'Why would they relocate him if he did it?'

'To cover up their mistake? It doesn't matter. The fact is, you *cannot* see him again.'

'But Archie . . .' I falter.

'Don't you understand?' Esther shouts. It is, I think, the first time I have ever heard her raise her voice. It frightens me. 'He's fucking *grooming* you, Melody Janie.'

'But Caleb Hawkins was . . . a boy . . . a man.'

'Boy, girl, man, woman, do you think that matters to monsters like him? Imagine how lucky he feels. He got away with Caleb Hawkins, maybe others too, and now he's found you, this young loner with no family. No one to notice if you disappear. *You cannot see him again.*'

She has begun to shake. I move in to hug her and she lets me. 'Okay,' I whisper. 'Okay. I won't see him again.'

When she pulls away from the hug, I can see the tears in her eyes. 'I think you should come to Bristol with me. Now. Tonight.'

'I can't do that.'

'For fuck's sake, Melody Janie, why not? We'll drive to St Petroc, we'll get some of your stuff from the house and then I'll take you with me.'

'I can't, Esther.'

'*Why not?*'

'I just . . . I just can't. Not yet. You wouldn't understand.'

Esther rubs at her eyes, smearing the tears from her lashes. 'Because of your mum?'

'I need a little longer.' A little longer to wait, to wait for her to come back to me.

'Then you have to promise me something else.'

I nod, the way I used to nod when she made me promise not to tell who she liked. Esther was always persuasive.

'Let me take you back to your house. Now. And then promise me you'll stay there. In St Petroc. You won't come back here.'

I finger the caravan keys in my pocket. The house's door keys are attached to the same loop. I nod again. It is the only way to appease Esther.

'Promise?'

'Promise.'

'Then let's go.'

The drive is brief. When we pull up outside the house, I tell Esther not to come in, to leave me here. We hug and she makes me promise the same promise again. I step out of the car, watch her drive away and then pass through the garden to let myself in.

The house is exactly the same as the day Little Sister Lucy and I left, only with more dust. The television on the stand, the throws on the couches, the books on the shelves, the sheets on the beds – all are covered with a layer of silver-grey dust. I wander through the stark rooms, listening to the hollow echoes of my footsteps. In Mum and Dad's bedroom, a picture has fallen from the wall: her print of Ophelia in the reeds. She adored that painting, said it was her favourite in the world. I pick it up from the floor and place it back on the nail protruding from the plaster, letting it swing gently into position. Then I walk along the hallway and into my own bedroom. My bookcase is there, but empty, for I took all my books with me when we moved into the caravan. It is no longer a library. It is lifeless. Like this whole house. Lifeless. There is nothing for me here any more.

I let myself out, lock the door behind me and begin the three-mile walk back to Bones Break. As I move through the dusky streets of St Petroc, the chilled air washing over my skin in smooth waves, I think about my bedroom in the house – the limp curtains, the dusty sheets – and fantasise about the bed waiting for me in the caravan. That bed, I love. I have been keeping it out more and more often lately, not forgetting but rather not bothering to transform it into the couches. I used to do it every day, but that was more for Little Sister Lucy than it was for me. Our first night together in the caravan, she woke from a bad dream and began to wail about monsters inside, monsters who wanted to kill her. I turned the lights on but it did not help.

'They're still here,' she said, and she began to beat her head with her fists ferociously.

It was only after I removed all the cushions from the bed and folded the wooden boards back into place to show her there were no monsters that she began to calm. From that day on, as long as I put the bed away the moment we woke up each morning, her talk of monsters stopped. Instead, ghosts took her focus, though it was a fascination borne of curiosity rather than fear.

'Do you believe in ghosts?'

'I don't think so.'

'Why?'

'Because I think that, if they did exist, there would be so many of them that we wouldn't be able to move.'

'That's silly. You can't *touch* ghosts. You can't see them either. They could be everywhere and you wouldn't know.'

'Well, then I suppose that if we can't feel them and we can't see them and we don't know they're there, why bother thinking about them?'

'Just because you can't feel or see someone, it doesn't mean you should stop thinking about them.'

She made a good point.

Cars flash past me on the road, their headlights winking in the dark. One sounds its horn as it whips by, its wing mirror inches from my arm, and I leap back into a wet hedge. The night is bitter, the wind high. Storm clouds gather above, faraway rumbles and brief flashes of light which make me hurry my steps.

It is almost midnight by the time I arrive back at Bones Break. The ocean roars. Rain has begun to fall. When I step inside the caravan, I close all the blinds and curtains, remove my sodden dress and then climb into bed with my new phone in my hands.

I hold it for a few moments, breathing long and deep, and then I turn it on, find the web browser, type in 'Nicholas Cartwright' and open the first search result.

Landlord questioned over Caleb Hawkins murder

The latest revelations in the murder of primary school teacher Caleb Hawkins have led to the questioning of his landlord.

Nicholas Cartwright (61), a former financial analyst in London, has lived in Manchester for the past ten years.

Yesterday, the reclusive property magnate was taken in for questioning related to the rape and murder of Caleb Hawkins in August. Mr Hawkins' body was found in one of Mr Cartwright's several properties, the flat he had rented from him for two years. He had been raped and repeatedly stabbed.

Suspects have been few and far between in the weeks since Mr Hawkins' murder, and the alleged discovery of samples of Mr Cartwright's DNA about the flat have led many to assume that the perpetrator has finally been found.

'We just want justice for our son,' said William Hawkins this morning. 'We will pray that it is delivered, so that our dear boy might find some peace.'

Originally from Manchester, Nicholas Cartwright returned to the area ten years ago to manage a number of properties across the city. Two of these properties, and Mr Cartwright's home, are currently being searched by police.

'He made me feel uncomfortable,' said Liam Crowley, a tenant of one of Mr Cartwright's student properties in Rusholme. 'He'd come round for spot checks. It was obvious he'd been drinking. He made these jokes which I found inappropriate.'

I swipe back to the search results, click on the next in line.

Where is Nicholas Cartwright?

They say that only the guilty run. What might they say about those who vanish off the face of the earth?

A constant face in the media since the brutal rape and murder of his tenant, Caleb Hawkins, Nicholas Cartwright has not been seen for the past two weeks. Where is he hiding? And, if his presumed innocence is to be believed, why is he hiding?

'This miscarriage of justice gets worse by the day,' said an unnamed family member of the victim. 'First they let him go, now he's probably relaxing down on the Costa del Sol with all the other criminals.'

I swipe back. Repeat.

Outrage as Nicholas Cartwright Walks Free

Police have confirmed that Nicholas Cartwright is no longer a part of their investigation into the death of teacher Caleb Hawkins.

The announcement has sparked outrage across the nation . . .

Swipe. Repeat.

Spotted – Nicholas Cartwright at the corner shop, buying his fruit and veg as if nothing has happened . . .

Repeat.

. . . the inhumanity of the man and the inhumanity of the authorities who let him go beggars belief . . .

Repeat.

. . . university professor reveals all about his five-year sexual relationship with Nicholas Cartwright . . .

Repeat, repeat, repeat.

. . . Do you believe Nicholas Cartwright? Call us now on 0800 777 6767. Have YOUR say . . .

. . . guilt is without doubt . . .

. . . rapist . . .

. . . murderer . . .

. . . monster . . .

I throw the phone down on to the duvet. It lands with a soft thump. I press my face into the pillow and think of Richard/Nicholas, of Caleb Hawkins and of Archie. And then I stare at the caravan ceiling and try to think of nothing at all.

A rumble, low and throbbing, wakes me. It feels somehow deep, as if it is beneath me, beneath the caravan, beneath the very surface of the earth. The volume builds steadily, first exquisite then maddening, still rising and rising. There is something very familiar about it: the sound, the sensation.

I climb out of bed. There is no doubt that it is continuing to build, perhaps travelling this way. A tractor? Too loud. An aeroplane? Too slow. The vibrations I can feel through the floor of the caravan are not a product of my imagination, not a hangover of my dreams. The kettle balanced on the hob has begun to rattle as it shakes on the metal. An earthquake? I have never heard of such a thing here before. The only similar event we ever had was . . .

I throw on my coat, open the door and sprint outside. The ground is saturated beneath my bare feet; muddy water splashes up my legs, casting streaks and dots. I emerge from the woods and run headlong into the wall of wind. It lifts my hair and flattens my coat against my body as I push on through it, past the Cafy and towards the road. The storm is thick overhead, but this is not where the noise comes from. Beyond the lip, the ocean is dark and choppy. I can see the swell lines all the way back to the horizon, building and rising, building and rising, gaining power and momentum in readiness to hurl themselves at Bones Break. I dart over the road and on to the grass, gaining speed myself, and then I see it.

A cleft in the lip. New.

I stop. The rumbling is beneath me, coupled with the incessant crash of wave on rock. I must be careful. This is unstable. It could all collapse below me at any moment. The ground beneath my feet.

I gingerly step forward. I can feel the ruptures vibrate up into my knees, can feel the fracturing and the splitting, the opening of the veins. Ahead, a crackling cracking, like long lightning, then the staccato machine-gun fire of splintered rock dispersing, striking water after an excruciating drop. My land is breaking.

Another crack, another rumble. Something shifts and then settles. The vibrations recede, the noise slips away beneath the waves. I lower myself on to my hands and knees and crawl forward, through the grass, towards the lip, towards its fresh wound.

From here, the new cleft appears to be meagre, forging inland for less than a foot, not as severe as last winter's damage to the eastern headland. It does not reach the coast path, and the wooden barrier which straddles its final inch remains standing. Nothing struck this, nothing carved it out: this portion of the edge has simply crumbled, crumbled under too much pressure. It is ugly, this burst lip, it has changed the face of my beloved Bones Break.

I flatten myself on to my belly, extend my arms and curl my fingers around the apex of the new cleft. It is sharp and wet. I want to tense my arms and pull myself forward, slide beneath the wooden barrier until my head hangs out over the opening, check the extent of the damage below. But the wind continues to howl and I dare not move any closer to the edge. Instead, I listen, listen to the waves as they roll in, listen as they crash against the cliff face I cannot see, listen as they bounce off it to rush back out into the ocean once more, colliding with new and incoming waves like hands clapping.

I pull myself up and move to the eastern headland to perch on its tip. Craning my neck, I peer down into the cove. The extent of the damage is clear from here. It makes me feel sick.

The new cleft is only the smallest part of it, the peak of a devastating rockfall that has transformed the entire cliff face below my land. The drop always bent back in on itself, culminating in the cave at its base, but now that curve is far more dramatic and precarious, a series of dents and jagged overhangs, so that the lip seems to float on thin air. When the waves drag themselves back in torrid washes, I can see that both the cave and the zawn, my favourite beach in the world, no longer exist. They are buried beneath a mound of fallen rock.

Bones Break will never be the same again.

I look in on the Cafy on my way back to the caravan. A single casualty lies smashed on the floor: a bottle of ketchup. It has shattered into an explosion of splinters, shards and thick blood-red dollops. I take the dustpan and brush from their cupboard in the kitchen, sweep up as much of the broken bottle and the spilled sauce as I can, empty the remains into the bin and then wash out both brush and pan with the kitchen hose before leaving them to dry beside the sink. I find the cloth and spray bottle of surface cleaner. I polish the floor until its tiles shine.

I make my way down into the storeroom. The cold weather has brought the temperature down in here significantly, yet that terrible, festering smell has not softened. If anything, it is worse. I find my necessary ingredients and climb the stairs back up to the kitchen to prepare a plate of Cornish Chow Mein.

I fill the kettle with water from the tap, light a burner with an extra-long match and then place the kettle on top of the blue flame to boil. I peel back the foil lid of the noodle pot and pick out the sachet, which I rip open along the 'Tear Here' line so that I can empty its contents over the block of dried noodles. While the kettle boils, I lean back against the counter and do very little.

The shrill whistle sounds. I gently pour the boiling water over the noodles, stopping when the level reaches the prescribed line, waiting for it to settle, for the noodles to absorb, and then topping up again. After resealing the foil lid I find a plate and then rummage in the drawer beneath Mum's pile of clothes to retrieve a pair of chopsticks. Closing the drawer, I pour myself a glass of water and carry everything through to the dining room. It takes me two trips. Once complete, I reopen the foil lid and, using a chopstick to guide the soupy entrails out of the pot, tip it all out on to my plate.

And then I eat my breakfast.

I wake with a grunt and sit up straight in the chair. I must have dozed off after eating. Unusual sounds filter into the Cafy: unusual because they are the sounds of people. I rise to my feet. A molten tide of acid indigestion erupts from my stomach. The Cornish Chow Mein is not sitting well. I take small sips from my glass of water. I have not been taking care of myself, I know that. My body craves more vegetables, more fruit. But my work here – taking care of the Cafy for Mum; taking care of Bones Break for me – is so all-consuming that I rarely have the energy to cook myself a healthy meal. It is far easier to rely on tinned foods, on noodles and pasta.

I walk over to the front windows and look out at the lip. It teems with people, perhaps twenty or thirty of them. Most wear hats and scarves, all hold cameras or phones in their gloved hands. Amongst the raincoats and ski jackets, I identify a few National Trust fleeces. They have come to inspect this new Bones Break, to assess its disfigured, weather-beaten face. They dot the lip from the western headland to the eastern, with most congregated about the new cleft. It is the busiest this place has been for a long time.

I let myself out of the door. The morning is crisp and clear, all traces of the storm gone. My breath billows. The puddles have iced over again. I need my boots. It only takes a few minutes to retrieve them from the caravan and then return. I cross the road and melt into the crowd, listen in on the criss-crossing conversations.

'They say most of this is going to disintegrate over the next fifty years.'

'Such a shame.'

'Climate change.'

'Then I suppose we'll be sending aid money down here too.'

I move through these people like a ghost – disregarded, as inconsequential as the seagulls. One of them, I realise, is my old art teacher from school. His eyes meet mine for a second as I draw close. He does not recognise me.

'Do you remember when we kayaked here? Petherick to Lantoweth.'

'Conn nearly drowned.'

'So did Alex trying to save him.'

'Woulda been a blessing. Poor bastard.'

An excitable hum hovers over everyone as they point down at the burial mound of rocks or photograph the crumbling lip or dare each other to approach the new cleft. I wish I could disappear into a hideaway without being seen, wish I could hop down on to the shelf, lie silently and listen to the myriad voices and their myriad proclamations. My land buzzes with life, it thrums and bubbles, and I want to lay down on the edge of it all, invisible, absorbing the collective energy of these interconnected narratives as they gather on the lip of my land.

'Excuse me, my dear.' The words bring me back to my senses. I turn around. At my side stands an elderly lady, shorter than the height of my shoulder. She holds out an old-fashioned disposable camera, waves it before my face. 'Would you mind taking a photograph of me?'

'Of course,' I say, taking the camera. She totters over to the wooden barrier in front of the lip, a small space free of any other voyeurs. She edges backwards uneasily, looking at the drop behind her as she does so, and then stops, faces me and smiles a broad, dentured grin. I snap the picture and, as she walks back to me, I wind the film on for her, feeling the whirr and the clunk of the hidden machinery.

'Thank you,' she says, taking the camera and tucking it away in her handbag. 'Would you like me to take one of you?'

'I don't have a camera,' I say before remembering that, in fact, I do.

She looks out over the view – my view – and sighs happily. 'It's such a beautiful spot, isn't it?'

'It was.'

'Have you been here before?'

'No,' I say. 'Never.'

It takes me a long time to jostle my way through the crowd to the eastern headland. When I finally reach it, I have an idea. I walk out to the edge of the headland, turn back and take my new phone from my pocket. I have already broken my rule to use it only to call Esther, and so this extra little transgression will not matter. I turn the phone on, find the camera function and then point the lens out over Bones Break and its swarm. I take a photo, and then another, and then yet another. It is, I realise, important, and exactly what I should be doing – recording, documenting, gathering evidence. These are the responsibilities of any good custodian.

Aiming the phone at the cliff face, I continue to snap, starting at the lip and slowly, systematically, working my way down until I reach the burial mound at the base. A group of people, perhaps a dozen or so, have noticed my vantage point and chosen to copy me, following me to the eastern headland and thrusting their own phones out in the same direction as mine. One – so characteristically inconsiderate he must be an emmet – steps in front of me, blocking my view to improve his own.

Anger flashes inside me. These emmets. They ruin everything.

I turn and walk away from them, east along the coast path. When I am far enough away for the noise of the waves below to drown out their stupid accents, I stop and resume my photography once more. The exercise is mesmerising. I experiment with different angles and contents and, when I discover the various filters, I feed photos through each of them, tweaking and toying with image after image, sometimes saving the same picture twice, once in Noir, once more in Vivid Warm, because I cannot decide which I prefer.

I try the panorama function, but it is difficult to get a smooth sweep; the resulting image always looks fragmented and unnatural and the emmets who remain on the eastern headland destroy every shot. I want my photographs unpeopled.

I walk further east, further away from them all, until they are out of sight and I can continue to capture the land and the land alone. I switch to the video function, discovering the beauty of slow motion, especially when applied to the waves which roll into the cliff face beneath me with a fluent but slumbering grace. A clean set comes in. I wait for it to pass, scanning the ocean for the telltale revelatory signs of which swell line will be the first to break. When I identify it, I point the camera and begin to film, following it all the way in, from the birth of its white water to its death against the cliff.

I watch the video back in slow motion, entranced, and then I repeat with another wave, and another, and another, hypnotised by the snail-like advance of white over turquoise, the smooth perfection of it all. I can *see* the energy, right there on my screen, the way the eddies and swirls flow into each other, join, rise, peak, break and wash, scattering spumes of froth which dance and linger in the air, devouring the water ahead, churning it into mountains and foothills in a flow both chaotic and somehow orderly, glinting brightly in the cold sunlight . . .

'Melody Janie.'

I know, without looking up from the slow waves on the screen of my phone, that it is Richard.

The moment I look at him, it is clear from the expression on his face that he knows. He knows that I know.

Archie picks up on the tension between us. He does not rise up to plant his paws on my chest, but instead shuffles forward and leans gently against my leg. I reach down and scratch the top of his head.

'You told me you didn't have a phone.' Richard is drunk. I can smell the alcohol on him, even from this distance, even in the open air. He sways ever so slightly on his feet. His eyes are red, his words slurred.

'I didn't. I do now.'

'You've been lying to me.'

'No,' I say. 'I'm not the liar.'

Richard laughs. Not a genuine laugh. A forced, sarcastic, mirthless laugh. 'You shouldn't believe everything you read in the papers.'

'I'm going to go now.' I turn my back on him and begin to walk away.

'I'm not the only one who's been in the papers, after all.'

I stop. Ahead of me the coast path stretches away into the distance. There is nobody in sight. Why did

I walk so far away? It was foolish of me. And it would be foolish of me to turn around, to face Richard again.

But I do it anyway.

'What did you just say?'

'You think you know all about me. You don't. You don't know anything. But I know about you.' He takes a hip flask from his pocket, opens it with his one free hand and takes a swig.

A familiar thought comes to me. *One little push.* The lip is close. I take a step forward.

'What do you know?'

'Not many Melody Janies down here in Cornwall. Not many anywhere. It's an easy name to search.'

'Unlike Richard Brown.'

This time his laugh is true. 'Precisely.'

I take another step forward, look away from Richard and towards the lip, consider distances, trajectories. Force. *One little push . . .*

'You're a monster,' I say.

'I've heard it all before.' The way he stands – shoulders back, unflinching, his face a drunken sneer – confirms everything for me.

'You're a rapist.'

'Heard it all before.'

'You're a murderer.'

'Heard it all.' He smiles. He has never looked uglier. It infuriates me.

'Why were you searching my name?' I say.

'Why were you searching mine?'

One little push . . .

Archie leaves my side and – tail low, refusing to look at me – stands between me and his master. He recognises violence, can see it from a distance.

'Is that where you keep it?' I say, pointing to the saddlebags which hang off Archie's sides.

'Keep what?'

'Your knife.'

Richard's eyes harden. 'It seems like you've got it all figured out.' He bends down to reach for the zip on the saddlebag closest to him.

One little push no longer seems enough. I take a step back, then two more. 'Leave me alone.'

'It's funny,' Richard slurs. 'I'm sure I said almost exactly the same thing to you the day you followed me. But you wouldn't, would you? You wouldn't leave me alone.' He takes the zip in his fingers and begins to pull it back.

'There's people,' I say. 'At Bones Break. Dozens of them. If I scream they'll hear.'

The zip stops: the sound of a bumblebee landing on heather. 'You're lying.'

'No. I'm not.' The phone is still in my hand. I turn it on and swipe through the photos until I find one which shows the emmets and voyeurs clustered across Bones Break. I enlarge it and then hold it up so Richard can see. My hand, I realise, is shaking.

Richard peers at the screen and then, stepping back from Archie, looks at me. 'If you tell them about me . . .' he whispers. I look down at his free hand. It is shaking too.

I begin to walk backwards, holding the phone out in front of me, the screen facing Richard, like a talisman. 'Stay away,' I say. 'Stay away from me.'

Richard nods once, slowly takes the lead from his pocket with his free hand and clips it on to Archie's collar. The two of them turn and walk east, back towards their house, their pace quickening with each step.

'Stay away from me.'

Richard disappears over the far side of the rise. The moment he is out of sight, I run, pounding along the coast path and then, once I reach the eastern headland, I take to the grass to avoid the crowd. A few emmets look at me with dubious curiosity as I make it to the road and then continue, never slowing, to pass the Cafy and enter the woods, stopping finally at the caravan. I let myself in, lock the door from the inside, close all the blinds and curtains and sit on the edge of the bed.

I breathe, long and deep.

My head is full of Richard. Those hard eyes. That drunken sneer. *Heard it all before*. The saddlebags.

I can feel the tremors in my hands begin to spread, making their way up my arms, towards my heart, towards my brain. I breathe more, try to hold on to the anger, to the violence deep inside, try to harden myself with it, but I can feel it slipping away from me, caught like driftwood in a riptide, carried out and away into an ocean of fear. I cannot shake the image of him from my head: I see that ugly smile, smell the alcohol which clings to his body, and cowardice swallows all. There is only fear. I want to retch with hopelessness.

If Mum were here, she would fight for me, just like

she did with the repulsive emmet and his hideous fingers two years ago. When she was well, she had the strength of ten Richard Browns. But if she was well, she would be here. And she is not. She is far away and my father is dead and my little sister too. I have nobody to protect me against Richard. Nobody to fight for me. And what if I can't fight for myself? *What if I can't fight?*

I try to force my mind elsewhere, not into memories – for Richard lives in them too – but into the present, the immediate, the sound of now: wind in the trees; the occasional shriek of a seagull; tyres crunching on gravel as vehicles pull into or out of the car park; voices, so many voices. Words remain unintelligible and I try to imagine dialogues over the drifting tones.

It does not work.

This world is populated by two people. Me and Richard Brown.

This cannot be life.

Hours pass. Somewhere within them I find a little peace, a semi-catatonia of stillness which I wrap myself in to hide from the fear. Perhaps this is where Mum went, this private world of nothingness. For the first time in my life, I can understand why she stayed there so long. Fear can drive you to terrible places.

When I emerge from the nothingness it is, perhaps, late afternoon. The voices from the lip have died, the slam of car doors and the low-level thrum of engines extinguished. I rise to my feet on stiff legs and make my way to the caravan door. I open it a crack: cool air caresses my face. Still no noise, only Bones Break's own – wind and swells and birds. I step outside and gently close the door behind me. Breathing long and deep, I venture forward through the woods, conscious of every twig snap and leaf crunch beneath my boots. I reach the periphery, the trees' shoreline, and peer out at the car park and, beyond that, the lip. They are empty.

I let myself into the Cafy, lock the door behind me. In the kitchen, I pour myself a glass of water and lean against the worktop, my back to the pile of clothes as I sip. The familiar sound of tyres on gravel comes and I move to the bar area to watch from the window. Although it is

Monday and Esther is not due to arrive until tomorrow, I find myself hoping it is her. I will tell her everything. But it is not a sky-blue Ford Fiesta, not even a car. It is a van, white, with a company logo painted on its side. Three men step out of it, all wearing high-visibility jackets and yellow hard hats. One opens the back doors and retrieves an array of instruments and appliances from the van's belly, handing them to his colleagues. The doors are closed, the equipment distributed evenly between the three men, and they leave their van to cross the road and make their way towards the lip.

I move back from the front windows towards and behind the bar, never letting the men from my sight. There is a trill of panic inside me that this is how it begins, that these men could be the harbingers of my greatest fear: property development on my land. But surely not. Not now. Not after the rockfall. Not even the richest or the stupidest emmets would risk building on Bones Break after what happened last night.

Nevertheless, I stay watching the three men. I do not want them to see me, am ready to duck out of view should they look my way, but they do not. Instead, they fan out from each other – one takes the eastern headland, one the western, the other dead centre – and, with my land divided into three, each photographs his allotted area. They bend low as they work, zigzagging back and forth across invisible yet seemingly fixed lines. They move slowly yet their fingers work with a hypnotic rapidity. I fixate on the one at dead centre, watch his hands as they deftly work the camera.

At some signal I do not notice, the men abruptly stop what they are doing and group around the signpost on the western headland. Turning back towards the cliff face, they take photos of Bones Break, swinging their lenses across the lip and then out and over the western headland itself. They will see my shelf, will take pictures of it. I wonder what they will think of it. I wonder if its utility will even occur to them.

Satisfied with the western headland they walk, as one, over to the eastern headland and repeat their actions, paying particular attention to the cavernous split which opened during last year's storms. Then they move to the new cleft to photograph and study and inspect and discuss it.

Grey pregnant clouds have begun to roll in from the horizon. They have not reached us yet – above, the sun remains out, unencumbered. It fires up the men's jackets and hard hats and polishes the white of their shirts so that, with the dark clouds behind them, they seem to shine, these three little men who move up and down my land with the routine motions of clockwork toys. I have a strange vision of myself out there on the lip, towering over them, watching them play and dance across the grass while I pat their little heads and whistle encouragements.

They stay until it grows dark, until hours after the sun has set, using their tripods and poles and wheels to observe and measure, flashing lights across to each other and back again, drilling holes so small I cannot see and always, before and during and after everything, taking photographs. I am mesmerised by the attention they shower upon my land. I should like copies of their photos, all of them, so that I might wallpaper the caravan with all those different angles, all those different viewpoints, from the grand panorama of the entire lip to the close-up of a single blade of grass.

It is late when they leave. First, they return to the van and unload the equipment they have carried back in their arms. Next, they take out three wooden posts, three sheets of metal and a large mallet. Crossing the road back to the lip, they walk to the eastern headland and one of them hammers the post into the ground while the other two hold it in place. I wince with each smack of the mallet.

Once they have tested the resilience of the post, ensured it is firmly in place in the earth, they walk a straight line down to the road and hammer the second post into the grass at its edge. The same happens to the third post, also by the road, in a straight line down from the western headland. One of them walks up towards the lip, takes out a thick roll of tape, loops it a few times around the coast path signpost and then allows it to spool out behind him as he navigates around each of the three posts he and his colleagues have inserted, being sure to loop the same line of tape around each as he passes. Once he is done, I can see what they have created. My land now stands within a cordoned-off rectangle, the four posts its corners, the tape – and the drop from the lip – its walls.

The men take the three sheets of metal, prop them up

on stands, and leave each beside the three barriers of tape: one facing the coast path leading in from Petherick; one facing the coast path leading in from Lantoweth; one facing the road, and the Cafy. I can read the moonlit sign from here.

DANGER
Unstable area
Do not pass

The men walk back to the van, climb in and drive away. I wait for a few minutes after they have gone, wait until I am sure they will not return, and then I run out of the Cafy and across the road to the band of tape which separates me from my land, bending down to pass beneath it.

I am inside the cordon. Inside the rectangle. The only one allowed here. The tape does not keep me out – this is my land, how could it? What it does is keep me safe within by *keeping everybody else out*. I will not cut it. I am pleased it is here, all of it, the tape and the posts and the signs. Even though they are unsightly, in stark contrast to the natural beauty of my land, it does not matter. I can accept them. I can warm to them. More than that, I can grow to love them. Because they preserve my land. They protect it. Maybe they will protect me too.

My phone rings. I fish it out of my coat pocket. It is Esther.

'Where are you?'

Before I remember that I am supposed to be at the house in St Petroc, I say, 'Bones Break.'

'What?' Her raised voice stings my ear through the phone's tinny speaker. 'You promised me you weren't going back there again. You know who he is. You know what he's—'

I interrupt her. 'There's been a rockfall. I had to come. To check for damage.'

The tone of anger in Esther's voice vanishes, replaced by concern. 'Is the Cafy all right?'

'It's fine.'

'So you're finished there?'

'Yes,' I lie.

'I'll come and pick you up. I can give you a lift to St Petroc.'

'Don't be ridiculous, Esther. I can walk home quicker than it takes you to drive here.'

'I'm in Treleven. I didn't go back to Bristol yesterday. Mum had to go to the doctor, so I said I'd take her.'

'Is she okay?'

'She's fine, absolutely fine. Getting better, actually. The doctor said she should be back to normal in no time.'

'That's good,' I say.

'Anyway, stay where you are, I'll be twenty minutes.'

I picture the dark road back from St Petroc, the cold winds and close headlights. 'Honestly, Esther, you don't need to worry about me. I can get back fine on my own.'

'I'll be twenty minutes,' she repeats and then hangs up before I can protest again.

I have another long walk ahead of me tonight.

When Esther arrives in the car park, I leave the Cafy, close and lock the door behind me, and walk out to meet her. She steps out of her car and hugs me. I remember how, when I mistook the workers' van for Esther earlier, I resolved there and then to tell her everything. Now that she is here with me, it no longer seems such a good idea. Secrets have come between us before. I do not want that to happen again.

'So how bad was this rockfall?' she asks, and I lead her over the road and up on to the eastern headland, where we stand and gaze down at the destruction, visible and ghostly by the light of the moon. 'It looks so precarious.'

'*Unstable*.' I point at the cordoned-off area and the sign which faces us. 'But it can't be that bad. Before they put all that up, there were maybe a hundred people here.'

Esther makes a whistling sound through her teeth. 'A hundred people? Shame Nicholas Cartwright wasn't walking his dog while they were here.'

I could tell her. Could tell her everything. Right now. I open my mouth. Nothing comes out.

'He'd probably never have got away,' Esther continues.

'Especially if they were from Petherick. They would have lynched him.'

The idea is strangely comforting. I feel ashamed to admit it, but that does not stop it from being true.

Esther turns and looks back at Bones Break, at its changed face almost iridescent in the moonlight. I follow her gaze, letting my eyes travel down to the incoming tide as it gently washes up and on to the mound covering my zawn.

'Are you okay?' she asks.

'Yes,' I say. 'I'm fine. Why?'

'You're quiet.'

'I always am.'

Esther half-smiles. 'Do you mind if I get a glass of water before we go?' she says. 'I'm parched.'

'Of course.'

I lead her back to the Cafy, unlock and hold open the door for her to step inside. We make our way into the kitchen where Esther fills a glass from the tap and gulps it down. 'That's good water,' she says, and then, with that mischievous glint in her eye, 'Got anything stronger?'

'What like?'

'Is there any wine left in the bar? We could have a glass before we go. Sit and talk.'

'No, I cleared everything out from the bar when we closed. I didn't want anyone looking through the window and seeing a load of stock they could break in and steal.' This is partly true. The alcohol was hidden away, but everything else – the cans and bottles and cartons of soft drinks and mixers and fruit juices – Little Sister Lucy and I squirrelled away in the caravan to consume at our leisure.

'Where did you move it to?'

Little Sister Lucy especially loved to mix pineapple juice with lemonade. She once called it 'Pie-n-ade', and I laughed so hard at how inappropriate the name sounded for a drink that she kept on calling it that, just to make me laugh again.

'Melody Janie,' Esther says. 'Where's the wine?'

'The storeroom,' I say, remembering the way she would crush the tip of the straw between her teeth, alternating between taking miniscule sips and blowing bubbles, the smell of pineapple on her breath at night before she disappeared beneath the duvet, nothing left of her but those two white feet dangling out over the edge of the bed. My softly snoring lump.

The sound of a door opening pulls me back into the present. I look about me, but Esther has vanished. Where has she gone? Has she left?

A foul stench drifts into the kitchen. I recognise it immediately. The storeroom. My stomach lurches.

'Esther?' I shout.

I hear her cough, and then, '*Jesus.*'

I run down the stairs to find her stood in the open doorway to the storeroom, one arm covering her mouth. 'Why does it smell so *bad*?' she says.

'It needs a clean.' My fingers reach automatically for the light switch, but the light down here has not worked for some time now. Small bottle-glass windows line the wall before it meets the ceiling – windows which sit just above ground level and look out towards the woods – and enough moonlight penetrates them to navigate the room. Esther walks towards the gigantic chest freezers, removes her arm from her mouth and opens one of the doors.

Her back arches and she seems to spasm twice before slamming the door closed and running from the storeroom and up the stairs. I climb back up to the kitchen and find her bent over the sink, her inhalations and exhalations forced and noisy.

'Melody Janie,' she gasps. 'The chicken in the freezer . . . it's *rancid*.'

I agree with her. Chicken is rancid. I do not eat it any more.

'How long has that freezer been off for?'

'I don't know. Since they cut the electricity. Five weeks? Six?'

'It's *warm*.' She coughs and holds her hand up to her mouth again. 'Haven't you seen the maggots?'

I walk back down the stairs and cross the storeroom to the chest freezer. I open it. Esther is right. The packets of chicken have burst and are crawling with maggots.

Which is precisely why I do not eat chicken any more.

The drive to St Petroc is quiet. Awkward. Esther seems angry at me but incapable of expressing it, as if she wants to yell yet forbids herself to do so. The few things she utters are strained, tempered by will.

'You could come back to Treleven with me tonight. Mum and Dad would love to see you. They ask about you all the time.'

'I'll see them soon. I promise.'

'If you need a hand cleaning the Cafy, you only have to ask.'

'Thank you. I will.'

'Are you warm enough at your house?'

'Yes. It's fine.'

She turns the radio on. We do not speak for the rest of the journey.

When we arrive outside the house, I unlatch my seat belt, hug her and open the door.

'Why won't you invite me in?' she asks.

I search for a convincing lie. I cannot tell her the real reason: that I do not live here any more. She would never forgive me. 'I'm embarrassed,' I say. 'It's a mess. Worse even than the Cafy. Once I get it tidied up properly, I'll invite you in. I promise.'

'I can help you.'

'Let me get started on it first. Do the worst bits. Then you can help.'

Esther moves her head to look at me, and the car's interior light reflects off her wet eyes. 'I'm worried about you, Melody Janie,' she says.

I lean over, reach for her hand and give it a soft squeeze. 'You don't need to be,' I say.

And then I close the door, walk down the drive and let myself into the house. I move into the living room and stand beside the window for the next five minutes until Esther finally drives away. I remain a few minutes more, breathing long and deep, before letting myself back out to begin the return walk to Bones Break – feeling foolish the whole time, but doing it anyway.

The thunder wakes me. It is still dark. The storm has returned and it is close, perhaps directly overhead, the crashes and cracks like stone hitting stone. As it recedes, from below comes the distant boom of waves. The surf must be huge, the tide high.

A flash. It lights up the inside of the caravan and I briefly glimpse my feet poking out from the duvet, ice-white and hard. Another flash, this one longer yet dimmer, fluctuating in intensity like a faulty bulb: a stream of lightning strikes, one after the other after the other.

I step out of bed, put my coat on to ward off the chill which has dug in deep across the caravan. I move from window to window, opening each curtain. Outside is black. My land has become auditory: thunder, waves, the splatter of heavy rain. Occasional flashes light the trees, but they are brief and unreliable. Beyond my concealing woods, out on the lip perhaps, the view must be spectacular – I could watch the forks descend over my land, over the ocean, watch the fluorescent lines explode into sparks, watch them carried away by the spray of the Atlantic. But the lip right now is too dangerous a place even for me. It is not the lightning that frightens me. It is the wind, which rampages through the trees and rocks the caravan from side to side like a ship on the sea. It is the kind of wind which could knock me over, send me sprawling. Carry me beyond the lip. Such thoughts keep me far back on nights like this.

There is another noise, distinct to the thunder and the waves and the rain on the roof, lower in the mix yet unmistakeably there, thinner, erratic, irregular but frequent. I listen, try to train my ears on to it. Pursue. Locate. Identify. It is loudest in the lulls, when the thunder drops, when the rain eases, when the last wave of the set has broken, but still elusive, impossible to define.

I must get closer.

I take the Cafy's keys from their place in the cutlery drawer and step out of the caravan and into the rain. Above me, the canopy of treetops sways back and forth, rainwater falling from it in waves. I am drenched before I have locked the door.

Another flash of lightning, followed almost immediately by a rolling, spitting bomb of thunder, its pulsing vibrations passing through my skin. I start to run. I have no fear of storms, only a healthy respect. Standing stock-still below one as violent as this is nothing short of pure stupidity. I reach the periphery of the woods and am about to launch out into the onslaught of rain, free from the shelter of trees, when I stop.

There, by the side of the Cafy, is Archie. He is barking: the noise I heard from the caravan. That I could not distinguish it comes as no surprise here – the violence of the storm transforms his bark into something alien, whipped by the wind and flattened by the shuddering acoustics of heavy swells. He sounds strangled, frantic, and yet he does not move more than a few centimetres from his position. I look closer and realise that he cannot move. He has been tied to one of the wooden benches.

I am about to run to him when I see Richard. He founders into view, ignoring Archie as he sways and stumbles around the Cafy. He lurches from windows to doors, banging his fists against them and shouting. His voice is drowned out by the storm, but I know he is calling my name. I press myself against a nearby tree, remain as still as possible. Droplets of rain burrow into my hair, make their way under my coat, crawl down my back. I breathe, long and deep.

Richard slips in a patch of mud, landing hard on his back. This seems to upset Archie yet further, and when Richard staggers back to his feet he lunges at the dog and grabs him with such force that I can hear Archie's yelp from here. Richard opens one of the saddlebags, reaches inside and retrieves something. It flashes silver in the night.

I run and I run and I do not stop, do not look behind me, until I reach the caravan. With one fluid motion, I enter, close and lock the door. I walk from window to window, peering out of each. Richard has not followed me. He did not see me. I pull shut all the blinds and curtains, building a blackout, until nothing penetrates the gloom of the caravan. In the darkness, I search for some form of defence. The knives I own are small and blunted, could never match the power of his, but I need something, anything, in case he progresses further than the Cafy, into the woods, in case he finds my caravan, in case he finds me inside it.

I open the cupboards above the sink, feel around amongst my meagre possessions. My hand settles upon a glass bottle of olive oil: a relic from those holidays so many years ago.

I take it down from the cupboard and clutch it in my hand as I stand beside the door. If he forces his way in here, I'll get to him first. I'll bring the bottle down over his head. And then I'll stick him, again and again, from his neck down to his feet, until the shards pepper his body. Like a little glass hedgehog. In agony.

Violence. I let it come, let it swell inside me, building and rolling like a set of waves. It washes away the fear. My palms itch. I will not fight the sensation. I will not breathe long and deep. I will let my heart race, let my brain cloud with adrenaline. I will let these urges come, these urges to bite, to swing, kick, squeeze and stamp. The charged prickles they send along my skin are exquisite.

I should not have run from him. I will not run again.

I stay beside the door. The storm continues. An hour passes. The sound of Archie vanishes. The bottle becomes a lead weight in my hand, and I can feel my raised arm weakening, jellifying. But I will not lower it.

He came on to my land. He came to my mother's Cafy. He pushed and he pushed too far and now this anger is here and it's more, more than anger. It has grown, bloomed, translated into hate, and hate can overcome anything. I will no longer be scared. I have been scared for too long. I will hate. This is my land. I will hate Richard Brown right off it.

I open the caravan door and step outside, bottle still gripped at head height.

I walk through the woods. I do not creep. I do not soften my footsteps. I walk.

I do not pause at the periphery of the woods, do not hide behind a tree. I step out into the rain. Present. Unashamed. Unafraid.

Archie is not there, no longer tied to the bench. I walk a calm and measured patrol of the Cafy's perimeter.

Richard has gone.

It does not matter. I will hate him. Now and tomorrow and all the tomorrows after that until he has left my land for good.

I return to the caravan. I lock the door but I do not close the blinds and curtains. I climb into bed.

I will never fear Richard Brown again.

I will hate him.

I will hate him and I will hurt him.

I wake with a head full of crystals: their illuminating clarity; their pricking, needle-sharp points. I get up.

Outside, the morning is bitter and still. I can see my breath. I walk through the woods and then out to the Cafy car park. There are no emmets here today. And, if Richard returned last night, there is no sign.

I move towards the road. The posts and tape remain in place on my land. Seabirds cluster on Gull Rock, soundless today, in mourning perhaps for the loss of our zawn. I do not walk out to the lip.

Instead, I make my way back to the Cafy and let myself in. A few moments after I close the door behind me, the phone sounds from within my pocket. I take it out. Esther's name is emblazoned across the screen.

'Melody Janie?'

'Hi, Esther.'

'It's Tuesday. Where are you? At the Cafy?' Her voice is impatient, antagonised.

'No,' I lie.

'Then where? I'm at your house right now.'

'Petherick.' It is all I can think to say.

'Are you okay? You sound . . .'

'It's Richard,' I say.

Esther's voice is hard ice. 'What's he done?'

I want to tell her about last night, about yesterday, but if I did she would know I was here, know I was at the Cafy. I search for an answer to her question. The pause takes too long.

'What's he done, Melody Janie?' Her tone demands a response.

'He's . . . he . . .'

'What?'

I settle on the only articulation I can muster. 'You were right about him.'

'I'm coming to pick you up.'

'No.'

'Yes. Where are you?'

'At the library.'

'I'll meet you there.'

'No. You don't need to do that.'

'I'll be there in ten minutes.'

It is impossible, without a car, to reach Petherick from Bones Break in ten minutes. I cannot agree to this. 'Esther,' I say, 'no. You don't have to meet me.'

'I'm meeting you.'

'At least give me an hour.'

'Why?'

'I'm reading.' Such pathetic excuses. She can see right through them, I'm sure.

'Reading what?'

'I'm reading about Richard. On the computer here. It's important for me, to know as much as possible. I'm trying to come to terms with it. The shock. You understand, don't you?'

Esther sighs. 'One hour,' she says. 'In the library.'

'Outside. I'll meet you outside.'

One hour.

I will have to run.

I arrive in Petherick with five minutes to spare, enough time to dart into the newsagent for the large bottle of water I crave. The bell dings as I enter. Paul Dunstan's mum stands behind the counter. She looks at me, taking in my heavy breathing, the sweat which stains the sides of my dress below my arms, my red, panting face. Her gaze remains longest on the thick scab which cuts its way across my cheek. Her eyes are heavy with something. Perhaps disdain. More likely, if she believes the same as her son, fear.

I turn away from her, walk to the fridge and open it. The feel of the cold bottle against my burning fingers sends trills of relief to my brain.

'One pound, please,' she says when I place the bottle on the counter.

I fish in my pocket for the money I stuffed in there before fleeing the Cafy, retrieve a £5 note and hold it out to her.

She does not take it. 'Anything smaller?' she asks.

'What do you think?' The sudden force of the words, the unexpected violence of them, surprises both of us. Her face turns crimson. She looks away from me, towards the door.

I want to ask her again. I want to ask precisely what she does think. But I suspect I know. She thinks I pushed Little Sister Lucy. Just like Paul Dunstan. Just like all of them here in this stupid excuse for a village. They can all go fuck themselves, her included.

She lifts her eyes to meet mine, but she cannot hold them, not for long. She mumbles to the floor. Her voice is so soft I can barely hear it, but I think she says *sorry*.

I leave the £5 note on the counter and turn to walk out of the shop without waiting for the change. When I slam the door shut, its pane of glass clatters with a violence which pleases me.

Petherick is quiet this morning. I make my way through its streets directly to the library and I pass no more than five people along the way. A solitary dog barks somewhere in the distance. Nearby, someone is cooking: smells of roasting meat linger in the cool air.

Esther finds me sat on the wooden bench opposite the library. I have composed myself sufficiently while drinking half the bottle of water, and I hold my arms at my side so that she does not notice the sweat stains as they dry.

'I don't understand why you had to come here,' she says. 'I gave you the phone. If you wanted to read about that monster, you could have used the internet on that.'

'You told me the mobile data was expensive.'

'Then use your Wi-Fi at home.'

'Cut off,' I say. I do not know if that is a lie. I suspect it is not.

Esther sits down on the bench next to me. 'How are you?'

'Unusual.'

She laughs, and then stops herself. 'Sorry,' she says. 'It's just . . . good word.'

I smile at her. She takes my hand in hers and we

sit side by side for a while without talking. It feels good.

'Let's get a coffee,' she says. 'Or, better yet, something stronger.'

'Okay.'

We stand and walk through the streets of Petherick together towards the tea shop. When we reach it, the lights are off and the CLOSED sign hangs from the shut door.

'Of course,' Esther says. 'I've only been in Bristol a year, but already I'm forgetting how things work down here. The season's over.'

'It'll start again.'

Esther smiles a smile that is not a real smile. 'Come on,' she says. 'We'll find somewhere else.'

I follow her as we walk out towards the harbour and, when we reach the pub, I realise that Esther means for us to go in. I feel a sudden stab of horror at the thought of seeing Paul Dunstan, but a quick glance through the window reveals it to be empty save for the solitary bartender.

The moment we enter, I feel the warmth and cosiness of this pub. It is what Mum has always wanted for the Cafy. The feeling that once you were inside, you would be safe, safe from the wind and the rain, safe from the ocean spray, from the noise and the drop, from the raw elements that make Bones Break so spectacular, so crucially vital. Yet they are impossible to reconcile: my land and her Cafy. Too at odds. You could build a castle there and it would never defeat the power of the place itself. Bones Break will always overcome.

Yet this pub, tucked away as it is in a bay, sheltered by the hills behind and its natural harbour and man-made breakwater ahead: this pub has nothing to fear. Its environment sings safety, and the diamond-patterned carpet and the sturdy oak tables and the framed black-and-white photos of fishing boats and crumbling houses and beach barbecues on the walls and even the bartender herself with her bleached hair and surfer's legs – all of it, all of it is so fixed, so *rooted*, that our Cafy could never, and has never been able to, contend.

Esther perches on one of the stools pushed up against the bar and I copy her. The bartender saunters towards us and offers a winning smile.

'Morning, ladies. What can I get you?' She is about our age and not from around here. If she were, we would recognise her.

'I'll have an Irish coffee,' Esther says and then turns to me. 'Same?'

'No,' I say. 'Just a cup of tea, please.'

'*Irish* tea?' I love the cheeky flash in Esther's eyes.

'I'll just stick with tea. But you'd better give the student her alcohol or she's likely to kick off. It's gone eleven o'clock in the morning.'

Esther laughs and so does the bartender and I am so glad – so very, very glad – to have my friend at my side.

The bartender flits about an oversized and steaming piece of machinery – toggling levers, bleeding spouts –

and returns to us with two tall and fancy-handled glasses. She makes a pretence of handing me the Irish coffee before clownishly correcting herself, declaring, 'Oh no, this is for the student,' and swapping the offending item with the weird glass of tea. I enjoy the charade.

Esther pays and we take our drinks to a table in the corner of the pub. The bartender beams her gratitude when Esther leaves behind the change, eighty pence, as a tip. 'So,' she says as we settle into the cushioned chairs on opposite sides of the table. 'How was the research?'

'You were right,' I reply. 'He's a monster.'

'I was thinking that maybe we should call the police.'

'What good would that do? He said he was relocated to Bones Break. It was the police who put him in Mrs Perrow's house.'

'That's only what he says. We don't know if it's for real, do we?'

'What do you mean?'

'I've been doing my own research. I've been reading up on him a lot. I haven't found anything that says the police put him here.'

'Of course you haven't. He's in witness protection, or whatever it is the police put wrongly accused people in. It has to be secret.'

'But he's not wrongly accused, is he? You know that and I know that. He's lied to you about other things . . .'

He's lied to me about everything, I think.

'. . . so why not lie to you about this as well? For all

we know, he needed to get away from Manchester because someone, or, no, that's not right, *everyone*, there knew he'd done it, and so he left of his own accord to escape it. Maybe he wasn't relocated at all. Maybe he bought Mrs Perrow's house knowing full well that it was hidden . . .'

Hidden. I remember being hidden. The sweetness of it.

'. . . and that he could hide out there alone . . .'

Alone. I like to be alone.

'. . . until it all blows over. Until some other monstrosity dominates the news and everyone forgets about Nicholas Cartwright . . .'

Nicholas Cartwright. Why can't I think of him as Nicholas Cartwright? Why is he Richard Brown? Still? After all I know?

'. . . and what he did and who he is. I don't think the police relocated him. Not for a second. I think he did it all himself. He's rich enough, isn't he? I read about all those houses he owns—'

'Properties,' I say.

'What?'

'He owns six properties.'

There is a difficult silence. Esther looks at me in a way I cannot comprehend. When the door opens I am, for a moment, relieved that I do not have to qualify my strange correction, grateful for the imposed break upon the conversation that comes as we both look towards the door, in the natural manner of locals, locals everywhere. Locals Only.

The relief lasts no longer than the moment it afforded. The door closes. Paul Dunstan steps into the pub.

He sees us a few seconds after we see him. The delay is enough for him not to notice Esther's rolled eyes, and he sheepishly makes his way to our table.

'Not seen you for a while,' he says to Esther. 'Heard you were living in Treleven.'

'I'm in Bristol now.'

'Any good?'

'Better than here.'

Paul snorts his disbelief but makes no comment. He turns to me. 'Hi, Melody Janie.'

'Hello.'

'You all right?' He points a dirty finger at my cheek.

'Fine.'

'Good. Mate of mine told me Bones Break took a battering yesterday. How's the Cafy?'

'It survived.'

He nods knowingly. 'Well built, that one. Solid. Bet it's never given you any problems.'

I shake my head.

'Look,' Paul says. 'Wanted to apologise to you. About Sunday. Was out of order.'

'What happened?' Esther says.

'Said some things I shouldn't. Was off my face.'

'It was barely midday,' I say.

'Sunday. You know how it is.'

'What did you say?' Esther will not relinquish her demand. 'What did you say to her?'

'Nothing,' Paul says. He has begun to shuffle nervously from one foot to the other. He will not look at me. 'Drunk talk. Didn't mean anything by it. Off my face.'

'Tell me, Melody Janie. What did he say to you?' Unlike Paul, Esther stares directly into my eyes.

'I don't know,' I say. 'What was it, Paul? A warning? Or an accusation?'

'Just what a few of the lads in the village have been saying. Don't believe it myself. Never would.'

'Then why was it so vitally important for you to share it with me?'

'Just thought you should know. That's all.'

'What . . .' Esther hisses, '. . . the *fuck* . . . did you say?'

I have never seen Paul Dunstan look so cowed. His shoulders are hunched and his hands are in his pockets, rattling coins together. Discomfort oozes from his pores. I am rather enjoying it.

'According to Paul—'

'Not me.'

'According to a few of the lads in the village, and maybe to Paul's mum as well . . .' Paul will not look at me, even when I mention his mother. 'According to all of them, Lucy didn't jump.'

Esther's jaws grind. She is not looking at me any more. Her focus is solely on Paul.

'Isn't that right, Paul?' I say. 'She didn't jump, did she? I pushed her.'

Esther leaps up so suddenly that her legs crash into the rim of the table, sending our glasses careening down on to the carpet, where they splash enormous brown stains across the diamonds. Her strength is magnificent, rocking this sturdy oak back and forth as she pulls herself free and, arms outstretched, pounces towards Paul. He darts out of reach just in time and, without stopping, turns and sprints out of the pub. Esther chases him – she *chases* him! – to the door, and then halts as it swings shut before her.

I rise and, along with the bartender, the three of us gather at the window, where we watch Paul Dunstan run his silly hopping run across the car park and over the road. And then we laugh. The three of us. We laugh so hard and so long that the notion of fear, of even the smallest speck of it, of ever feeling it again for the rest of my life, suddenly seems as unreal to me as snow on a summer's day.

'They don't really believe it,' Esther says as we walk to her car. 'It's just stupid boys making up their stupid stories. The same as they used to back in school.'

'I know, Esther,' I say.

'They're bullies, the lot of them. They haven't got a clue what they're talking about. Don't let them get to you.'

'I won't, Esther.'

'And you can stop that too,' she says with a smile.

'Stop what, Esther?'

'*That.*'

We reach her car and halt. She hugs me.

'Are you sure you're all right?' she whispers into my ear.

'I'm fine. Honestly, I am.'

'Jesus,' she says, pulling herself away. 'It's just the sheer fucking insensitivity of it. I mean, who says something like that? Who is really so fucking lacking in even a shred of sympathy that they can say something like that? And then say it to *you*?'

'Most people are like that.'

'But that's just it, Melody Janie. Most people aren't like that at all. It's this place. It's poisonous. You've got to get away from here. Come with me to Bristol. Please. See what the rest of the world is like.'

'Bristol's hardly the rest of the world.'

'But it isn't *here*. Please, Melody Janie. Why won't you come?'

'You know why.'

'I know, I know, you need more time. I'm sorry. I shouldn't hassle you like this. Now I'm being insensitive.'

'I don't think that's even possible for you.'

Esther looks suddenly sad. 'I have been though, haven't I? Ever since we moved to Treleven. It was my fault we lost contact. I should have been around for you more. And I'm so sorry about that. Really, I am.'

'It wasn't your fault,' I whisper.

'What?'

'It wasn't your fault. That we lost contact.' It was my fault. I should tell her. I want to tell her. Yet there are some things I cannot say to anyone, myself included. Instead, I hug her. She feels light in my arms, the way Little Sister Lucy used to. 'But it's all okay,' I say. 'Because you came back. That's all that's important. You came back.'

Esther offers to take me to St Petroc, but I tell her I want to return to the library to read some more. She believes me and does not put up a fight.

'See you Saturday?' I say as she climbs into her car.

'I'm going to try and make it back earlier if I can,' she says, shutting the door and opening the window. 'Maybe in a couple of days?'

'That'd be nice.'

As she pulls out of the car park and on to the road, she keeps one hand out the window, waving the whole time until she vanishes from view. She will come back, I know that.

I aimlessly wander the streets of Petherick for a while. I have no intention of visiting the library, but I want to stay here in case Esther has forgotten something and turns the car around. Should she call me to ask where I am, I do not want to be back up on the coast path, halfway home.

Somehow, I find myself on the edge of the new estate. No locals live here. There are only holiday lets and purpose-built second homes. I walk along its streets. The tarmac is the same here as anywhere else in Petherick; the smell of the sea and the sound of the shrieking gulls, it is all as familiar as the woodsmoke which drifts from the pub's chimney. And yet this estate could not be more alien. It is not merely the stark and imposing buildings, their straight lines and enormous panes of glass, their lifts and air conditioning units, their signs with tariffs and rates and phone numbers and professional photographs of gorgeous people on gorgeous sand. It is the complete absence of life. This estate is empty. There are no children playing in the street, no cars carefully making their way around them, no cats perched on gateposts observing it all. One of the Three Lauras – I cannot remember which – used to live in Polmennor before she moved to St Petroc, and she would tell Esther about the winters when her village would transform into a ghost town, and how when she was little she used to run up and down the streets pretending she was the last person on earth. That is how it feels here, in this estate, like an abandoned outpost or an old movie set of one, like some post-apocalyptic wilderness, like hibernation.

I leave the estate and make my way towards the front, towards the coast path. I have been in Petherick long enough. It is time to go back to the caravan, to go back home.

From around a corner, Paul appears, walking in my direction. When he sees me, he stops. I approach him. He looks like he is thinking about turning around, retreating the way he came, but he stays put.

'Where is she?' he asks when I stop before him.

'Are you scared of Esther?'

'Course not.'

'Maybe you should be.'

Paul does not reply to that. I look at him for a long time. Why was I so intimidated by him when we were children? This man I see now is nothing, not even a bully any more, just a sad, slobbish waste of space who looks like he should be turning forty next year rather than twenty. Doing nothing with his life except going to the pub early on a Tuesday afternoon. Does he even have a job? What else does he do? What is the point of Paul Dunstan?

I remember yesterday's conversation with Esther. *Shame Nicholas Cartwright wasn't walking his dog . . .*

'How's your dad?' I ask.

'All right. Why?'

'No reason.' I let the awkward silence hang for one moment, two moments, three, and then I say, 'Have you ever heard of Nicholas Cartwright?'

'That nonce scum from the news? Course. Everyone has.'

'He moved into Mrs Perrow's old house the other day.'

I let myself smile the moment I turn my back on Paul Dunstan. I am pleased with myself. Mum would be pleased with me too. She would have done something similar were she here. She would have dealt with it, just like the way she dealt with that repulsive emmet two years ago.

I can still remember his face: the lingering eyes, the wet sneer, the fluff of a beard he could not properly grow. The way his fingers brushed my arm when I handed him his bottle of beer, and then my palm when I gave him his change. He sat in the dining room, but close to the doorway so that I could see him from behind the bar, and he could see me. Mum clocked him immediately.

'Looks like you've got a little admirer,' she said when we were both in the kitchen.

'Him?' I tried to say the word with disgust, but instead it came in a tone of surprise. I was not used to being admired.

'He's cute. He's about your age. Why don't you talk to him?'

'He's not cute. He's . . .' I searched for the right word. 'Repellent.'

Mum laughed. 'Fair enough, Melody Janie. If you don't like him, you don't like him.'

There was an awkward pause.

'Don't you?'

'Mum,' I said, 'I *don't* like him.'

'Okay, okay.' She waved her hands in mock defence. 'Whatever you say.'

Twenty minutes later he came back for a second bottle of beer. And then a third. And then a fourth. Each time, the same touches on my hand and arm. When I served him his fifth beer, he placed his fingers over my wrist and said, 'Show me the real Cornwall.'

I wrenched my arm away and backstepped right into Mum. I did not know she was there.

'She won't show you the real Cornwall,' Mum said, 'but I will.' She leaned over the bar, palms flat against the counter, shoulders firm. She looked thoroughly menacing, sinister even, and I loved her for it. 'Here it is,' she said in a voice barely louder than a whisper. 'Finish your beer and fuck off out of my Cafy.'

The emmet's shock was instant, his eyes widening into white circles and his jaw slackening. He seemed like he was about to say something, but could not find the words, nor the ability to form them. He did not look at either me or Mum again. Instead, he looked down, at himself, at his hands as they pushed him up from his bar stool, at his feet as they flattened on to the floor. He turned from us quickly and left the Cafy yet quicker. We watched him through the window as he hurried off to his rental car and drove out of the car park, away in the direction of Petherick. We never saw him again.

Once the car was out of sight, Mum turned to me. 'Are you all right?' she asked.

'How did you do that?' I breathed. 'He was *terrified* of you.'

'He harassed my daughter. He was right to be terrified.'

'But you said he was cute.'

Mum looked at me for a moment and then a thunderstorm of laughter burst from her, so violent she had to hold on to the bar for support. I tried to laugh with her, but the shock of it all, of everything, of what they had both done, made it difficult for me to even muster a smile.

Mum eventually composed herself. 'Just because I think something,' she said, 'it doesn't mean it's true.'

I remember lying in bed that night, confused by all the emotions which kept me awake. Shame and pride; hope and helplessness. That Mum stood up for me with such magnificent, composed strength. That, had she not been there, it would have fallen on me to stand up for myself. And could I have? Was I capable? I felt torn between my adoration of her and my deep, deep terror that, without her, I would have been nothing but a victim.

I wish I could tell that seventeen-year-old me what I now know. Because Mum is not here. She has not been for a long time. She left me with the bittersweet burden of Little Sister Lucy and the trauma of my father's death. And, yet, I have endured. Alone. Fending for myself.

Making the choices I've needed to make. Seeing them through. When she returns, Mum will find me a different woman. A woman more like her.

And the next time someone makes advances on me I'll tell him to fuck off myself, and Mum and I can laugh together.

To my surprise, the sun comes out the moment I step on to the coast path and begin the ascent up and away from Petherick. The terrain levels before my calves start to ache, and I walk west, towards my home, with a quick stride which is fierce in its purpose. The sky before me is a thin, autumnal blue, the brilliant-white clouds which populate it high and solid, starkly outlined. The air is fresh in my lungs and sharp – but sharp in a gentle way: a knife pressed lightly – on my cheeks. Below, swells build and approach, clean and glassy in the sunlight, splintering into broken white and hurdling over rocks semi-submerged in the green water. Two seals have beached themselves on the zawn halfway between Petherick and Nare Point. One lies flat on its back, its belly to the sun, while the other flaps its tail and sniffs at the sand.

From afar, I catch my first sight of Richard's house. I picture myself walking past it with a slow and measured step, staring towards it as I do so, so that if he should look out the window and see me he would see precisely how unafraid of him I am. Because it is the truth. Richard does not scare me. Not any more. I have dealt with him. It is only a matter of time before he is out of my life forever.

Nevertheless, I must remain sensible for the time being. He owns a knife, after all, and he has used it before. It is growing late in the afternoon and he may have begun drinking. Should he see me, it is impossible to predict how he might react. To evade this, I leave the coast path at the public entrance to Trethewas Woods. A few cars are parked here and the familiar shouts of playing children echo beneath the leaf canopy. I use the wooden walkway to cross the boggy marsh near the entrance which floods the moment there is a drop of rain and then, once the ground is solid again, I step off the walkway, leaving the prescribed visitors' route, and go it alone, west through the trees.

I do not see Richard's house as I pass it from behind, but I am habituated enough with these woods to know roughly when I have drawn level with the rise. I scramble out towards the road. When I appear back in the sunlight, my precision delights me. The rise is there, directly ahead. I cross the road and rejoin the coast path.

Before I continue, before I tackle the last leg, it feels pertinent to stand atop the rise and quickly scan the coast path from west to east, to check from this, the best of vantage points, who might be up here with me. From Nare Point to the eastern headland of my land, there is no one. Satisfied by the emptiness, I push on.

A tern shoots out of the cleft the moment I step on

to the eastern headland. It barks its annoyance at me before wheeling away to land on Gull Rock. I stop at the edge of the cleft to examine it for nests or eggs. Nothing has been deposited there, but the fact that the birds have begun to use it is a good sign. They are slowly accepting the changed face of Bones Break.

I make my way along the lip to the new cleft. No birds appear from it to swoop off into the distance, but it does not matter. These things take time. The birds will learn to love it when they are ready. As will I.

I continue along the lip until I reach the enclosure. The posts remain in place, as does the tape between them – though it has begun to sag a little, stretched and contorted by the wind. I turn from it, walk across the road and on to the gravel of the car park, then make my way past the wooden picnic benches to open the front door of the Cafy.

It sticks as I push it.

I squeeze through the gap and find an envelope wedged between the door and the entrance mat. My own name, long and looping letters in blue ink, is written across its front. I pull the envelope free, close and lock the door and make my way to the kitchen, away from the windows. I lean back against the cooker, both support and anchor, and open the envelope.

Dear Melody Janie,

I will keep this letter short, but there are some things I must tell you.

The first is how very sorry I am for our conversation yesterday. I was drunk, and I suspect you know that. I have been drinking too much lately. My way of coping with all that has happened to me. I can only hope you will forgive me, and especially so when you read what I have to say next.

When I returned home that afternoon, I did so to some wonderful news. My lawyer called to tell me that the murderer of Caleb Hawkins has finally been found. This news is set to be released to the public first thing tomorrow morning, when you shall see for yourself. This time, I hope you _will_ believe what you read in the papers.

What was strangest to me was that, as soon as I heard, I wanted to tell you. You may not have realised it, but you have been a good friend to me – and to Archie – while we have been here. An immensely good friend who has helped us more than you will ever know. Last night, after waiting for the crowds you described at Bones Break to disappear, I went to the Cafy in the hope of seeing you. It was a foolish enterprise – it was very late and you, of course, must have been at home. I thought to write this letter to you then, but was so drunk I could barely put pen to paper. I am embarrassed to admit that I even fell over, and when I got home I was caked in mud.

Today, however, I woke with a clear purpose. While it is deeply important to me that you know the truth, what you choose to do with it is, of course, up to you. It goes without saying that, now my name has been cleared (or will be tomorrow morning), I can return to Manchester once more, which I plan on doing as soon as possible. Before that, I would dearly like to see you again, and I know Archie would too. We shall both miss you greatly when we leave. Nevertheless, if you feel it would be best not to see us, for whatever reason, then I of course understand. So long as you at least read this letter, I can be content with that.

Your friend,
Richard

I walk back to the caravan, close all the curtains, turn on the lights and open up my phone. My search for the name Nicholas Cartwright returns no new results, nothing supporting his supposed innocence. And why would there be? By his admission, the news will not filter out until tomorrow morning. Yet all of this, everything he has told me so far, has been by his admission. Why should I choose to believe this new declaration? Perhaps this letter itself and everything written in it is just another ruse, a trick to lure me to his house where my screams will go unheard.

But what if it's the truth? What then? If Richard is innocent, then what have I done?

No. He is lying to me. I know it. He has seen how I've changed, how I've grown. He knows what I am capable of. He fears me. He *should* fear me. Who even is he anyway? This Richard Brown, this Nicholas Cartwright? Whether or not he is what they say he is, or what *he* says he is, maybe it doesn't even matter, because he's still an emmet, still another emmet crawling all over my land as if it belongs to him. He says I have been a friend to him, but why are we friends? Why? And why is friendship itself so important? What does it matter, really and at the end of it all, what does it matter why your friends are your friends or if they are genuinely your friends at all? Because friends – even true friends, even real friends – friends can still neglect, friends can still disappear, friends can still leave you. So why this need for friendship? Isn't friendship itself a lie, a lie we tell ourselves to make our stupid, meaningless lives better? A lie just like any other, just like all the lies we tell ourselves over and over and over again until they are as ingrained, as stamped in, as truth, mashed into our skulls, hanging there deep inside the consciousness like the smell of fresh bread? If he is lying to me now or the papers lied to all of us, what does it matter? Why does any of it matter, what he did, or what I've done, or what any of us have done and will do and then will continue to do again and again until the nausea of repetition finally works its way into our hearts and lungs and begs us – no, *forces* us – to just stop, to just stop it right now, to just *please let go*. And then there's the letting go. Why is that so prized? Why can't we *hold on*? What's wrong with *holding on*? Isn't that a part of friendship too? To hold on, no matter what? To hold on because if you don't it'll all just float away, off the lip, down into the bone-shattering chasm?

I close my eyes. Breathe. Long and deep.

I have a choice to make, a choice that must exist out there beyond the realm of belief and lies. Tomorrow, the truth will come: a statement will or will not be released to the press. Whichever occurs, I will know. But, until then, things might happen. Things which, should they occur, will be of my doing. I saw the plans forming in Paul Dunstan's eyes the moment I told him. They came from me – I expected him to make them, wanted it. And the crux of it all is this: if those plans are carried out tonight, and if I discover Richard's innocence tomorrow, I know that I will never forgive myself. Of that I can be certain.

Another thought nags at me. A thought I cannot displace. If Richard is telling the truth, he has been wrongly accused. And *I* have been wrongly accused. By the very people I may have stirred into action against Richard. The stupid men of Petherick. They think I did it, think I pushed Little Sister Lucy off the lip. I know what it is to be wrongly accused.

Tonight is only one night. Tomorrow, the world can do what it wants.

If I do this, it will just be what I do every day and every night anyway. I protect my land, protect it by watching.

All I need to do is watch.

I find my old school rucksack buried amongst the mounds of bedding in the overhead storage unit. I stuff it with a cushion, two blankets and three bin bags. There is room left in the bag only for a bottle of water, which I fill from one of the large bottles in the bathroom, a tin of ravioli and a fork. I pull on a pair of jeans under my dress and then a thick jumper and my coat over it. Three pairs of socks are all that I can squeeze into my shoes. My woollen bobble hat squashes hair against forehead and cheeks. It will be a cold night tonight, cold and long.

Outside, it is dark already. I lock the caravan door and make my way through the woods, past the Cafy and across the road. Wind whips at the barriers of tape as I bend low and pass beneath. The tide is high and the swells are rising with it. I stand at dead centre and look down, watch the white water clamber up the burial mound of fallen rocks, feel the spray lift up to douse the uncovered parts of my face. It all feels different, denser perhaps, and it sounds different too. The familiar booms and thumps of the waves crashing against the cliff walls remain, but there is a scrabbling, wrenching crunch which underpins it all: loose stone pushed forward and then ripped back again.

I move away, ducking beneath the tape on the eastern edge of my land, and follow the coast path towards the rise. Beyond it, Nare Point is empty. No cars. I breathe a sigh of relief. Above, a seagull screams by in the briny air. The chill is mounting: sharp fingernails dragged over skin.

I reach the car park and look over towards Richard's house. There are no lights on. Perhaps he has left already. Perhaps he could not wait. Perhaps he is halfway to Manchester.

Perhaps. It does not matter. This is where I will spend the night.

It will not be the first time. I have wild camped often this year, ever since Little Sister Lucy and I first moved into the caravan – never here at Nare Point, but on my land, close to the lip. Neither the cold nor the dark ever bothered me – if anything, they made my makeshift bivouacs, the blankets and the pillows and the wet grass beneath them, and the wetter air above and around them, cosier. I lay back and I watched the stars and I listened to the surf and I thought of my dead father or my vanished mother or both. Once, I brought Little Sister Lucy out with me. I thought she might enjoy it as much as I did, thought she might find the same peace which I found in the night air. She lasted less than an hour. First came the boredom, then the shivering, and finally the tears. She cried so loud I had to unearth us from our blanket mound and lead her by the hand back to the caravan. I did not try again. Whenever I did it next, I did it alone. It was easy enough to leave her in bed in the caravan. She liked to sleep deep under the duvet with only her feet exposed, and once they stopped twitching I knew nothing would wake her until the morning. For a little girl, she was good in that way. I used to wake at the slightest interruption when I was as little as her.

I continue walking along the coast path until I reach the pocket at the northern aspect of the car park. I check my watch. It is half past eight. I crouch down beside the pocket, unzip my rucksack and remove the three bin bags. I unroll them and lay them out flat so that they cover the muddy ground within the pocket. I crawl in on top of them and pierce the deepest parts upon the sharpest points of the knotted weeds, the poking twigs and thorns. Then I roll back out into the open air and retrieve several stones from the car park to use as ballast along the exposed edges of the bin bags. A gust of wind passes through, and I watch eagerly to see if everything holds in place. It does, all of it: these constituent parts of an excellent groundsheet. They may not be a perfect fit, but from the way I have positioned the bin bags they do not poke out into the open air, and this means at least that no flapping edges will attract the attention of anyone who happens to come to Nare Point tonight.

Next, I take the cushion from my rucksack and place it atop the groundsheet at the northern end of the pocket, the end closest to the lip, so that when I lay my head upon it I will be able to see the rest of the car park and the road. Richard's house will remain out of sight from there, but anyone coming up here tonight will arrive by car on the road or by foot on the coast path. I will see them. And, even if I do not, I will surely hear them.

Only the blankets remain. I remove the first from the rucksack and lay it out flat across the bin bags, pressing my hands down on to it at various places to check for any semblance of dampness. None occurs. The blanket remains dry. Taking the second blanket from the rucksack and bunching it up into a ball in my hand, I climb into the pocket and lie across the first blanket, pulling the rucksack in after me and placing it at my feet, being sure to retrieve the water bottle first and positioning it beside the cushion. Flat on my back with my head propped up on the cushion, I unfurl the second blanket and gently throw it out over me, kicking it into place with my feet, tucking it beneath my legs and hips and rolling into it until I am fully covered and no gaps remain for the wind to pass through. I stretch out, feeling somewhat languorous all of a sudden, content and comfortable here in my little nest. Waves crash and winds howl. I shimmy on to my right side, making sure not to disturb the careful arrangement of my bedding, pull the sleeves of both coat and jumper down over my hands, and nestle my right cheek into the cushion.

And then I watch.

'I don't like it here. Let's go back to the Cafy.'

'Just a little while longer.'

'It's cold. I'm cold.'

'I told you to bring your coat.'

That silenced her. She became stubborn, knowing I was right, refusing to acknowledge it. My little bundle of defiance.

We walked on together, passing The Warren and continuing on towards Pedna Head. It surprised me we had made it even this far. Normally, Little Sister Lucy began to grow impatient by the time we reached the western headland. Only once had she let me take her all the way to Lantoweth, and then our planned afternoon at the beach had been cut short when she stood on a sharp pebble moments after kicking off her sandals and dissolved into a temper tantrum. I remember pulling her back up to her feet and being shocked, even then, despite how little she was, at how light she felt, at how easy it was to right her. It threw me so much that I forgot to tell her off.

'How much longer? How much further?'

'Let's just make it to Pedna Head. Come on. Walking is good for us.'

'It's good for *you*.'

When she left the caravan, Little Sister Lucy only wanted to go to the Cafy. She was Mum through and through. I remember once trying to get Mum to join me on a walk, just a short walk, to Nare Point and back. She had given up before we even reached the rise.

'I'm just not made for walking, Melody Janie,' she had said. 'Not like you.'

'What are you made for?' I remember the defiance in my voice when I asked her that. It reminds me now of the defiance I used to hear in Little Sister Lucy's voice. We are all just a spiral of each other.

'The Cafy,' Mum had said. 'I'm made for the Cafy. My dream come true.' It was a familiar line.

When we reached Pedna Head, me and Little Sister Lucy, I asked her to sit with me, just for a minute or two.

'I need a wee,' she said.

'Go in the bushes,' I replied, pointing at the thicket behind the coast path.

'*Ewww*, no.'

'Tiny little bladder for a tiny little girl,' I teased, and she beamed a wide and toothy grin and sat next to me, laying her head on my shoulder. She loved it when I made reference to her size, when I called her little, as if it affirmed everything she felt about herself.

'Mellijane,' she said. 'It's like you're my mum now.'

Her words made my palms itch and I did not know how to reply. For a moment, I nearly lost myself in this vortex of mothers and daughters and mothers. But it did not matter, because a pod of dolphins appeared to distract us both, a hundred metres out to sea, dipping and rising, their backs and fins glistening as they made their tranquil way towards Lantoweth and beyond.

I may have slept. I cannot be certain. My nose is wet and frigid. I raise my hands up and out of the blankets to my face, cup them around my mouth and nose and breathe into them. Mist plumes out from the cracks between my fingers.

A taut line runs from my right shoulder down to my right ankle, a path of aches and twinges. I wriggle to offset the stiffness: jagged, frozen spikes prickle through my bones. I am unnaturally cold. It occurs to me that all my previous wild nights were undertaken during the summer season. It occurs to me that it is now somewhere near the end of October.

A will that is thoughtless, instinctive, pushes me out from the pocket and pitches me, lurching a little, to my feet, the blanket still wrapped around my body. I need to stretch, to walk, to run even, to activate the warm blood, to pump it through my numb frame. Knees crack as I clumsily step on to the coast path; muscles return to life in a way that is both painful and delicious. Fog clears from my brain. I check my watch. It is ten past one in the morning.

I jog on the spot for a dozen beats and then, keeping the blanket around me like a cape, walk the length of the car park down to the road, back up again, and down once more.

I stop. There is a noise. It occurs to me that there *has* been a noise, ever since I awoke, perhaps even the cause of it. I look up the road, in the direction of Petherick. Two headlights appear, flashing white as they round a corner: the peak of the hill ahead.

I run back to the pocket. Dive in. Bury myself beneath my blanket cape. Thrust my head into the cushion. Watch. Listen.

The car nears, slows.

I breathe, long and deep.

It appears in view, its headlights coursing across Nare Point as it turns into the car park, and then continues on, into my blind spot, where it stops. I cannot see it, nor whoever might be inside.

Another car appears, and then another. They park beside the first. Engines are killed and doors opened. I hear no voices, but the sound of bottles being opened and clinked together is unmistakeable.

Three more cars arrive, and then a fourth, and then another two. They all park together. No lights shine in my direction. I shimmy out from beneath the pocket's overhang to improve my view. There, milling about the cars, are at least twenty people. Bottles of beer are passed around. Cigarettes are lit. They are all men. Amongst them, Paul Dunstan.

They speak softly and I cannot make out their words, but their purpose here is as clear as if they were shouting it into the wind. Backs to me, they face Richard's house.

I discern a cricket bat in one hand, what looks like a glass ashtray in another. A golf club and a length of wood. Cylindrical piping which glints metallically in the moonlight. Yet despite their weapons, the men are hesitant, unsure of themselves. They stay close to their cars, drinking their beers, smoking their cigarettes. There is no laughter, only mutters and mumbles. Another car approaches, does not slow down, and they shrink from it, huddle together as it passes.

I watch them all. They do not know I am here.

Around twenty minutes pass. I have begun to shiver. The cold has returned, penetrating my blanket, penetrating me. But I will not leave. Not until they leave first.

The signal, the spur, is a bottle, thrown to the ground with such force that it smashes with surprising volume. More follow, and a din of splintering glass fills the night air. And then, as one, they move.

The shouts begin once the men have crossed the road, as they step on to the pathway in single file, as they spill in different directions across the garden, as they surround the house.

'Murderer.'

'Rapist scum.'

'Monster.'

'Monster.'

'Monster.'

I climb out of the pocket and creep across the car park. Not one of the men sees me. They face the house. Their shouts transform from accusations into threats, overlapping each other with sloppy imprecision.

'. . . come out . . .'

'. . . someone your own size . . .'

'. . . fuck you up . . .'

'. . . break your neck . . .'

'. . . kill you . . .'

'. . . kill you . . .'

'. . . kill you . . .'

I reach the road in time to watch one of the men swing his cricket bat at a window. There is a cheer as the glass breaks. He pokes the bat into the opening and swipes at the remaining glass until it shatters to nothingness. Another man approaches the window, those around encouraging him on with calls and claps. He starts to climb through, stops, pulls back, holds his hand up before his face. Blood pours down his sleeve. Some laugh, others grow furious, as if this too were Richard's fault.

'. . . get out here . . .'

'. . . stand up . . .'

'. . . monster . . .'

'. . . kill you . . .'

'. . . monster . . .'

Another window is broken. Men beat at the door with their bats, with their metal pipes, with their fists, their feet, their shoulders.

I take a step on to the road and stop. I cannot go any further. I cannot get any closer. This is too much. I cannot stop this. What am I doing here? What was I thinking? This is beyond me. I take a step back into the car park again. I should not be here. I cannot see this, cannot watch what is going to happen, cannot bear the sight of it. I came here to protect by keeping a lookout. But my protection means nothing. Things have gone too far, have transformed into something I must not, under any circumstances, witness.

I retreat yet further, towards the coast path. I take the phone from my pocket, hold it up and, with a shaking hand, key in 999. What use will it have? They took an hour to get here last time, an hour to rescue me and Little Sister Lucy. In an hour this will all be over.

Another window falls to the onslaught. I hear the rain-like cascade of glass. If Richard had any sense, he would have left already, slipped out the back and hidden in the woods. Surely he has; surely he fled the minute he heard all those accumulating engines outside his house. He is not there. I will tell myself this, repeat it again and again until it becomes truth – *it doesn't matter, Richard wasn't there, the house they raided was empty, he got away.*

A long and low howl pierces the air, a sound unlike any I have ever heard before. It rises, breaks up an octave and then plummets back down again, dense with fear and heartbreak, pure pain made auditory. The men freeze, and for a moment the howl is all I can hear. The weight of it pushes on my stomach. Archie. It is Archie.

I run: across the road, up the pathway, to the door, shove and barge the men aside, push at shoulders and strike at faces and kick at knees until they have cleared around me, my back to the door, the howling behind me, the men before. I hold my arms out, make a cross with my body, a barrier, breathing heavily, and when one of the men begins to approach, I scream, '*Get back!*', and he does.

The howling stops. Everything stops.

'You shouldn't be here, young lady.'

I look at the man who has spoken. He is an ape, a barbarian.

'This is my land,' I say.

I spit in his face.

His response is instinctual, reactive: the raised fist.

The response of all stupid, weak little men everywhere.
He holds his fist at shoulder level. But I am not scared,
and he can see it. I will not be scared. Not any more.
The fist unclenches, lowers.

'Leave,' I say. I can feel the shine in my eyes. 'Now.'

'That man in there,' he says, 'is a monster.'

Behind him, accord ripples through this paltry
crowd of Neanderthals. Murmurs, assent. But they
remain still. Only one moves, slowly treading across
the grass towards the door, towards me and this man.
I keep my arms out. I do not blink.

'You need to get out of the way. Leave us to it. Go
home.'

I spit at him again.

He lunges. His hand does not become a fist this time,
but reaches out, for my throat. My saliva drips from
his eyebrows. I do not move.

Two arms catch him around the waist before he can
take me, pull him back. He spins awkwardly; the same
arms push him to the ground. This other man nearly
topples after him, but rights himself in time. He turns,
looks at me.

'Fuck's sake, Paul,' the man says from the ground.
He gets back up on to his feet, brushes his clothes down.
Paul Dunstan leans in close to his face, mutters something into his ear. The man looks at me, horrified. Then
he retreats, and more mutters pass from him to others
and then to yet others until all of these men share the
same look, that same horror, a recognition somehow
both awful and humbling. As one, they begin to back

away, off the grass, down the pathway, on to the road, towards their cars.

Paul Dunstan remains. 'Sorry, Melody Janie,' he says. 'Didn't know you were . . . that you . . .'

'Go away, Paul,' I say.

'I will . . . we will,' he stutters. 'Because of you. Here. But . . . but you know who he is, don't you? What he did?'

'I know exactly who he is.'

'We're coming back for him.' Paul begins to sidestep down the pathway towards the road. 'And you shouldn't be here when we do.'

I notice, at my feet, the glass ashtray, dropped in the frenzy. I pick it up and throw it at Paul. It whistles past him to shatter on the road.

'I'll always be here,' I say as he turns and hurries away. 'Always. This is my land.'

Richard opens the battered door the moment the last car has disappeared.

'I think,' he says, 'that you may have just saved my life.'

Archie appears through Richard's legs. I sink to my knees and let him run into my outstretched arms. He shakes and whimpers. I hold him until he is still, quiet.

'How did you do it?'

I let Archie go and stand up. 'Do what?'

'How did you get them to leave?'

Archie remains by my side. Tremors come and go, prickling his fur. I rub my hand along his ribs, kneading out the spasms and twitches. 'They're coming back,' I say.

'When?'

'Maybe tonight.'

'I've called the police. They'll be here soon. Nothing else will happen tonight.'

'And tomorrow?'

'Tomorrow the news will be out. Everyone will know.'

'So you say.'

'Oh.' Richard's shoulders fall. 'You still don't believe me.'

'I'll find out tomorrow,' I reply. 'If it's not in the papers, don't expect to ever see me again.'

'Of course.'

Archie's breathing has begun to slow. He sits beside my feet and pushes his head into my hand until I scratch the top of his nose. It occurs to me that this might be the last time I see him.

'If you don't believe me,' Richard says, 'why did you come here tonight?'

'I was just passing.'

'I don't think that's true.'

'I don't care.' I look down at Archie. His wet eyes stare back into mine. 'I heard Archie howling. I couldn't let them hurt him.'

'I would have done my best to stop them.'

'With what? Your knife?'

'Oh,' he says. And then, quietly, 'My knife.'

'I saw it in your hand. Last night. At the Cafy.'

Richard looks at me, the same weird and intense look I've squirmed under too many times. I will not squirm any more.

'I'm not afraid of you,' I say.

'Nor should you be,' he replies.

'And everything you know about me, everything you *think* you know, you should forget it. Like you said, don't believe everything you read in the papers.'

Richard holds my gaze for a few moments and then looks down at the ground. 'Sometimes,' he says, 'I think I'm the one who's afraid of you.'

'Good,' I say. 'You don't know what I'm capable of.'

'You're right. I don't.'

I reach down and give Archie one final stroke, but

I make sure to keep my eyes on Richard. He keeps his on the ground. When I turn and leave, I do not look back at him. But I stay alert, waiting, waiting, for the sounds of feet on grass, of flailing arms and a swooping blade.

They never come.

I take the coast path back to the Cafy, hurry through the woods and let myself into the caravan.

I crawl into bed, thinking about Richard, about what truths or lies will be uncovered tomorrow, but I am tired and my mind soon drifts, away from him towards Mum, and then finally towards Little Sister Lucy. My Little Sister Lucy broke my heart the first time I saw her, she broke my heart. She was so fresh, so new. Even then, that first time, I saw all of us in her face – myself so much, and Mum especially. I remember her, I cannot stop myself. I remember her all the time.

I think about the morning we played behind the bar while the sun rose, the light creeping in through the windows, the day beginning.

'Do you think people will come today?'

'I hope so.'

'I hope so too.'

The storm was beginning to pass, moving inland. A night storm. Thunder and rain hammering so loud on the caravan roof that Little Sister Lucy had cried and I had taken her into the Cafy. The windows rattled harder there, but the certainty of concrete, the Cafy itself, always made her feel safer. To distract her, I had initiated a game of I spy, one which she was finally growing tired of.

'What time will we open?'

'The usual time. Ten.'

'Maybe we should open earlier.'

'I don't think it'll help.'

'Why?'

'Probably no one's coming today anyway.'

'Why?'

'It's a bad season.'

'Why?'

'I don't know, Lucy. I don't have the answers.'

'Why?'

'I just don't. So no more questions.'

Sparse rain remained, sparse rain and thick cloud cover. I could not see out of the window from that angle, sitting on the floor behind the bar, but I could tell from the quality of light settling across the room that the sun was obscured.

'Is it Mum's fault, Mellijane?'

'What do you mean?'

'Would it be better if she was here?'

The wind played around the windows, howling along the panes, whistling through the brickwork.

'Yes,' I said. 'It would. Wouldn't you like to see her again?'

'I don't know.' Little Sister Lucy thought for a while, and then looked at me with a hopeful smile. 'I like it just the two of us.'

When I wake, the caravan is cold and my duvet stiff. I raise myself up on my elbows to look out the window: the day is grey and miserable. I feel for my phone. It has been charging overnight and, to my surprise, proves to have used far less of my valuable electricity than I had supposed. Opening it, I click on the news app preinstalled on the home screen. *Manchester Man Confesses to Caleb Hawkins Murder*, runs the main headline. I scroll down for details. No name or photos have been released, but the scant information available reveals the murderer to be thirty-eight years old, married, a father of two, an electrician. Nicholas Cartwright is not mentioned.

I feel something close to dizziness, a light-headed distance which is not sickening but is instead warm, a comfort. Relief. A slow swirl of oxygen and abatement. Richard was telling the truth. He is innocent.

I think, he said, *that you may have just saved my life.*

Perhaps I did. Perhaps I genuinely saved his life last night.

I saved someone's.

I forget breakfast. I do not change my clothes. There is no need. They are dirty but they are dry. I let myself

out of the caravan and head towards Richard's house.
I do not stop at dead centre.

I watch the ocean as I walk east: there is a storm
coming. It lingers over the horizon, shedding its load
in faint grey streaks. The swells stretch far back. I can
see them building from miles distant, gaining weight,
gathering force. A burst of wind cannonballs in from
the ocean, making me lurch to the right. A low rumble
of thunder succeeds it, far away, watery. Then more
wind, smacking and buffeting me away from the lip,
lacerating my skin and calcifying my lips.

I quicken my pace. A bee launches itself from the
heather before me. If Archie were here, he would chase
it. I will miss Archie when he leaves. Will he miss me?
Will he miss this coast path, the lip, Nare Point, Bones
Break? What dog would not? Surely this is canine
heaven?

Perhaps it is time I started to think about adopting
my own dog, a rescue pup, some poor hopeless
mite desperate for the home and the love I can give.
A friend who would curl up at the foot of my bed in
the caravan; who would sit patiently out the front
of the Cafy and greet the customers; who would join
me on long walks along the coast path; who would
keep me company while I wait for Mum.

I wonder what will become of Richard's house. I
must keep an eye on it, on whoever moves in there
next. My neighbours. I hope they will not be emmets –
this house should be for locals: their first home; their
only home. Locals with a dog. A family would be best,

not too large, two parents and two children. Enough for me to work with. I will warn the dad to drive with care on the road; school the little girls about the hideaways and vantage points; show the mum the way down. Yes, a family would suit here. There should be more life. There should be more love.

Nare Point is empty. I crunch my way over its gravel, cross the road and walk up the pathway through the garden. If Paul Dunstan and his men returned last night there is no sign. Lengths of cardboard have been taped over the broken windows. The house is as quiet as the air. I knock on the door.

Archie barks. I wait for twenty seconds and then knock again. Archie replies once more, but Richard does not. I stoop down, open the letterbox with my fingers and position my mouth a few centimetres from it.

'Richard.' I keep my voice soft. 'It's me, Richard. It's only me.'

'Are you alone?' His voice is close.

'Always.'

As Richard undoes the locks, I can hear Archie thudding against the door, desperate to get to me. He bounds out the moment the door is open enough for him to squeeze through, finds his way to my right hand, licks it frantically and then threads his way between my legs and wiggles from side to side. I lean over and scratch his hips. His tail wags with such force it fans my hair back. 'I've come to believe that there is no greeting in the world quite like that which you receive from a dog,' Richard says.

Still scratching Archie, I look up at Richard. 'So I read an article today.'

'Good.'

'Why didn't you answer the door? You're innocent. The world knows.'

'Only the part of it which reads the news.' Richard holds the door open wide and steps back. 'Would you like to come in?'

The hallway is narrow and dark. There are no pictures on the walls. A black metal stag's head with keys hanging from its antlers is the only adornment save the wallpaper. The carpet is haunted by the telltale circular imprints of cigarette burns. One piece of lonely furniture stands in the corner, a tall and narrow table, over which Richard's coat is draped. The single light suspended from the white ceiling is a bare bulb, switched off. Archie leans against my legs and nudges his nose into my palm.

'Should I call you Nicholas?' I ask.

'You can call me whatever you like.' He closes the door behind me. 'At least it won't be *monster* any more.'

'I'm sorry.'

'Apology accepted. And, to better answer your question, I think I prefer you to call me Richard.'

'Why?'

'You've been a friend to Richard. You've been kind to him. I'd like to keep it that way.'

'Me too,' I agree. 'Richard it is.'

He smiles. 'I've just made some tea. Would you like a cup?'

'Yes. That'd be nice.'

All doors leading off from the hallway are closed, all except one. We walk towards and through it, into the dining room. Like the hallway, it too is plain and bland, devoid of any semblance of character, of personality. A television, not flat-screen, sits on the floor in a corner, a Freeview box next to it, facing the wall. Both are covered in a film of dust. Aside from the oval table and, around it, the four chairs, no two of which match, there is only one other item of furniture in this room: an ancient and imposing chest of three large drawers, each with a lock above its handle. Behind the chest is a window, veiled by lace curtains.

Richard gestures for me to sit on one of the chairs. In the middle of the table is a ceramic teapot, steam issuing from its spout. Next to it is a small cup, perched on a cork coaster. 'I'll get you a cup,' Richard says. He closes the door behind him. I sit. Archie coaxes his head between my shins. Richard returns, sits on the chair opposite mine and pours tea from the pot into the cups. He hands one to me and I take a sip. It is too sweet.

'I suppose you'll be going back to Manchester soon,' I say.

Richard picks at the rim of his cup, loosening a speck of dirt with his fingernail. 'In a couple of days, I hope. It's not like I have much to tie up around here.'

'Don't you want to just go, right now? After last night? What if they come back?'

'It's a possibility,' he says, taking a long draught of the sugary tea. 'But I'm certain the main threat has passed.'

'The news never said the man's name.'

'They can't. Not just yet. Legal reasons. But he's confessed, and that's out there. I think that's enough for now. I'm quietly confident my days of harassment are over.'

'Do you know anything about him?'

Richard hesitates. 'Yes,' he finally says. 'I've been privy to certain information the press doesn't have. Perhaps the only perk of this entire ordeal.'

'Who is he?'

'Nobody,' Richard says. 'That's what surprised me the most. I thought that, if they ever caught the killer, it would come with a big twist. Like all along it had been his brother, or a jealous ex, or a serial killer who struck again, was caught and retroactively linked to Caleb. But it was nothing like that. From what I've been told, Caleb was out in town that night and met the man when he'd left his last bar. The man was hanging around on the streets and they got talking. He was drunk and, when he found out Caleb was gay, he admitted to him that, even though he was married, he'd always fanta- sised about being with another man. Caleb took him home, but he must have had a change of heart when they got there because he told the man he wouldn't sleep with him. That's when it happened. The man was never questioned because nobody knew he had any connection to Caleb. And then, on Monday, the guilt all got too much for him and he walked into his local police station and confessed. That's it. It feels so insub- stantial. So hollow.'

'They've convicted him on his confession alone?'

'He had kept the knife. God only knows why.'

'I bet you can't believe your luck.'

'You think I've been *lucky*?'

I meet Richard's eyes. He is not angry, but nor is he happy. There is only resignation there. Remorse for time lost.

We sit in silence for a few moments. Archie switches back and forth between us, taking his head scratches where he can get them, moving on when they dry up. Richard stretches his free arm up to rub at the back of his neck. 'You know,' he says, 'when the police came for me, it wasn't even a surprise. And they were perfectly professional and reasonable. I was called in a few times, but they established my innocence and I presumed that would be the end of it. The police believed me. The media . . . well, the media did not.'

I say nothing, let him speak.

'The press pegged the murder on me from the first time I stepped out of the police station, and they wouldn't let go of it. They hounded me. Harassed me. The eccentric landlord. I was never charged with the murder, didn't even have to go to court, but that didn't matter to the papers. They dragged my name so deeply through the mud that I never thought I'd get it clean again. That was it. In the eyes of the public, I was a rapist and a murderer. Of a young man, and possibly men, because there was plenty of speculation about others too. And I tried to stay, to put up with it, with the bricks through my windows and the graffiti on my walls, with all the dirty looks and the spitting and the name-calling in the street, even with the death threats through the letterbox. But then I was cornered in an alley. Beaten with a golf club. They broke my arm. I couldn't stay after that. I had no choice. I appealed to the police for help. They got me out of Manchester. They put me here.'

Richard looks at me. It is not the usual look, the one which leaves me so agitated, but a sorrowful look, begging understanding and forgiveness, somehow hopeless.

'I'm sorry I didn't believe you,' I say.

'I don't blame you. I wouldn't have believed me either.'

'But you scared me.'

'When? I never did anything to you, Melody Janie. Never.'

'The morning on the lip, when you were drunk. And then again that night, when you came to the Cafy.'

Richard raises his free hand to his mouth. 'Oh God,' he says through his fingers. 'Of course. You said last night you were there.'

I nod. 'I saw the knife.'

'The knife.' The hand drops from his mouth, rests in his lap. He sighs. 'You talked about *my knife* last night, too. It was a cruel thing to say. Why would I have a knife? Why on earth? After what happened to Caleb?'

'But I saw it. I was watching you from the woods.'

'What did you see exactly?'

I think back, picture that horrible scene: Archie's

yelp, Richard's slip and fall. 'I saw you . . .' My voice
falters. Hesitant. What *did* I see exactly? Silver glinting
in the moonlight. And then the trees as I ran through
them. 'I saw you take . . . I saw you take *something* from
Archie's saddlebags.'

'Oh, Melody Janie.' His voice is light, compassionate
even. 'That was a pen. My favourite pen. I brought it
and some paper so I could write you a letter, tell you
about my news. I kept them in Archie's saddlebags to
keep them dry from the rain. Not that it mattered. It
was so wet and I was so drunk that I couldn't write a
word. That's why I went back to the Cafy yesterday.
Although that time, I wrote the letter before I left home.'

Something is not right. I feel faint, lost amongst all
these truths and lies. 'But that can't be . . .' I stutter.
'It doesn't make sense . . . is that all you keep in
Archie's saddlebags? You said they were security. You
were going to take something out of them when we
argued on the lip . . . I watched you . . . you were going
to . . . you stopped when I said there were people at
Bones Break . . .'

Richard stands up and leaves the room. When he
returns, he holds the saddlebags in his hands. He places
them at my feet and sits down. 'You're right about security,' he says. 'But I have never carried a knife. Look for
yourself.'

I reach down and slowly unzip each of the saddlebags. Between them, they hold a small assortment of
items. I take them out, one by one, standing them on
the table between us. A large bottle of whisky. 'In case

my hip flask runs dry,' Richard says. A much smaller
bottle of pills labelled as diazepam. 'In case the whisky
doesn't work.' A mobile phone. 'In case of emergency.'
A can of pepper spray. '*Security.*'

I stare at the four objects on the table. 'So when we
were arguing on the lip,' I mumble, 'you were just trying
to show me you didn't have a knife?'

Richard looks at me. That stare. That same stare.
'Maybe not just that,' he says. 'I might have taken out
the pepper spray.' His free hand returns to his face,
flittering around his eyebrows.

'You were going to pepper-spray me?'

'No,' he says. 'I was going to threaten you with it.'

'But why?'

He does not reply.

'Why, Richard? Why did you want to threaten me?'

'Because you scared me.' His voice is a whisper. 'I
told you that last night. You scare me, Melody Janie.
You always have.'

'But why?'

'Because . . .' Richard sniffs twice, clears his throat
and then wipes at his eyes with his free hand. 'Because
of your mother.'

It surprises me that my words come with ease. I spit them out. 'What do you know about my mother?'

Richard moves for his cup of tea and, when he picks it up, I can see that his hand shakes. 'I know everything. I'm so sorry, Melody Janie. I should have told you I knew. I've been concerned about you ever since we first met. I didn't find out right away, but then we went for a walk that evening, and you kept asking me questions, questions about my past, and after that I thought I should look for yours.'

'Look where?' The tremors in my voice match those in his hand.

'Online. I searched your name. It came up.'

The walls are beginning to move. I dig my nails into my chair. 'Tell me what you saw. Tell me what you know.'

Archie, sensing the change in atmosphere, disappears under the table. A thin whine issues out from somewhere around my legs.

'All of it. But of course I wasn't going to say anything. How could I when—'

I slam my hand down on to the table. 'Stop it!' I shout. 'Just tell me what you know about my mother.'

I stare at him until he has to look down, masking it by pretending to search for Archie, who remains beneath the table, his whimpers growing increasingly maddening.

Finally, Richard looks back up at me. There is nothing in his eyes. 'She's dead.'

The world falls away.

I stagger to my feet. A thin but consuming whistle resonates through my eardrums. Richard is saying something, but it is too muffled to hear. Archie is barking. I lurch against the table, sending the teapot and cups crashing to the floor – wet splashes which soak through my shoes and weigh heavily on my feet. Richard stands, approaches me. I push at him, both hands on both shoulders. He cries in pain and clutches at his broken arm. Archie's barks grow louder, though they remain dulled inside the cacophony of my head.

And then I fall.

My head bounces off the carpet. My neck twists and my shoulders wrench and my spine shudders; wrists and ankles contort into unnatural angles, lungs squeeze out air, something trickles from my ear. And I think – *this is how she looked.*

Archie rushes to my side, licking my face and whining at the same time. Two arms gently place themselves beneath mine, coaxing me up and backwards, so that I am sitting on the floor. Richard holds his face close to mine and slowly, ever so slowly, I begin to understand his words.

'Melody Janie. Are you okay? Are you okay, Melody Janie?'

'She's not,' I whisper. 'She's not dead. She can't be.'

'I thought you knew. The article I read, it said you were there. It said you were the one who called the coastguard.'

A part of me wants to plug my fingers into my ears and chant nonsense like Esther and I used to do at school when we would pretend not to listen to each other. But my arms are limp at my sides, and I feel as if I might never be able to lift them, nor anything else, ever again.

'That damn press,' Richard is saying. 'It's lies, all of it. They feed off it. The soulless bastards.'

I look at Archie. There is so much love in his eyes, and it reminds me of her, how she became, how heart-breakingly beautiful those eyes were.

'They didn't lie,' I say.

Richard falls silent. I do not look at him. I focus instead on Archie, draw from his love. Fixate on it. Make it my own. It is the only way to say what I need to say. Finally, after all this time. I have to say it. Archie will help me find the words.

'She wasn't my mum. She hadn't been. Not for a long time. She was my little sister. She was my Little Sister Lucy.'

I want to scream, I want to sleep, I want to scream and sleep simultaneously, but the pain in my chest is so exquisite it sends me lurching to my feet. I stagger to my side and Archie appears beneath my outstretched hand as if by magic, lending me support precisely when and where I need it. I right myself, look at the room about me. The table is upended, one of the chairs with it. Crockery lies broken across the floor.

'I have to leave,' I say. My voice is a shattered mirror of itself.

'You're in no fit state.' Richard approaches me with his free arm outstretched. I swat it away, and the motion lends itself to a wave of dizziness which threatens to topple me once more.

'I have to leave,' I repeat. The room stops spinning. I see the door, make my unsteady way towards it.

'Melody Janie, please.' Richard stays back from me, though Archie does not. 'I can't let you go anywhere like this.'

'I have to leave.'

'Just tell me who to call.'

'There's no one.'

'There must be someone. You can't be alone.'

'There's no one!'

My scream rocks the air. In its wake is only silence. Both Richard and Archie retreat a few steps.

'Okay. You can leave.' Richard's free hand is raised, palm out, facing me, supplicating, pleading. 'But sit down for a few minutes first. Just a few minutes. Please.'

I breathe, long and deep.

'Just a few minutes,' I say.

Richard drags a chair over the stained carpet towards me and then steps back. I let myself drop into it.

'I'll get you some water.'

He leaves the room. Archie pads slowly towards me, torn between his learned wariness of violence and his innate compassion. I hold a hand out and he nudges his wet nose into it, just once. The touch rips six months of pain out of me in a heartbeat, and as the first sob comes, loud and ugly, he presses his whole body against me, so that his weight anchors me to the world. I burrow my fingers into the coarse fur along his back and nuzzle my forehead into his neck and feel the way he breathes, long and deep, through my chest. We stay like that, pressed together, for a long time. He never moves.

I raise my head. The fur across his neck has matted, tamped down and soaked by my tears, so that it reveals dark and lumpy skin beneath. I look about me. Richard is not in the room. Beside me, a full glass of water sits on the righted table. I lightly take one of Archie's floppy ears in my hand and lean back in to kiss it. He grumbles something pleasant.

I kiss him again, and then hold his ear open and whisper into it, 'Stay.'

He does, never moving an inch as I rise to my feet, tiptoe out of the room and down the hall, open and close the door as quietly as I can, and then swiftly walk down the garden, across the road, through the car park and on to the coast path.

The wind is violent. I sway from side to side, punch-drunk. A gust catches me and I stumble forward, gathering momentum which carries me towards and then over the rise. Rain begins to fall, a sudden onslaught as if tipped from a bucket. These clothes – this hat and coat and jumper, these shoes and thick pairs of socks – they suffocate me. I need to feel my land, I need to now more than ever. I rip them from me as I walk, leaving each offending item suspended upon the thickets of gorse and bracken which seem to grow before my eyes in this drenching rain, curling their tendrils out and over the coast path, greedily snatching up everything I have to offer. I come to a stop by the cleft on the eastern headland, raise my newly bared arms for balance and grip the gravel with my toes while I look over the ocean. Out in the swells, a black shape bobs: the head of a resting seal perhaps; though, in this weather, more likely a rene-gade buoy, slipped from its anchor. I glance upwards. The sky moves like the sea, black and crushing. The rain cools my scorched head and plasters my hair to my face. There is no thunder. Not yet. But it will come.

Foundering down towards my land, I find that one of the DANGER signs has been blown over. I prop it back up and then duck beneath the tape to walk to the lip, where I gaze down at the burial mound. It may be my imagination, but the pile of rubble seems smaller. I console myself with the thought that, one day, it will all be washed away, and I will have my zawn back again. The rubble will disappear, just like Richard, just like Archie, just like Little Sister Lucy, just like Mum, dispersing and reeling, clinging to whatever safety and shelter they can find. Bones Break gave them all both, but it was temporary. It could only ever have been that way.

I walk forward, slow and steady strides, deliberate, defiant against the wind. My arms have lost their feeling. My head, cooled and dripping, approaches a similar numbness. All focus has gravitated towards my legs, which move and move and move, over grass sodden and marshy from the rain, out to the lip.

I stand in position. Precise. Dead centre. It is vital to know where my feet are. The left an inch closer to the lip than the right, both angled slightly inwards, heels up. For this is where my mother, Lucy Rowe, stood, naked, at three o'clock in the morning.

'Tell me about Mum.'

'No.'

'Tell me.'

'I don't need to. She'll be back soon. She can tell you everything herself.'

'She won't.'

'She will. And it'll be better if it comes from her. You know her even better than I do.'

'Tell me anyway.'

So I did. I told her a story, the story I wanted to believe. I never told her the truth. Perhaps I should have. Perhaps I should have told her everything. But I never knew her the way Dad did. I never knew how to bring her back. I couldn't buy her a Cafy. I couldn't save her.

Not that it matters any more. I only have myself to tell now. And so I do. I tell myself the real story: the story of my mother, the story of Little Sister Lucy. The same story.

Lucy Rowe was a strong woman. Tough. Resilient. She had to be. At the age of nineteen, her world transformed, became a place both terrifying and incomprehensible. She had to learn how to adapt to it, and adapt quickly. This new world had no patience. It swallowed her from the inside out. But my mother fought it, she fought it hard, and after those three months in the Centre, she discovered how to manage this new world. She overcame. She re-emerged.

Her disorder was always her biggest enemy, and when she had to fight it again, eight years later, her enemy had been preparing all the while, and this time it took longer, much longer, and it took some of her with it. She re-emerged once more, but she had not overcome, not entirely. The enemy, and her fight with it, had destroyed a part of her. She was never the same again.

But she kept trying – maybe for my sake, maybe for Dad's, and certainly for her own. When the Cafy became hers, she had a new tool, a new weapon: that of a dream come true. She brandished the dream and, despite what she had lost, she used it to flourish. To succeed in a life which only wanted to harm her. She could have retreated, could have returned to the Centre, but she refused. She fought.

It is my belief that she would have won, that she would have kept on succeeding, had my father not died. When that happened, she gave up. She retreated. From the moment the police officer appeared at our door to tell us the news, to the day of Dad's funeral, Mum slipped and slipped and slipped. I did not know where she was retreating to, and perhaps neither did she, but she vanished during the night after the funeral, and when I woke in the morning I found a new being in my bed with me, curled up beneath the duvet, a softly snoring lump.

I woke her. She rubbed at her eyes with balled-up fists.

'Are you okay, Mum?'

She giggled shyly. 'I'm not Mum, silly.' Her voice was weak, babyish. Mischievous and undeniably adorable with it. 'Mum's gone away.'

'Where has she gone?'

'Dunno. She didn't tell me.' She yawned like a tiny hippo. Hair fell into her mouth and she spat it out with puerile disgust. 'Yuck.'

'How long will she be gone?'

She began to sing then. '*Gone gone gone goooooone.*' I took her gently by the shoulders. She stopped singing and looked curiously at me with her enormous eyes.

'Mum, what's happening?'

'It's not Mum, Mellijane,' she said, giggling again. 'It's me. Me. Don't you recognise me? I'm your Little Sister Lucy.'

What shames me perhaps more than anything else is how severely I fell in love with my Little Sister Lucy. She was so happy and compliant and full of fresh, unconditional love that I could not help but take part in the role play and even begin to enjoy it. I gave into all her infantile demands: I sang nursery rhymes to her; I fed her by hand; I washed her clothes and cleaned her down in the shower after accidents; I stroked her hair until she fell asleep. And I did it all not because I felt she needed it, not because I thought it might somehow offer her some respite from her world so that she could re-emerge from it once more, herself, my mother, again – no, I did it because I liked it. I loved it. I loved my Little Sister Lucy.

And I wanted her to be happy. We moved into the caravan because there the memories of Dad did not linger with as much pressing force as they did in the house. I took her for walks along the lip, her hand in mine, so that she could see the seals or play in the grass and make us daisy chains. I kept the Cafy open for the next month because, even as a little girl, she still loved to sit inside it, often perched on top of the bar, swinging her legs and plaiting her hair. Most of the customers we had during that time either ignored her or humoured her. Only once was there a problem. There was a family in, two young parents and their three girls, all below the age of ten. I had been cleaning the coffee machine when I heard the mother shriek. I looked up and out the window. Little Sister Lucy was bouncing up and down upon one of the wooden picnic benches, two of the girls beside her and the third in her arms. She was throwing her into the air with each leap and catching her with each descent. The mother ripped the girl from Little Sister Lucy's arms and the father grabbed the other two by the hands. The youngest girl began to cry, and so did Little Sister Lucy. The family left immediately, stomping back to their car. They had not paid their bill.

I closed the Cafy the following day. Little Sister Lucy cried and said she was sorry, but it did not take long to convince her that, between the two of us, we could not keep it open.

'Okay,' she said, wiping her nose with her knuckles. 'Mellijane knows best.' And then she beamed at me.

Despite it being closed, we would still visit the Cafy most days to clean it, and this kept her happy. It wasn't until sometime in early September that she began to withdraw from me. I never knew what it was that triggered the decline – maybe the onset of the cold weather, maybe the subconscious knowledge of our worsening situation, or maybe it was just the degenerative nature of her disorder unchecked by medication. All I knew was that the pain of that was even worse than when Mum had first vanished, and I did all I could to coax her back to me, singing her songs or telling her stories or offering her treats salvaged from the subterranean storeroom. It was no use. The distance between us grew and it broke my heart. She began to sleep for days at a time. When she admitted that she would dream of Dad, and that she liked to sleep so that she could see him again, I began to let her. Once, she did not open her eyes for five whole days, not even when I urged water or Cornish Chow Mein between her lips.

I should never have told her I was going to call the Centre. I should have just done it. They would have come. They would have taken her. They would have helped her. But I could not let her go without some sort of warning. That has always been the problem with my mother. I have never been able to let her go.

Our last conversation was an argument. Short and screamed. I called her 'Mum'. I told her what I was going to do. She wailed imprecations at me and then she flung herself beneath the duvet and then she never spoke to me again.

When she began to snore, I let her sleep. I resolved to call the Centre from the Cafy's landline the following day. I just wanted one more night with my Little Sister Lucy. I crawled into bed next to her. I could feel her warmth on my legs. I fell asleep. When I awoke, at three o'clock in the morning, she was gone.

I do not know when she left the caravan. I do not know how long she was out there. All I know is that, whatever she did during those lost hours, she spent some time in the Cafy: long enough to remove her clothes, fold each item neatly and place them piece by piece on the kitchen worktop, topping the pile with her faded green slip-on shoes. And then she walked, naked, to the lip.

If the cold made an impression on her, she did not show it. Nor the prospect of the drop. The tide was at its lowest. No water awaited her down there, only black sand.

I have often wondered what she thought of in those last moments. I like to believe that if she thought of anything, it was of my land, of the overwhelming beauty of it from the lip. And then I hope she thought of nothing at all. Because there is peace in that.

I had no time to shout. I was halfway across the road when I realised. By my next step, she had jumped. I watched her disappear out of sight beneath the lip and, still, I did not shout. I wanted to, I wanted to scream, but something stopped me. I did not know what it was at the time, but I do now. It was already too late. She had left, her action irreversible, and the last thing she needed to hear on the drop was my scream. Then she would have known that I had seen her. Seen *it*. I could not give her that as a final thought. I wanted peace for her. I always have.

I did not shout but I did run. Her footprints remained in the grass at the lip and I nestled my own feet into them. I looked.

She lay face down on the black sand.

I look up.

Thunder, low and resonant, cascading ripples ending in a whip crack. It heralds extra rain, an upgrade in intensity. My shivering has become violent, rattling my skull, the convulsions uncontrollable, impossible to stop. I cannot think. I am pure physicality. Is this how Esther used to feel as she slipped towards a seizure?

I retreat from the lip, edge back to the caravan. Inside, I take my towel from the bathroom and rub my hair. It floats outwards from my face and my shoulders. I wrap the damp towel around myself and perch on the bed, feeling the shivers subside.

I know that the death of my mother was reported in the newspapers, because people came to the Cafy. Not many, but people nonetheless. I hid in my caravan. Nobody found me. I heard their cars and their voices but I never saw them, and they never saw me. I went into the Cafy only for food or to make the few phone calls that were unavoidable. The police. The coroner. The funeral directors. I spoke with the company who had provided their service for Dad, and I explained I wanted the same for Mum. That is, the least possible. The lady I spoke to on the phone, I think she might have cried when I told her. She said she remembered me.

It was only after I left the Nankervis crematorium with Mum in my hands that I realised I had not paid the directors. That, in fact, they had never asked for a penny. I considered calling them with apologies and thanks, but refrained. It may have been a mistake on their part and if it was then I did not want to remind them, for I had not the means to pay.

I stayed in the caravan, alone, for four days. It was hunger which forced me out. I made my quiet way through the woods and let myself into the Cafy. Mum and I had kept up with the cleaning all through the summer, but there had been so much rain that mould had begun to spread across the walls and leaks had sprung from the ceiling. The electricity had been cut off three weeks earlier and when I descended to the subterranean storeroom and opened the freezers the billowing smell almost made me sick. I could not stomach opening them again after that.

Esther came. I did not hear her car approach, did not even see her face as she peered through the window and spotted me. When the door swung open and she appeared, it felt something close to magic. She told me she had been looking for me, had been to the house dozens of times, had asked all over St Petroc and Petherick for news, had been to the Cafy as many times as the house, but could find no sign of me. There was an accusatory tone to her voice as she blurted all this out, but then she stopped talking and she looked at me properly for the first time, and that was when she forgot about her own horror and saw mine instead, and I saw her pull everything back into herself, I saw her *withdraw*, not from me, but from her usual self, and the sight of it was too much to bear and the weight of a thousand convulsions took over my body and she ran to me and held me for a long time.

I did not speak. I couldn't. I wanted to tell her everything – about Mum, about Little Sister Lucy, about the caravan – but no words came, only tears. Finally, I was able to wipe my eyes and gaze into hers, but there was so much grief there, grief which almost matched my own, that the tragedy of it all sent us both into a fit of sobbing which neither of us could pull ourselves out of until long after the October sun had set.

When, hours later, Esther got up to leave, it was with a score of apologies. 'I'll come and see you again,' she said.

'When?'

'I've got lectures all day tomorrow, but I can drive down first thing on Saturday morning.'

'Okay,' I said. *Please do*, I meant.

'I'll be back then. Do you need anything?'

'No.'

She left.

I was alone again.

I looked around me. At the Cafy. It was disgusting. Mum would have been horrified. I let myself out and, leaving the door unlocked, walked across the road and on to my land, through the grass and then over the barrier to the lip, to dead centre, finding the exact position with my feet.

I looked down. The tide was high and the water calm. I pictured the sands of the zawn below it all, and if the outline of my mother was washed away, which it surely was, it stayed etched into the contours of my mind. I wondered what it felt like to stare down into that, to know it would be my final view, an ever-present memory. To drop, to *just drop*, and watch it race upwards, those final fractions of a second, eyes stinging and arms outstretched. I knew then, as I know now, that I could never do it. Pure cowardice dismembered any possibility of it. I had climbed down but I could not jump. The drop was, and always has been, too much for me. Only my mother had that kind of strength.

And so I turned from the lip, and I walked back to the Cafy, and I let myself back in through the unlocked door, and I remembered my Little Sister Lucy as my Little Sister Lucy, and I remembered my mother as my mother, and I began, right there and then, to clean the Cafy for her, because if I could not save her then I could at least wait for her, and I could make sure the Cafy was clean for her, was ready for her, was tidy for her, for when she came back, and all the while I could keep an eye on Bones Break, could protect it and nurture it and care for it as I protected and nurtured and cared for the Cafy, could keep it all, all of my land, safe from the emmets and the ramblers and the voyeurs – because if I did not then who else would? Who else would?

Afternoon bleeds into evening into night. Outside, the storm worsens with each passing hour. I am cold. I stand up on unsteady feet, walk the few steps from the bed to the kitchenette. Taking the box of matches from the drawer beneath the sink, I open up the gas valves, press one of the dials down and strike a match, holding the flame close to the cooker's largest burner. It bursts into blue life and I repeat the action with the other two burners and the same flame. The match burns down to my fingertips and I drop it into the sink. I hold my hands for a while above the three circular fires, heating the blood in my wrists, letting it pump around my body, imagining myself back into warmth. Then I retrieve the kettle from the overhead cupboard and take it into the bathroom, where I fill it from one of the bottles. I close the door to the bathroom, re-enter the kitchenette and place the kettle on to the largest of the burners. I find a clean cup in a different cupboard and take out my pot of teabags and hold one above the cup . . .

And then I stop. There is no need for this. Not any more. This mindless description of everything I do to keep myself on track, to block out the insistent nagging of thoughts I do not want to think – all of it, all of it is useless now. The pretence is over. My mother is not coming back. My mother is dead.

I am alone here.

I turn off each of the burners, walk back to the bed and lie on top of the duvet. I do not have the energy to lift it and crawl underneath. I do not have the energy for anything any more. I do not have energy.

I close my eyes. There is an itch on my left elbow. I do not scratch it. It will go away soon. Everything does. First, will. Second, action. Finally, thought. I long for that latter, ache for it. I never want to think again. If I must live, if I must be the only one who has to, then let it be without thought. Let me be free from reaction and recollection, let me slide into something other. Let me find some peace somewhere.

Let me forget.

Let me sleep.

This is not thunder. I know this noise. I remember it. It does not come from above. It comes from the earth.

The caravan rocks from side to side as a tremendous crashing builds and sustains. I stumble to my feet, resting hands against cupboards and walls to steady myself. The wood panelling and linoleum vibrate beneath my palms. The noise has grown deafening, the long crashes topped by staccato crackles. Not a melody: a harmony.

I know what is happening.

I open the door as the ground shakes. The caravan bounces beneath me and I fall out, landing on my side in the mud and puddles.

There is no pain.

The noise subsides; the ground steadies. I push myself up and grope my way through the woods, past the Cafy and towards the road. I stop.

The lip has gone.

There is no more graceful curve. Instead, a diagonal line, so straight it seems drawn with a ruler, streaks back from the western headland, stopping just short of the road. The edge – the new lip, if I can call it that – is no longer a precipice but a peak, below it a slope like a hillside, an embankment, an almost walkable decline of shattered rock and debris.

Such beauty transformed into such mundanity.

The eastern headland is broken in two, cut along the fault line of last winter's cleft. I want to cry when I look at it, half of its face missing. Tortured, abused. Deformed.

The coast path signpost on the western headland remains, as do the two new posts at the road. But the third new post has fallen. The severed tape flaps against the ground like the wing of a dying bird.

I look out to sea. Gull Rock is no longer there.

There is a crack, so quick and sharp I feel it in my throat. Then the booming begins again, deafening, maddening. I scream but cannot hear myself. I look over to the western headland and it vanishes – does not fall or slip or recede, just disappears right before my eyes. So much rock has fallen that white water sprays up as it hits the sea, sprays up over this new lip, this crumbling, retreating lip, this traitorous, cowardly lip; the water sprays over it, splashing my face and arms.

My land. My land is leaving me. Like everything else.

The shudders of the ground are erratic, sending jolts of grinding pain up through my bones. The lip is not so much falling as dissolving, eating itself up as it hurries towards the road, towards me.

Suddenly, there is a shift, a change of gears some-where below, and the world tilts, sending me sprawling to the ground. I hit the concrete heavily and wait it out, for things are slowing, quietening. Is it the end or merely a pause, like a clean set between waves?

I stand up.

I look out at Bones Break.

I understand.

My land is gone. All of it. My headlands and my stretch of coast path, my soft grass, my shelf, my beautiful, beautiful lip. Gone.

I understand.

This is help. This is an offer. I have known my land intimately, and my land has known me likewise. It knew I could never jump. It knew I would never be capable. And so it has sacrificed itself. And I know now what I am being told. That all I have to do is stand still. All I have to do is remain here, be at one with my land, and it will take care of everything for me. It has not finished yet. Its self-destruction remains incomplete. All I have to do is wait.

I hold my arms up above my head, stretching out my limbs and tendons. I roll my shoulders, first back and then forward. I rotate my head in a clockwise motion, my neck crackling and popping under its own seismic contortions. And then I look down at my feet, my bare and mud-caked feet. Both are angled slightly inwards, heels up.

'Melody Janie.'

Keeping my feet in place, I turn my head. Richard is here.

'Don't,' he says.

I look back out to the ocean. Its proximity is astonishing. 'I don't have to,' I murmur. 'I just have to wait.'

'Please. Don't.'

The water is bright. Hungry.

'Melody Janie, please, this is senseless.'

'Everything is.'

'No,' Richard says. 'Not everything.'

I do not reply.

He walks forward and stands beside me. Archie appears from behind his legs. His tail is looped down and tucked beneath his body. His ears are flat against the sides of his head. He is petrified. He does not understand all this noise, all this tumult. He wants to run away: the deep, deep angst in his eyes is as clear as hunger, or pain. Or love. He wants to run away but he does not. He remains. He remains for me. He presses his wet nose into my leg.

I cannot help myself. I unleash a sob as sudden and violent as vomit. Archie tilts his head. Richard reaches out and, so softly I can barely feel it, takes my hand in his.

'Come on, Melody Janie,' he says. 'Come on.'

I let him lead me away, off the road and towards the side of the Cafy. The gravel is suddenly sharp beneath my feet, the air suddenly frozen around my bare arms, and when I slip I do not fight it, but let myself fall. Archie comes, whines, licks my face. I wrap my arms around him, bury my face into his fur and cry for a long time. Archie stands still and lets me.

I open my eyes. I am in bed, in the caravan. I close my eyes.

I open my eyes. I hear snoring. I prop myself up on my elbows and look over the lip of the bed. Archie sleeps on the floor, one ear flopped back and hanging open, revealing pink skin and grey fuzz. I close my eyes.

I open my eyes. Richard is here.

'What's there to be scared of?'

He jumps a little at the sound of my voice. 'I didn't realise you were awake.'

'What's there to be scared of?' I repeat.

'What do you mean?'

'You said you were scared of me. Why? What's there to be scared of?'

I can almost hear Richard thinking through the silence. 'Do you remember the first time we met?'

'Yes.'

'You were hiding in a bush. And then, the second time, you were doing this strange dance and shouting something about randy spiders.'

A thin and unexpected smile breaks across my lips, and then vanishes just as quickly as it appeared. 'Strange,' I say, 'but not scary. You said you were afraid of me.'

'When I searched your name online, I found out what happened to your mother, and then I found out what happened to your father. Anyone who has lost their parents so recently, so *tragically* – well, anyone like that is . . .'

'Someone to be concerned about. Not someone to be scared of.'

Richard does not reply.

'There's more,' I say. 'Tell me. Tell me why you were afraid of me.'

'It was in one of the articles.'

'What was?'

'What happened to your mother. *Before* she jumped. Her history. Her illness.'

'And?'

'She was nineteen when she first went to hospital.'

'And?'

'And I think that's about how old you are.'

'There it is,' I say. 'That's it.'

I close my eyes.

I open my eyes.

'How are you feeling today?'

'Tired.'

'Hungry?'

'A little.'

'Let me cook something for you. What would you like?'

'Anything but noodles.'

Richard fires up the cooker in the kitchenette, lighting a burner and then the grill underneath. He takes a plastic bag, not one I recognise, down from the cupboard above the sink, and removes a frying pan and some ingredients from it.

'I brought this over from my house. Do you like egg on toast?'

'Yes.'

'Fried or scrambled?'

'Whatever you're having.'

'Fried it is.'

I sit up. Archie plods over to my side and leans against the bed, watching Richard as he pours oil into the pan, cracks eggs and slides slices of bread below the grill. Butter appears from the plastic bag, salt and pepper grinders after it. The interweaving smells are delicious.

'You're still here,' I say.

Richard nods, reaches below the grill to flip the slices of bread over and then turns his attention back to the eggs, which spit and pop in the pan.

'When are you leaving?'

He shrugs. 'Soon.'

'A new life.'

'Maybe. But an old home.'

I think about that word. *Home*. Without land, is it possible to have a home?

'How did you find my caravan?'

'You told me.'

'When?'

'After I found you on the . . .' He searches for the right word.'. . . on the lip.' It is not the right word. Not any more.

'I don't remember that.'

'I'm not surprised. You were in a bad way. Understandably.' He butters the slices of toast and lays them on to paper plates. The eggs come next, draped over the dripping butter. He hands me a plate and a plastic knife and fork. I tear into the eggs, ravenous.

'What will you do?' Richard asks quietly.

'What?'

'Now. What now? What are you going to do?'

I think for a moment. 'I don't know. My land is gone.'

'The Cafy is still here.'

'It didn't fall?'

'No. The collapse didn't reach the road.'

It surprises me to realise that I do not care. 'The Cafy was never mine,' I say. 'It was Mum's.'

The mention of her silences him, which in turn silences me, and we eat on. Archie sits beside me, staring at my hand as it moves up to my mouth and then down to my plate. Every now and then, his front paws perform a little expectant shuffle.

'I don't think you should stay here. In this caravan.'

'Where else is there?' I think about the house in St Petroc, but the prospect of setting foot inside it fills me with angst and sorrow. I cannot go there.

'Don't you have anyone, Melody Janie? Don't you have anyone at all who can care for you when I leave? You shouldn't be alone.'

Alone, I think. *Am I alone? Have I really been, all this time?*

'What about family? Or friends? Someone?'

Someone. A friend.

'Esther,' I say. 'Esther is my friend.'

'Where is she?' He carves off a slice of toast, dabs it into the yolk of an egg and throws it into Archie's mouth. He seems energised by this new prospect, by this discovery that I have a friend. Another friend besides him.

'She lives in Bristol. For university.'

'Can she come here? To see you?'

'She comes here all the time.'

'Really? I've never seen her.'

She's seen you, I think, and the image of her legs poking

out from beneath the weeds of the pocket almost makes me laugh. Almost.

I find my phone somewhere deep beneath the folds of the duvet, take it out, turn it on and hand it to Richard. 'Her number's here,' I say.

'Shall I call her?'

'Yes. Call her.'

I eat what remains on my plate, put it on the floor for Archie to lick clean and lie back down.

I close my eyes.

I open my eyes. Esther is here. She sits upon a chair in the kitchenette, reading my copy of *One Hundred Years of Solitude*. I recognise the chair, she must have brought it in from the Cafy. She looks up as I yawn and stretch.

'Nice caravan,' she says. 'Cosy.'

'I'm sorry I didn't tell you.'

Esther shrugs, smiles sadly. 'Don't be sorry,' she says.

'There's other things I haven't told you. About . . .' I take a deep breath. 'About Mum.'

'I know.'

'Richard?'

'Yes.'

'I'm so sorry. I should have told you.'

Esther shrugs again. 'Don't be sorry. About anything.'

Propping myself up on my elbows, I look around the caravan, notice the absence. 'Where's Archie?'

'Nicholas took him home.'

'Manchester?'

'No. They haven't left yet. But I think they will soon.'

'I have to say goodbye.'

'I know. And he knows too. You will. He promised me that.'

'Thank you.' I can feel energy build inside me. Esther always has been an enlivening source. I shimmy out from beneath the covers and stand up, legs shaking beneath me, feeling like an infant about to take its first fledgling steps towards its mother. 'Did Richard phone you?' I ask.

'Yes. And he said you were still calling him that.'

'Did you see the news?'

Esther nods. 'It makes me feel awful, how wrong I was about him.'

'You weren't alone.'

She looks away from me, out the window. 'You were, though, weren't you?' she says quietly. 'Alone. All this time.'

'No. I wasn't alone. She was here. She may not have been herself, but she was here with me. And then, after the drop – well, then you turned up. You were here.'

Esther continues to look out the window. I think she may be crying – crying or trying hard not to. 'I should have turned up earlier. I knew about your dad. Mum told me about it back in April. I could have come to see you then.' Her voice is cracking. 'But I didn't.'

'Why not?'

'I guess I didn't feel I knew you any more. We were friends, like, four years ago. I don't know, it's probably stupid, but, you know, you went off me in Year 11, so I figured you didn't like me any more. I didn't think you'd want to see me.'

'I probably would have hidden from you.'

Esther does not reply. I notice a slight tremor in the shoulder angled towards me. She is crying.

I breathe, long and deep. It is time to let everything go.

'Do you want to know why I stopped talking to you? Back in Year 11?'

She turns to face me, fixes me with her red, wet eyes. 'I don't know. Do I?'

'I overheard Mum tell Dad she thought I was becoming like her. That maybe I had the same thing. She said she could see it in me. I messaged you about it. You never replied. I found out later you had lost your phone. By then it was too late. Neither of us were talking to each other and I didn't have the courage to break the silence.'

Esther sniffs. 'Fuck me, Melody Janie,' she says. 'Are you serious?'

I try to smile. It does not work. 'You were my only friend. And I let you go. I'm an idiot.'

'We're both idiots. It's not like I put up much of a fight, is it?' She runs the back of her hand over her eyes, sniffs again. 'Was I really your only friend?'

'You know you were. I wasn't popular like you.'

'Popular? I don't know about that. I guess I had quite a few mates. But I used to think you were my best friend.'

Best friend. Two simple words. They send crackles of electricity across my skin.

'And that's why I'm so sorry about not being here for you through all this . . . all this . . . *horror* you've had to deal with.' She lowers her head into her hands. 'I just keep thinking about all those times you just asked me to come for a fucking *walk* with you, and I didn't even do that . . .'

My legs are buoyant as I stride forward and slide my hands into hers, peeling them back from her tear-streaked face. 'Then let's go for a walk,' I say.

'Now?' Esther looks up at me. Her eyes are so beautiful. She is so beautiful.

'Yes. Now.' I peer out of the window. The light is low, colourless. 'I need to see it.'

We pass through the woods in silence. It is only as we begin to emerge that I first hear the noise. Engines and voices. Hand in hand, Esther and I step out from the trees to walk up alongside the Cafy.

The car park is full. Some have double-parked, others squeezed so close together it is a wonder they can open their doors. A man dressed like a lumberjack opens his boot to take out the most expensive camera I have ever seen; his girlfriend, impatient with him, has begun to move towards the road, already taking selfies, ensuring her heavily tattooed arms are in each shot. She is oblivious to us. I look around at the rest of the car park. They are all oblivious to us, everyone here, climbing out of their cars or back into them, the parents and the lovers and the ramblers and the children and the emmets and the teenagers, all oblivious to these two girls walking amongst them – and why wouldn't they be? The new face of Bones Break is the draw here; it absorbs the attention of all.

I stop, feel Esther's hand in mine, the weight of it, the tactile connection, the pathway through which we can both communicate without words, the give of accordance and the resistance of reluctance, sometimes one and sometimes both and sometimes neither, like the lead which spooled out between me and Archie, its twitches and vibrations telling us both when and where we were, when and where we are.

I let go.

It is time to let go.

I breathe, long and deep, and then I look out at what was once my land. With both headlands vanished and the old bay-shaped curve of the lip gone with them, there is not even an absence of Bones Break any more. There is simply nothingness. Like it never existed. The coastline has rewritten itself, and Bones Break was chosen for deletion. Photos will remain, and so will memories, but not for long, not without the physical facts, or the retold stories, behind them. This place is no longer Bones Break. It will not be renamed. There is no name for nothingness.

Two old ladies have sat down on one of the wooden benches. I walk towards them.

'Are you opening?' one asks, pointing at the Cafy.

'No,' I say, and then move on. Forward. Esther follows.

The road crawls with people. I spot the three funny little men amongst them, doing their best to take their measurements and their photographs in the midst of the heavy throng. There must be a hundred people here, more perhaps. I hold my head up and walk into the crowd, alone. People jostle against me as I push my way through. Someone tuts as a child cries close by.

I reach the new lip, which begins just a few feet from

the road, and look down. There is no zawn, no cliff face, no Gull Rock, no headlands, no longer even any birds wheeling above or swooping and diving below. There is just rubble and mud and dust, a bank of it sloping down from my feet to the water, which no longer seems so far away. This place used to be a masterpiece; now it is no better than ordinary. I look at the enormous crowd around me, look at them cooing and bleating as they gaze across the new landscape.

They can keep it, I think.

The coast path begins again a few metres along from where the eastern headland used to be. I step on to it and walk towards the rise. Esther follows. From here, facing east, the world appears untouched: the cliff faces intact, the zawns open and unburied, the coast path itself no different. It seems that mine was the only land to fall. The sole change out here, away from Bones Break, is the sudden absence of life. There are no birds above or seals below. Perhaps the fragility of this place has grown too much for them to bear. Perhaps they were right to leave.

We reach Nare Point. The car park is full; the cars themselves empty. Everyone is at Bones Break. Everyone but me.

Archie's bark comes before I knock on the door and, when it opens, he ignores Esther and rises up to thrust his front paws into my hands. We perform a little dance together. At its conclusion, I bend down so that he can lick my face.

'Cup of tea?' Richard says.

We walk inside. Four large suitcases stand against the wall of the hallway. I wonder if Archie's saddlebags have been packed into them.

Richard opens the door to the kitchen, stops and says, 'Oh.'

'What?'

'I've just realised. I only own two cups.'

'I'm all right without,' Esther says.

'Me too,' I say.

'Are you sure?'

'Yes.'

'Okay.'

We stand, the three of us, hovering awkwardly in the hallway. Esther breaks the silence. 'Actually,' she says, 'I'd better call my mum. I'll do it outside.' She slips out through the front door.

It occurs to me that Richard and I are not looking at each other, and perhaps it occurs to him too, for we make eye contact at the same time and then, a moment later, we laugh at the same time too.

'I just came to say goodbye.'

'I'm glad.'

I can hear Esther talking outside, can hear my name mentioned.

'So when are you leaving?'

'Tomorrow, I think. First thing.'

'Straight to Manchester?'

'Straight to Manchester.'

Archie nudges his wet nose against my leg. I scratch him behind the ears.

'And you?' Richard says. 'Any plans?'

'I think so.'

'That's good.'

I take a step forward and reach out my hand. Richard takes it and we shake gently. 'So,' I say. 'Goodbye then.'

'Yes. Goodbye, Melody Janie.'

I let go.

'Thank you.'

'For what?'

'You know.'

'Thank you too.'

'For what?'

'You know.'

I lower myself to the floor and sit cross-legged. Archie rests his front paws in my lap and nuzzles his face against my cheek. '*And thank you,*' I whisper to him. '*Thank you the most.*'

'I think,' Richard says, 'I'll have a cup of tea anyway. Take your time. I'll just be in the kitchen.'

Archie watches him as he walks from the hallway, and then turns his attention back to me. Tail wagging, he pushes his head against my shoulder and I roll on to my back. He flops down on to my stomach, forcing air from my mouth in a gasped laugh, and when I wrap my arms around his body he wriggles into position so that his head lies on my chest and his eyes gaze up into mine. Jets of warm air funnel from his nostrils to tickle my chin.

'Thank you,' I say out loud.

Slowly, his eyes begin to close. We lie there together, not moving, only breathing, breathing long and deep.

Back on the coast path, I speak to Esther.

She says, 'Yes.'

But first she needs to collect her mum from the train station and take her home. She will be back, she promises me, within the hour.

I help her negotiate her way out of the car park and through the crowds still teeming across the road. After I wave her off, I walk through the woods, let myself into the caravan and busy myself transforming the bed into the two couches and packing all loose items away into the overhead storage units. Then I step back outside, make my way around to the front, open up the exterior compartment to turn the gas off at the bottle and take out the collapsible ladder and small tool bag Mum left in there. I use the ladder to clamber up on to the roof and use the screwdrivers from the tool bag to disconnect the solar panels. It is an easy task. Mum did a good job. I place the ladder and the tool bag back inside the exterior storage compartment, lock it, and then stack the solar panels inside the bathroom.

I look around me. I am ready. It has taken less than an hour. Esther has not yet returned, and so I walk to the Cafy, let myself in, sit at a table in the dining room, take out my phone and, for the first time, search for the name 'Lucy Rowe'.

The scarcity of reports I can find about her drop surprises me. Those that do exist are vague and often inaccurate. In the few that feature my name, it is rarely spelled correctly: 'Mrs Rowe leaves behind one daughter, Melody Janey (19).'

I continue to scroll through her search results, click on the links: the donors' page of a website fundraising for MIND; a (flattering) review of the Cafy by a local blogger; the Facebook group for Three Stones School Class of 1991. This last becomes my favourite. Mum did not post anything there herself, but I grow addicted to trawling through the tags of her, enlarging the scanned photographs, where she appears – never in the foreground, but never in the background either – smiling and confident, surrounded by friends. She is so pretty in those photographs. It takes my breath away a little.

One member of the group has painstakingly scanned and uploaded every page from their leavers' book and I click through it over and over again, visiting and revisiting two pages in particular. The first is a list of awards, of superlatives – best smile; most optimistic; cutest couple. Mum won one: 'Most Likely to Succeed'.

The second page is a photograph, taken in Year 9 while she was at school camp. The photograph reveals a bright day at the beach, the yellow sand and the blue sky dazzling. Mum, thirteen years old and clad in a wetsuit, sits cross-legged, a lollipop stick poking out from her smile. She has her arm around another girl, blonde and freckled, also in a wetsuit, and this girl leans into Mum, pointing at the camera. She is saying something, her mouth open, and it is hard to tell what, though it is clear that she is laughing, that they both are. It is gorgeous.

The image fades from the screen, replaced by the name ESTHER emblazoned on a black background. The phone screeches. I press down on the green circle.

'I'm outside,' Esther says.

I leave the Cafy, lock the door behind me, spot the sky-blue Ford Fiesta and walk towards it.

'Are you ready?'

'Yes. Follow me.'

I hear the tyres on the gravel behind me as I walk towards the woods. Nobody pays any attention to us.

We pass along the side of the Cafy and reach the trees. Esther performs a three-point turn and then, making sure she can see me in her wing mirror, I begin to guide her backwards, into the woods. Branches scrape the sides and roof of her car as she squeezes through the trees, trees which have seen no traffic other than feet since Mum and Dad and I cleared this path and brought the caravan down it all those years ago.

We reach the clearing and, using shouts now as well as gesticulations, I guide Esther slowly backwards until her tow bar sits directly beneath the caravan's hitch. She stops the car, cuts the engine and steps out.

'Are you sure the caravan will make it through?' she

says as I lock the hitch into place and connect the electrics. 'My car barely fits.'

'It'll be fine,' I say. 'We got it in, we'll get it out.'

'Then at least stay in the car with me.'

I shake my head. 'This is the only way I can do it.'

I remove the flywheel, release the handbrake and wind each of the legs in. Esther starts her car back up and crawls forward a few inches. The caravan creaks slightly, but otherwise passes the test. Nothing breaks, nothing seizes. She's strong, my caravan. I walk to the car and open the passenger door. I smile at Esther. She smiles back. I shut the door, walk to the caravan, climb in, sit down, and I breathe. I breathe long and deep.

I hear the soft rev of Esther's engine, and then feel the caravan lurch forward. It rocks from side to side as we find the track, and the cacophony of branches begins, the squeals of protest resonating throughout the interior. We make it through, and the caravan rocks again as the surface changes to gravel. I look out at the Cafy through the window. I wonder how long before it too falls down.

Esther crosses the car park, slowly navigating through the parting crowd. We crawl out on to the road, the caravan lurching unsteadily on to the tarmac, and then we stop. I look through the front window, can see the back of Esther's head above her seat. She does not look around at me. She remains stationary.

Then I understand.

I turn and look out of the side window. This was all I had. All of this was mine. But it is gone.

All of it is gone. The coast path signpost, the western headland, the jagged but perfectly curved lip, dead centre, the warning sign, the eastern headland, the sheer cliff face, the field of untamed grass, Gull Rock – my land, my *world*, all of it perished. Irrevocable.

There was no better place.

A slight tug, and the caravan is on the move again, trundling forward, away. I leap up from the couch and run to the back of the caravan to look out of the rear window. We speed up. I place one hand on the window. The bend in the road is coming soon. I force myself not to blink. We lurch around to the right. There are only seconds left. A single wave breaks. And then the turn is complete, and it is gone, out of sight, forever, this land without name, without owner.

ACKNOWLEDGEMENTS

The first person to read this was my 'critical friend' Tom Coles. His insights were invaluable. Without them, Charlotte Van Wijk may never have taken an interest in my submission to PEW Literary and passed the manuscript on to Eleanor Birne – and that would have been a shame, because Eleanor is a tremendous agent, and I'm deeply grateful for all her work (and for Charlotte's early edit).

For stripping down the engine, and then for helping me rebuild it with care and consistency, thank you to Kat Burdon, Charlotte Robathan and Cari Rosen, and likewise to Rachael Duncan and Emma Petfield for letting the world know about it. Crucially, thank you to Lisa Highton for giving Melody Janie her perfect home at Two Roads.

For me, writing a novel turned out to be far tougher than writing non-fiction. Things doubtless would have been tougher still were it not for the support of the kind and lovely people I have in my life – Mary; Jodi, Cassie, Rini and Clara; Kel; Josh and Liv; Aaron; Adrian; and, of course, my wonderful wife Michelle. They get all the love.

Finally, thank you to books, to music and to home.

ABOUT THE AUTHOR

Charlie Carroll is the author of three non-fiction books: *The Friendship Highway* (2014), *No Fixed Abode* (2013) and *On the Edge* (2010). He has twice won the K Blundell Trust Award for 'writers under 40 who aim to raise social awareness with their writing', wrote the voice-over for the TV series *Transamazonica* (2017), and is one of the *Kindness of Strangers* storytellers. *The Lip* is his first novel. He lives in Cornwall.